The Blood Moon Murders

Also by Patrick C. Walsh

The Mac Maguire detective mysteries

The Body in the Boot

The Dead Squirrel

The Weeping Women

The Blackness

23 Cold Cases

Two Dogs

The Match of the Day Murders

The Chancer

The Tiger's Back

The Eight Bench Walk

A Concrete Case of Murder

Stories of the supernatural

13 Ghosts of Winter

The Black Vaults Experiment

All available in Amazon Books

Patrick C. Walsh

The Blood Moon Murders

The twelfth 'Mac' Maguire mystery

Garden City Ink

A Garden City Ink ebook
www.gardencityink.com

First published in Great Britain in 2021
All rights reserved
Copyright © 2021 Patrick C. Walsh

Cover art © Patrick C Walsh 2021
Garden City Ink Design

"Everyone is a moon, and has a dark side which they never show to anybody."
— Mark Twain

For Halloween, ghost stories and things that go bump in the night...

The Dream

It was night time and he was lost. He had no idea where he was or where he was going. Something invisible lay ahead in the darkness, something that filled him with dread. A path appeared in front of him and, even though he wanted to run the other way, his feet still took him relentlessly forward. Crippled trees bent over the path and, between the branches, he caught glimpses of a blood red moon high in the sky.

Something screamed in the near distance, a high-pitched note that made him shiver. The scream spoke eloquently of both despair and horror. Still his feet moved him inexorably forward. He looked anxiously around as the hair on the back of his neck stood up. Something was moving in the blackness beyond the trees, tracking him, something he didn't want to ever see.

He walked on down the path as the blood moon got bloodier. He was aware of rustlings and whisperings in the darkness on both sides of the path and he desperately wanted to run, to run away as fast as he could but his feet stayed anchored to the ground. Then he saw her.

She was lying just to the right of the path. The red rays of the blood moon illuminated her broken body like a spotlight. He moved towards her. She was dead, he somehow knew this to be true. Her body was just an empty shell that had once contained a living being. She was so young, too young to be lying there dead in the night. Despite his gnawing fear he moved closer.

Her face was made up and she wore blood red lipstick on her full lips. Her eyes were closed as she there lay unmoving. There was something written on her forehead in blood, a word perhaps, but he couldn't quite make it out. He moved closer and bent down.

He was only inches away, still trying to make out the word, when her eyes opened...

The New Moon...a time of unknowing but also a time for reaching out from the darkness, knowing that the light will soon come. A time for reflection and a time to decide who or what you want your magic to affect in the next cycle..."

Diana L. Selene, Wicca – The Deep Magic of the Wondreth Coven

Chapter One

Saturday

Mac awoke with a start. His heart was thumping and his mouth felt dry. It took him a while to work out where he was. He sat up and rubbed his face with his hands.

It was that dream again. He had been having it on and off now for the last three weeks or so. At first, he'd thought that it was just one of his lucid dreams but now he wasn't so sure. The lucid dreams, caused by his pain medication, were strange and surreal but they had never repeated themselves before. He'd had this one several times now and it was always the same. Of course, when he was in the dream it was all new and happening to him for the first time.

The dream faded away but vestiges of the dread he'd felt remained.

He turned on the light and looked at the clock. It was nearly seven o'clock. He remembered that it was a Saturday and that he had nothing special to get up for. He sighed. There had been no good reason for him to get up early for quite some time now. The last job he'd had was over five weeks ago now and that had only lasted for a few days. He wondered if he should just go back to sleep. He wasn't meeting his friend Tim until later that evening so he could sleep all day if he wanted to.

He had a sudden flashback to the months after his wife's death when he'd lived in the dark tunnel of a deep depression. He'd slept for days and, sometimes, weeks on end. A sudden fear of going back there again made him sit up.

He rubbed his face with his hands again before slowly standing up and checking his back. There was just the usual background pain so that, at least, was good. The room was a little chilly so he put his dressing gown on and turned up the thermostat in the hallway before heading towards the kitchen.

He passed by his dog Terry who was curled up in his basket. He opened half an eye as Mac went past and then went straight back to sleep.

He poured himself an orange juice and stared out of the kitchen window. Dawn was slowly getting underway and, to his left, the darkness was being fractured by fingers of pink light. It quickly grew and he could see small birds starting to congregate around the feeders. He smiled at their gymnastics and he was glad that he'd refilled the feeders just the evening before.

The sun grew ever brighter and it looked as if it might be another crisp and bright autumn day. The forecasters had been predicting a long spell of dry weather which was unusual for late October. While it would be sunny, it would be cold out too. This was confirmed by the grass in Mac's back garden. It was frosty white. In fact, the whole garden looked as if it had been covered in icing sugar.

He busied himself by making a pot of coffee. He took a cup and some toast into the living room and sat on the sofa. Terry opened half an eye again and then roused himself enough to sleepwalk to the sofa, climb up and then lie down next to Mac. He went straight back to sleep again.

He turned on the TV and watched the news for a few minutes before he turned it off again in disgust. He'd never known the news to be so consistently bad. Surreal as they were, his lucid dreams made a lot more sense than what seemed to be going on in the world at the moment.

He sat there in silence listening to the clock tick as the light grew ever stronger outside. He felt that he should be doing something but what? He looked at the clock again. It was still only seven thirty. He could always go to the office, he supposed, just in case there was any post. He knew that there probably wouldn't be but it would be something to do.

Once again, he thought of Leigh Marston. He and Tim had visited her just a couple of days ago. She was getting on really well but it was slow going. She had been hoping to be on crutches for his daughter's wedding but she'd had to settle for a wheelchair. Tim had enjoyed being her driver though and it had been a really good day.

Unfortunately, a week after the wedding, Leigh had a setback. During 'The Case of the House That Wasn't There'[1], as Mac liked to call it, she had been shot three times and, while the wound in her chest had been the immediate concern at the time, it was her knee that was causing all of her long-term problems. Leigh was desperate to get back to being a police detective but then she was told by the doctors that she would need another operation on her knee. The operation went well but Mac could see that the delay in getting back to work was getting Leigh down. He wished that there was something he could do for her.

On a cheerier note, he thought of his daughter Bridget and it brought an immediate smile to his face. She was seven months pregnant now and she was doing well. She had kept working until last week and it was a relief to both him, and her husband Tommy, when she had finally agreed to stop.

Bridget and Tommy's wedding in August, and the months of preparation before that, had been a real

---

[1] A Concrete Case of Murder – the eleventh Mac Maguire mystery

antidote to the dark times following Leigh's attempted murder. Mac had smiled at Bridget's decision not to change her name. In his day it was something that was always done but she said that she just couldn't be bothered changing her passport and a hundred other things and so she was now officially Ms. Bridget Maguire. Tommy didn't mind a bit. All he was thinking about was the child that was to come.

He and Mac had a few drinks one night and Tommy had confided to him that there were still times when he had to pinch himself. He still thought that Bridget was the most beautiful woman he'd ever met and now a child was on the way, his child. He said that he just couldn't believe his luck. Mac had assured him that it wasn't just him that had gotten lucky, Bridget had too.

He finally roused himself from his thoughts and tried to get busy. He spent a little time on his laptop checking his emails and deleting the spam. It was still only eight fifteen when he'd exhausted this activity.

After sitting in a deafening silence for a few minutes, he decided that he needed some fresh air. He'd take his time getting dressed and then he'd take Terry for a walk but first he'd go and talk to his Nora. He needed to tell her how Bridget was getting on.

When he'd been on holiday in Cyprus, he'd started walking every day and he found that he could do a little more than he'd have thought possible. Bridget said that the trick was in keeping it up. She'd suggested Radley Meadows as a good spot because it was a nice country walk that had picnic tables all along its length. That meant that he could sit down and take a rest if it ever became too much for his back. Terry loved too as it was popular with dog walkers and had lots of trees and bushes to him to sniff.

He got himself dressed and peeked in the living room. Terry was still stretched out on the sofa. He took the dog lead from its hook near the front door and when he re-entered the living room Terry was sitting up, his head on one side and his tail wagging. When he saw the lead, he was off the sofa in a flash and a second later he was waiting excitedly for his owner by the front door.

It was now a bright new morning as Mac made his way to his wife's grave. As usual, he gave the gravestone a good clean and then sat down on a little fold up chair and had a chat with his wife. He told her everything that had been going on and he could hear her replies as clearly as if she'd been standing next to him. After thirty years together you really get to know someone.

She told him not to buy anything for the baby until it was born as it would be bad luck and, anyway, you would need to know if it was a boy or a girl. She asked him if they had decided on any names yet. Mac said no and assured her that he'd tell her the minute that he knew.

Although talking to someone who is dead might sound like a slightly crazy thing to do, it had actually saved Mac's sanity when he'd been in a very dark place. He said his goodbyes and Nora told him to enjoy his walk but not to overdo it.

Mac smiled at this. He always felt a little less lonely after talking to Nora.

It was a short but very nice drive to the Meadows. The houses he drove by were a mixture but most had the Letchworth Cottage stamp on them; white rendering, distinctive oblong windows and peaked rooflines. No two were the same though which only made the drive more charming. He passed by the garden centre and that was his cue to turn right. He drove up a narrow country road and turned sharp left at the entrance to a farm. He then turned left again and drove past a sign that said 'Radley Meadows – Welcome!'

He'd lived in Letchworth Garden City for many years but he'd never known that this place existed until his daughter had told him about it. As usual she had been right. It was a nice peaceful walk and the picnic tables were a godsend if ever the pain in his back got too bad. It also meant that he could complete his daily exercise in easy stages. He drove into the little car park and noticed that there were already a couple of cars parked there.

It was a sort of country park in miniature but it was more than big enough for Mac. He normally came a little later in the day but thankfully it never got overly busy, not even during the school holidays. As they started their walk, a sharp gust of freezing wind made Mac shiver. His mother would have called it a 'lazy wind'. He remembered asking her why when he'd been a child. He could still clearly hear her reply in his head.

'Ah, now that's because it doesn't go around you like most winds do,' she'd said in her rich Donegal accent. 'A lazy wind just goes right through you.'

The memory made him smile.

He walked around a large circular area of grass allowing Terry to sniff at every tree and bush that they passed. This was where the summer picnics were usually held. It was really nice to see whole families sitting on blankets while the younger children ran around in the security of the grassy circle. There was plenty for the older children to explore in the woodlands that surrounded them.

There were woven sculptures of characters from The Wind in the Willows dotted all around the walk. Although they were aimed at entertaining the children, Mac found them quite delightful too. He was just about to sit down and take his first rest when he heard a scream.

It was just like the one in his dream.

He hurried towards it and came to a path that was darkened by the branches of the low trees that hung over it. He had the surreal feeling that he was back in the dream again. He moved on and he saw a small dog up ahead sniffing a tree. It had a lead on but no owner at the end of it. He went on and saw a woman stumble out onto the path.

'Help her,' she pleaded. 'Help her, please.'

She pointed to the side of the path. Mac looped Terry's lead over a tree branch and went closer. In amongst the trees a young girl was lying on her back. Her right hand was lying palm upwards so Mac quickly felt at her exposed wrist for a pulse. There was none. Her flesh felt icy cold. He backed off a few steps and looked at her.

He shivered but this time it wasn't the lazy wind.

She was so young, too young to be lying there dead. Unlike the dream there was nothing written on her forehead and her eyes were already open. He found his gaze drawn to her open lips.

They had blood red lipstick on.

Chapter Two

Detective Superintendent Dan Carter walked quickly up the path. DI Andy Reid came behind him, trying to keep up. They could see Mac up ahead looking at something in the trees.

'What have you got?' Dan said when he was still twenty or so yards off.

He'd been planning on going shopping with his wife when he'd gotten the call. He'd only been told that a body had been found in Radley Meadows. Andy had gotten the call too and they'd arrived at almost the same time. He knew just from looking at Mac that it wasn't going to be good.

Mac didn't answer, he just nodded to his right.

Dan stopped and looked down. There lay the unmoving body of a young girl aged around fourteen or fifteen. She had long black hair and red lipstick on. There was another splash of red, a stream of blood that had trickled out of her right ear. She had a long black dress on over which she wore a fur-lined black denim jacket. Patches on the jacket said 'Bauhaus', 'Sisters of Mercy' and 'Christian Death'. The dress was made of black velvet. It was long and should have gone down to her ankles but instead it was rucked up just above her knees. She wore black lace-up work boots that clashed with the dress. He supposed that was the point. There was a black waterproof blanket on the ground, half of which was trapped underneath the body.

'Christ!' Dan said to no-one in particular. He turned to face Andy, 'Can you get on to Operations and see if anyone's been reported missing?'

11

He looked at the girl once more and then turned to Mac.

'Who found her?'

'She did,' Mac said pointing to a woman who was sitting on a bench some fifty yards away.

She was in her late twenties and she was being consoled by an older woman. Two dogs were sniffing around each other nearby. Terry wanted to join in too but his lead was too short. Dan marched towards the two women. He introduced himself and showed them his warrant card.

'Was it you who found the body?' he asked the younger woman.

'Yes, I was just walking my dog Bonnie, I do it most mornings at around this time. I was just taking the path through the trees back to my car when I saw her...'

She stopped and shook her head as she tried to stop the tears coming. Dan waited for her to collect herself.

'I thought that she was asleep at first but her eyes were open and then I saw the blood. I've never seen a dead person before. I'm afraid that I just went to pieces.'

'What did you do then?'

'I screamed, I think, then the man with the crutch there came,' she said pointing to Mac. 'He took me away, sat me down here and then called the police.'

'Did you touch the body or anything around it?' Dan asked.

'God no!' she replied giving Dan a horrified look. 'I couldn't believe what I was seeing so I took a few steps towards it. I thought that she might have been asleep but, when I saw the blood, I didn't go any closer.'

Dan turned to the older woman.

'What about you?' he asked.

'I haven't been anywhere near it, thank God,' she said. 'I heard the scream and the gentleman there

12

asked me to look after this lady. She told me that she'd found a dead body and, believe me, this is as near as I want to get to it.'

'Can you both please wait here until someone comes and takes your names and addresses,' Dan said. 'You'll both also need to make a statement.'

He walked back towards Mac.

'Thankfully, it looks as if the crime scene hasn't been contaminated. Forensics should be here fairly soon. What do you think?'

'While it's always possible that it could have been an accident of some sort, the position of her dress suggests something of a sexual nature, rape or attempted rape perhaps,' Mac replied. 'We'll know for sure once forensics have a look. Then there's the fact that she was a Goth.'

'A Goth?' Dan said. 'Oh yes, the black clothes. There was a case a while back, wasn't there?'

'Yes, around ten or twelve years ago, two young Goths were assaulted in a park up North somewhere,' Mac replied. 'They were assaulted just because of what they were wearing. A young girl died from her injuries. She was only twenty and she'd been kicked in the head repeatedly. Five very brave young men went to prison for it.'

'Yes, the blood coming from her ear suggests some sort of head trauma, doesn't it?' Dan said. 'Do you think that this might be some sort of hate crime then?'

Mac had no idea so he just shrugged.

Andy joined them.

'I'm sorry but it took me a while to get through. We've only had one missing person call and that was for a young man in his early twenties. I've asked them to call me straight away if they get anything else.'

'She's so young. Someone must be worried that she's not come home,' Dan said with a frown.

13

'It's early yet and it's Saturday,' Mac said. 'They might not have noticed that she's missing yet.'

'Perhaps,' Dan said. 'Andy, the uniforms should be here soon. Can you get them to mount guard at the entrance to the car park? Also tell them that nothing comes in or out of the site without my authorisation. Get them to close the road for a couple of hundred yards either side of the entrance and tell everyone to park there. After that I'd like you to have a quick scout around and see if there's somewhere close by that we can use as an incident room,' Dan asked. 'I'll call the team and tell them that their weekend has been cancelled. As of now all other cases are to be parked.'

Andy walked quickly off in the direction of the car park.

When Dan turned around, he saw that Mac was still staring at the dead girl. She was so like the girl in his dream, in fact he started to wonder if she actually was the girl in his dream but he dismissed this thought quickly. He didn't believe that it was possible to see the future but it troubled him nonetheless.

'Are you alright, Mac?' Dan asked.

Dan had never seen him quite so affected by a murder. He supposed that the girl's young age might be the cause. He also thought that Mac looked a little disoriented for a moment, as if he'd just woken up or something.

'I'm sorry but I didn't sleep well last night. I'm just feeling a bit tired, that's all,' Mac said.

Dan took his excuse at face value. Mac wasn't about to tell him why he couldn't sleep though.

He looked up as four men in white all-in-ones marched up the path towards them in single file. They were all carrying black cases of varying sizes. Mac recognised the lead figure as being Bob Yeardley. He'd worked with him on a few cases now and he felt grateful that he was in charge of the forensics team. He wanted whoever killed the girl to be caught and he knew that Bob was very good at his job.

Bob took a quick look at the crime scene.

'Do we know who she is?' he asked.

Dan shook his head.

'Anyway, I'm glad that you had the sense to park your cars out on the road,' Bob said. 'We've taped off the entrance to the car park so tell your people that no-one else is to enter the cordon until we've finished. Whoever did this may have driven here and, if they did, they might have left some tyre marks. Do you know who the cars out there in the car park belong to?'

'One of them is mine and the other two belong to those two ladies sitting up there,' Mac said.

'Well, the cars will have to stay where they are for the time being. I'd like to get some casts of their tyres,' Bob said. 'Oh, talking of casts, can you ask the two ladies to drop their shoes into the station? Oh, and I'll need yours too, Mac.'

'No problem,' Mac replied.

'Call me straight away if you find any ID on her,' Dan said.

'We can get back to the car park this way,' Mac said pointing towards where the two women were sitting.

Mac untied Terry from the tree and went after Dan.

'Could you both please follow me to the car park?' Dan said to the two women. 'Please walk off the path behind me in single file.'

They collected their dogs and followed Dan back around to the car park. There, they could see that two uniformed officers were already guarding the entrance and that they'd deployed a large 'Crime Scene – Do Not Enter' sign on the roadside. A car pulled up on the road. It was Andy who was back already.

Dan asked the two women to wait on the other side of the tape.

'We're in luck,' Andy said as he climbed out of his car. 'There's a farm just over the road and they have a building that they use for auctions every now and then. It's just a big barn really but it should be perfect for us.'

'And we can start using it straightaway?' Dan asked.

'Sure,' Andy said as he produced a set of keys.

'Okay, I'll arrange to get some office equipment and a data hook-up moved in,' Dan said.

'What about them?' Mac asked nodding towards the two women.

'The incident room will take a few hours to get up and running,' Dan replied. 'When I get a minute, I'll get someone to take them to the station. They can make a statement there.'

'I'll go with them, if you like,' Mac volunteered. 'I need to hand my shoes in too.'

He knew that he wouldn't be missing much. Dan would be busy for the next few hours just getting the team up and running.

'Thanks, Mac,' Dan said. 'I'll get a car to you as soon as I can.'

Dan went off with Andy to have a look at their new incident room. Mac turned around and introduced himself to the two women.

'My name's Emma,' the younger woman said. 'Emma Dawson.'

'And I'm Genny Albrighton,' the older woman said. 'It was lucky that we had a policeman to hand. I was wondering why you able to react so quickly. I hadn't got a clue what to do and I didn't even see anything.'

Emma gave her a look that suggested that she too wished that she hadn't seen anything.

A few minutes later a police car pulled up. The young policewoman behind the wheel confirmed that she was their lift to Letchworth police station. Both Emma and Genny seemed to be grateful to be leaving the Meadows behind them. Their driver looked a little surprised when she found out that her passengers were six in all. Emma and Genny sat in the back and, luckily, their dogs seemed to get on well with each other. Mac sat in the front but Terry didn't seem to like the arrangement at all. He kept looking towards the back seats with soulful eyes and letting out mournful little whines. He did this for most of the drive back.

Mac decided that they should go by their houses first so that they could drop their dogs off and swap their footwear. He asked the two women for their addresses. Emma lived nearby in Norton on the fairly new Drymanshouse Estate while Genny lived just around the corner from the police station in Letchworth which was very convenient.

'So, what happens now?' Genny asked.

'We'll drive you both home where you'll need to drop your dog off and then swap your shoes. Our forensics team will need the ones that you're wearing as a comparison just in case they find any footprints,' Mac replied. 'After that we'll take you to the police station in Letchworth. Once we're at the station, I'll get a uniformed officer to take your statements. They'll also give you some contact numbers in case you might need any support such as counselling. While you're doing that I'll need to go home and change my shoes too. However, please remain at the police station until I tell you that you can go. I'll need to check that the police team doesn't have any further questions for you.'

'Okay,' Emma said. 'I just want to get it over with.'

She turned her face to the window, muttered something about a 'bloody nightmare' and then didn't say another word until they pulled up outside her house.

Chapter Three

Mac looked around while he waited. Emma's house was one of several very large houses that were tucked away down one of the many discrete and strange-sounding streets that comprised the Drymanshouse Estate. The little cul-de-sac that Emma lived on was called 'Swmhagan' and Mac thought that it sounded vaguely Scandinavian. He made a mental note to find out what it meant.

The estate was landscaped so that every house had its privacy and he had to admit that, from what he'd seen, the houses themselves were quite impressive. What he hadn't been so impressed with was the huge metal gates that kept the hoi-polloi out of the estate. Emma had to take her phone out and touch the screen a few times before the gates opened to let them in.

Mac had always wondered at the very rich. They always seemed to prefer the company of other rich people for some reason. Personally, he'd found that a lot of really well-off people tended to be quite boring as all they seemed to be interested in talking about was money.

Emma's house had at least six bedrooms. Mac idly wondered if she was planning for lots of children or something.

'Well, someone's worth a pound or two,' Genny said as they waited for Emma to re-emerge from her house. 'I came and had a look at one of these when they were building them a few years ago.'

'Why, were you interested in buying one?' Mac asked as he turned around in his seat.

'Oh, God no!' Genny replied with a laugh. 'I'm a retired office manager, I couldn't possibly afford anything like this.' On seeing Mac's puzzled expression, she continued. 'On the odd Sunday me and the husband like to go and look at a few houses that are up for sale and see what we think of them. It's always interesting and, followed by a nice coffee and a piece of cake at David's Cafe, it makes for a good day out.'

'So, you're not thinking of moving then?'

'Oh, God no!' Genny said again. 'I've got a lovely little two-bedroomed bungalow on The Quadrant and I've got the loveliest neighbours that you could ever have. Why on earth would I want to move?'

Mac smiled and shook his head. He'd heard of people who went looking at houses for sale with no intention of buying but he'd never actually met one before. He supposed that they viewed it as a sort of free entertainment.

The front door opened and Emma came out carrying a backpack. She climbed into the car and then turned her face away.

She didn't look very happy, Mac thought. Then again that was understandable given the circumstances. She didn't speak until they were just coming into Letchworth.

'How long do you think we'll be?' she asked.

'Not too long. An hour or so I'd guess,' Mac replied. 'Do you have to be in work or something?'

'No, I've called my husband. Saturday's normally quite a busy day for us but he told me to take the day off. We normally work together, you see. My husband owns a company that gives financial advice, you know, tax and investments and so on,' Emma explained.

'Is he coming to pick you up?' Mac asked.

'No...no, he won't be coming. He's got some very important meetings you see and he can't...'

Mac never got to hear exactly what her husband couldn't do as Emma wiped away a tear and turned her face away to look out of the window. Genny gave

Mac a glance that told him that she was less than impressed with Emma's husband. He noticed the older woman take hold of her hand. Emma gripped it tightly.

Genny's house was just as she'd described it. However, as small as it was, it looked like a real home. There was a neat little garden in front with a well-trimmed hedge. The outside of the house was a gleaming white and that, combined with the distinctive peaked roof and an old-fashioned wooden door painted dark green, meant that the house could only be in Letchworth.

Genny quickly went inside and returned a few minutes later without her dog but with a plastic carrier bag which Mac guessed contained her shoes. The police station was literally just around the corner.

Mac got out with the two women and explained to the duty sergeant what they were doing there. The sergeant took possession of the women's shoes and said that he'd get someone to take their statements straight away. Mac told him that he too would need to make a statement after he'd dropped his dog home.

Terry gave a sad little whine as Mac closed the front door behind him. Mac knew that he would only have a couple of hours to wait until his neighbour Amanda came to give him his daily walk. It didn't stop him feeling any less guilty though.

Emma and Genny were waiting in the lobby when he came out of the interview room having given his statement.

'I've already called my boss and he said that it will be okay for you both to go home for now,' Mac said. 'We'll be in touch if we need to ask any further questions.'

The two women looked at Mac with some relief.

'So, what do we do now?' Emma asked looking a little lost.

'Well, I don't know about you, love, but I'm going for a drink,' Genny said. 'I should think that we both deserve one after the morning that we've had.'

Emma was just about able to manage a smile as she said, 'Well, that's the nicest thing anyone's said to me today. Come on, I could do with a really stiff one myself.'

Emma started walking towards the Magnets.

Genny turned to Mac and said, 'Don't worry, I'll look after her.'

Mac watched her as she caught up with Emma. They linked arms as if they were old friends. He made a mental note to contact Genny in a day or two and find out what had happened. Sometimes the people who find murder victims can be more involved than they let on. However, Mac didn't seriously think that this was the case here. He was just curious about Emma, that's all.

After making his statement, he asked his driver if she could drop him off at the new incident room. Mac guessed that it should be well on the way to being set up by now. They pulled up outside what looked like a barn. It looked like a barn from the inside too. Mac had worked in places like this before. Even with a couple of industrial-sized heaters it could still be cold and draughty.

Desks had been set up on the concrete floor and workmen were installing some partitions in the far two corners of the wide-open space.

For interview rooms, Mac guessed.

Most of the team were already there and they were gathered around a whiteboard that had been set on an easel. Two women stood uncertainly at the edge of the scrum. They were both new to Mac.

Dan waved at Mac to come over. He pulled him over to one side away from the team.

'You're just in time, Mac,' he said in low voice. 'We're about to have our first briefing. I've been thinking and I want to ask you for a favour.'

Dan quickly explained what he wanted. Mac told him that he was more than happy to do as he was being asked. They returned to the whiteboard.

'I'd first of all like to introduce Inspector Jean Watson. She'll be our liaison with the uniformed police for the duration of the investigation.'

Mac, and the rest of the team, turned to look at the new member of the team. She gave them all a nervous smile back.

She was snub-nosed and quite attractive. She was a little taller than Mac and her blonde hair was screwed up into a tight bun at the back of her head. He guessed that she was in her late thirties although she could have been younger.

'And I'd also like to introduce the newest member of our team. She'll be with us until Leigh is ready to return to work. This is Carrie Mortimer,' Dan said gesturing towards a young woman who was clearly embarrassed being under everyone's gaze.

She was about the same height as Mac and her brown hair had been cut into an efficient bob. She had large black-rimmed spectacles on and an expression of mild puzzlement. For some reason he could easily picture her behind the desk in a library.

'Carrie has joined us from the Cambridge detective team and she comes highly recommended. I'll leave you all to introduce yourselves later. Okay, let's start. Mac, perhaps you can kick us off and tell us how the girl was found,' Dan said.

He took them through the surreal events of the morning in as much detail as he could. He didn't mention his dream though.

'What's your take on the two women who found her?' Dan asked when he'd finished.

'They seemed genuine enough,' Mac replied, 'but I'll follow up on them anyway. Do we know who she is yet?'

'Not yet,' Dan replied. 'She had no identification on her and she only had these in the pockets of her jacket.'

He stuck a photo on the whiteboard. It showed around six pounds in coins, a half-empty packet of paper tissues and a tube of lipstick. Mac guessed that it was bright red.

'What? Where's her phone?' DI Jo Dugdale exclaimed in some surprise. 'Girls at her age seem to have their phones permanently glued to their hands, don't they?'

'I agree that's a bit strange,' Dan replied. 'They haven't found a phone as yet but we have a contingent of uniforms doing a fingertip search of the area.'

'Perhaps her killer took it away for some reason,' DS Kate Grimsson suggested.

'Yes, that thought occurred to us too. It's highly likely that she might have known her killer and, who knows, she might have even had a photo of them on her phone so it's important that we find it,' Dan said. 'Anyway, our first priority is to identify our Jane Doe. Martin over there is putting the finishing touches to a photo of the dead girl.'

Mac glanced over and saw Martin Selby, the team's computer and data specialist, in a corner hunched over his laptop. He smiled. He hadn't noticed him there.

Dan continued, 'It's likely that she's a local girl and, with the help of Jean's colleagues, I'm hoping that we can get an ID fairly quickly. They'll be interviewing everyone in the adjacent area. Once we know who she is then we can really get to work.'

'What about using the press?' DC Gerry Dugdale asked.

'I suppose it won't be long until this leaks out and we'll be descended on,' Dan replied. 'However, I'd like to try and get a quick ID before we give any details out to the press. I don't want her parents hearing about their daughter's death through the TV or from the front of the newspaper, if I can help it. However, if we don't get a quick ID, then we may have no choice but to get them involved. Anyway, the main point of this briefing is to discuss how we're going to organise ourselves going forward. I'd like us to stay in our teams of two and we'll keep the current pairings of Adil and myself, Kate and Tommy and Andy and Gerry. Carrie, you'll be with Jo.'

Carried nodded and smiled over at Jo.

'I take it that, for a case like this, we'll be pulling in some help?' Andy asked.

'Absolutely. However, I'm keen to keep it all under our control. Some of the local detective teams will be helping us out but I don't want anyone going off half-cock and so the local detectives will work directly under you. They'll report directly to you too so, in effect, you'll be managing your own sub-teams. You can also call in as many uniformed officers as you'll need at any one time and you can do that through Jean here. Ask for whatever you need, our bosses are quite willing to throw the kitchen sink at this one.'

The team all gave each other a thoughtful look. This investigation was obviously going to be a little different.

'I've decided on doing it this way after how we reacted to Leigh's shooting. Our response, at least in part, was a bit of a mess and I don't want that happening again. However, something good did come out of it and that's how Martin and Mac here handled the inform-ation coming in. So, while you can call me at any time if you need a decision about anything, everything else has to go through Mac and Martin,' Dan said. 'That's everything; every report, request, document, photo, witness statement, note, even any suspicions or ideas that you might have.'

The team turned to look at Mac. He'd been thinking about Dan's request to act as part of the information hub for the team again and he was glad that Dan could see the value in it. If they didn't get a quick result then it would inevitably turn into a sprawling and possibly disjointed investigation. In that case, lots of information could disappear down the organisational cracks if they weren't very careful. Dan's idea should help with that. Anyway, Mac knew that he would be more useful sifting the information as it came in rather than running around knocking on doors. It would also be a lot easier on his back.

'Make sure that you tell the people working under you to do the same. Also warn them that, if they fail to do as asked, I'll take them off the case immediately,' Dan said as he gave the team a look that assured them that he meant what he said. 'Mac and Martin will once again be working as a team on this one so, if you have any data-based requests, you can contact either of them. Jean will also be working with them as the third member of the team to ensure that we have good communication with her colleagues who will be doing the majority of the door to doors and other interviews. I'll trust Mac and Martin to pass on anything that I should know about and I'll also be asking them to update us at every briefing. This could turn out to be a long and very drawn-out investigation and, with the amount of manpower that we'll be throwing at it, I want to make sure that nothing gets missed.'

'So, how is that going to work in practice?' DC Tommy Nugent asked.

'That's a good question,' Dan replied. 'Martin has put together a sort of data timeline of the whole investigation and he and Mac will be electronically logging everything we get in, whatever it is, against that timeline. Martin's also set up a search form that we can all use so we'll be able to filter the data in lots of other ways too; by location, by witness, by document type, by team and so on. The chances are that the really useful information is going to come to us in bits and pieces and so I'm trusting that Mac will be able to pull a few needles out of some haystacks for us. He'll be reviewing everything that comes in and, luckily for him and us, that's something he quite enjoys doing anyway.'

Dan was interrupted by Martin as he ambled over to the group.

'What do you think?' Martin said as he handed Dan a photo.

'I think that you've done a great job. We'll go with this one,' Dan said. 'Jean will tell you who you'll need to send copies to.'

'No problem,' Martin replied.

Jean followed Martin back to his desk.

Dan turned and stuck the photo to the whiteboard. Everyone in the team came closer to get a better look.

The girl he'd seen in the woods had been made ugly by death but this girl was alive and she was very pretty. She had a long symmetrical face with eyes of piecing blue. Her face was framed with long jet-black hair parted in the middle. Mac guessed from her complexion and eye colour that her hair had been dyed. The eyes seemed to be looking at him, asking a question.

Unfortunately, Mac had no answers.

Yet.

Chapter Four

The team busied themselves setting up their desks and laptops. Once that was done then all they could do was wait. Everyone just sat there, still with their outdoor coats and jackets on.

It would take the heaters quite a while to warm up such a large space, Mac thought. If they ever did that is.

Mac made a beeline for Tommy. He wanted to know how his daughter was getting on.

'Oh, she's fine but she really doesn't like being at home all the time,' Tommy replied giving Mac a glum look.

'I'd guess that she's getting a bit snarky at times, isn't she?'

Tommy nodded.

'She always hated being bored but, don't worry, it will pass. Her mother was the same towards the end of her pregnancy so just stick with it.'

'I know but it all seems so...' Tommy said ending his sentence with a sigh.

'I know, the waiting is the really hard part but it won't be long now.'

Tommy didn't look all that convinced.

Mac made his way to Dan's desk.

'I take it that there's nothing else from forensics yet?' Mac asked.

Dan shook his head.

'Bob said that he'd call if he found anything we should know about.'

Mac could see that Dan was fidgety. He guessed that, like the rest of the team, he felt somewhat helpless.

They desperately needed to know who the girl was before they could jump-start the investigation.

They all ended up sitting at their desks waiting. Just waiting.

Jean's radio woke up. She spoke to someone and then passed it to Dan. He said 'Yes' as few times and Mac thought that he could detect the hint of a smile. Something had happened. Dan went and had a quick word with Martin before returning to the team.

'We've got an identification,' Dan said as he passed the radio back to Jean. 'A man called Edward Lewin, who lives just up the road from here, has identified our dead girl as Rhiannon Brodeur. He says that she lives on the Drymanshouse Estate but he's not sure exactly at which house.'

Dan looked at the team before continuing.

'Adil and I will go and have a word with Mr. Lewin ourselves but he's also told us that Rhiannon was a pupil at St. Hilda's School in the town. Andy, can you take the rest of the team and start looking at the school? If you can confirm that she was a pupil there then get her address and pass it on to me straight away.'

Dan was interrupted by Martin.

'The address is The Clapper Board, Cifesborene on the Drymanshouse Estate. A Mrs. Angelica Brodeur is listed as living there on the Electoral Register.'

'Thanks, Martin,' Dan said with a smile as he turned back to Andy. 'Okay then, start tracking down her classmates and anyone else at the school who knew her. As I said, keep in touch with Mac and Martin. Now that we have an address, we had better break the news to her family before they find out for themselves.'

Mac intercepted Dan as he made his way out.

'Do you mind if I join you?' he asked. 'There won't be anything coming through for a while.'

'Sure, come on,' Dan replied guessing that Mac was no better at twiddling his thumbs than he was.

A few minutes later Dan pulled up outside the electronic gates that barred their way into the estate. He gave them a sour look before pulling down his window and pressing the button on the intercom.

'Yes?' a tinny voice answered.

'Police. Open the gates,' Dan said tersely.

There was a silence before the tinny voice said, 'Well, I don't know...'

Dan gave Mac a disbelieving look.

'My name is Detective Superintendent Dan Carter and if these gates aren't opened in the next ten seconds, I'll get a team here to take them off at the hinges and we'll sell them to the nearest scrap metal merchant.'

There was no reply other than the gates silently sliding open.

'The address is just given as The Clapper Board, Cifesborene, whatever that is,' Dan said. 'Let's hope that the satnav knows where it's going.'

Luckily it did. They caught glimpses of some truly grand houses as they slowly rolled down the road. Dan turned into a narrow road that had a discrete sign saying 'Cifesborene' and he slowed right down as they all looked for a house called 'The Clapper Board.' Adil saw it first. It had an actual clapper board as used in the movies hanging on a piece of rope. They only saw the house once they pulled into the driveway. It was discretely hidden behind a man-made hillock.

Everything about this place is 'discreet', Mac thought.

They pulled up outside a large house built of a cream-coloured stone that had clearly been kidnapped from the French provinces and dumped in Hertfordshire. The mini-chateau had long decorative windows, a black slate roof and even a little round tower at one end.

Dan looked for a doorbell but couldn't find one. He hopefully pulled on a piece of rope and an actual bell rang. The door was opened by a young Filipino woman dressed in a loose blue blouse and jeans.

'Is Mrs. Angelica Brodeur in?' Dan said as he held out his warrant card.

The young woman looked at it carefully and then gave Dan a worried glance.

'She's still in bed but I can wake her if you like,' she replied.

'Please do,' Dan said. 'It's very important.'

She led them into a marbled lobby that had a grand staircase at the far end.

'You can wait in here,' the young woman said as she opened a door.

They walked into a room that was illuminated by several long windows. Antique tapestries covered large parts of the cream-coloured walls while the furniture was ornate and quite delicate looking. Mac didn't sit down as he honestly didn't think that the chair would take his weight. As he looked around, he couldn't help thinking that the clapper board outside was quite appropriate. Indeed, the whole place looked like a film set.

A woman with tousled hair and sleep-filled eyes burst into the room. She had a pink dressing gown on and a pair of striped pyjamas underneath. She looked at the three policemen with some apprehension.

'Is it Marc?' she asked. 'Has something happened to him?'

'Who's Marc?' Dan asked.

'My husband. Well, my ex-husband, I should say.'

'No, it's nothing to do with your husband. Well, not directly anyway. We're here about Rhiannon.'

'Rhi?' she said giving them a puzzled look. 'What could you possibly want with my daughter? Has she been up to something?'

'Do you know where she is?' Dan said ignoring her question.

She pulled a phone out of her pocket and swiped through a few screens.

'She's upstairs in her room. Do you want me to go and get her?'

'Yes, if you could. Would you mind if we went with you?'

She gave the policemen a strange look but she didn't say no. They followed her up the staircase and along the corridor to the end.

She opened the door a fraction and shouted, 'Rhi, there's someone here to see you.'

There was no sound from the other side of the door.

'She's probably still asleep,' Angelica said. 'Like most teenagers she could sleep for England at times.'

She went inside and closed the door behind her. A minute later the door opened again. Angelica stood in the doorway with a worried look on her face. She had a phone in her hand.

'It's Rhi's phone. She never goes anywhere without it.'

Dan pulled an evidence bag from his pocket.

'Could you place it in here, please?' Dan said as he held the bag open.

'What's going on?' she asked in a near whisper as she dropped the phone into the bag.

'We just need to have a quick look in your daughter's room first, if we may?' Dan said as he nodded to Adil and then to the stairs.

'Yes, yes of course.'

Adil escorted her back downstairs while Dan put on some disposable gloves before opening the door again. Dan ensured that the room was indeed empty. He looked in the large wardrobe and under a bed that looked as if it had been made out of scaffolding tubes.

Mac stood in the doorway and looked on. The room was round. It was obviously in the tower that they'd seen as they drove up. It was totally unlike the rest of the house though. The walls and ceiling were painted black and the ceiling had little glittery stars all over it. The room was untidy with clothing piled up on one side and the dressing table was covered with items of make-up, books and some unopened cardboard boxes. The walls were mostly covered with posters of glum-looking musicians but amongst them Mac noticed some that were a little different.

One contained a series of circles with a five-pointed star in the middle. It said 'The Wheel of the Year'. Another featured what looked like the phases of the moon inside an ornate circular design. Yet another again featured the five-pointed star within what looked like a maze. These posters interested Mac. He took his phone out and took some photos.

'Well, she's definitely not here then,' Dan said looking somewhat disappointed. 'Have you spotted something?'

'Those posters, I've come across something like them before. Can you tell me what the books are about?' Mac said pointing to the dressing table.

Dan bent down so he could read the spines without having to touch the books.

'The top one's called *The Wiccan Book of Spells* and there's also *Wicca: The Guide to Founding Your Own Coven*, plus *Wicca – The Deep Magic of the Wondreth Coven* and lastly *The Book of Thoth*.'

'That would explain these posters too. It looks like Rhiannon was a witch or, at least, she was aspiring to be one. Can you take a photo of the books?' Mac asked as he held out his phone.

Dan took a photo of the spines of the books.

'Do people nowadays really believe in that stuff?' Dan said with a look of disbelief as he handed Mac his phone back.

'They do and I believe that it's growing as well. I saw a programme about it on the TV not long ago,' Mac said. 'They were saying that, while many mainstream churches are reporting falling attendances, more people are turning to alternative religions like Wicca and other pagan beliefs. It's even accepted as a recognised religion, at least as far as the census goes.'

Dan just shook his head in disbelief.

'Anyway, let's leave the bedroom to the forensics team,' Dan said as he shut the door behind him. 'Come on, let's go and tell Mrs. Brodeur that her daughter's dead.'

Mac could tell from Dan's expression that he wasn't looking forward to it.

Angelica stood up as they entered the room. She was about to say something but Dan stopped her. He pulled out his phone and got Martin's photo up.

'Mrs. Brodeur, is this your daughter?'

She looked at the photo and then gave them a puzzled look.

'Well, it certainly looks like her but why are you showing me this? What's she done?'

The penny, however, was beginning to drop and, for the first time, Mac could see real fear in her eyes.

'This is the photo of a girl who was found early this morning in Radley Meadows,' Dan said. 'The girl was dead.'

She looked at Dan as though he'd just grown another head.

'Dead? Rhi can't be dead, I only saw her yesterday. She can't be. You've made a mistake. That's it, it's all a mistake.'

Her face said otherwise and started crumpling as the realisation hit home.

'We had an argument yesterday before I went out. We shouted at each other. We shouted...'

She then broke down completely. Dan sat down beside her and offered her a shoulder to cry on.

'Adil, can you see if you can find the young woman who let us in?' Mac asked.

'Yes, sure.'

He returned a minute later with a surprised looking woman who immediately took Dan's place and started comforting the newly bereaved mother. He managed to get her doctor's name from the young woman.

The three of them left the two women alone and stood in the lobby. Dan called the doctor and then made another call.

'The doctor should be here soon and I've also called Stella,' Dan said. 'Luckily, she's not got much on at the moment.'

'That's Police Constable Stella Ajunwa?' Mac asked.

'Well, she's Sergeant Ajunwa now,' Dan replied. 'We need a good Family Liaison Officer and she's just about the best I've come across.'

Mac could only agree. They'd worked with Stella during the Natasha Barker kidnapping case[2] and she'd done an excellent job.

'I guess that we won't get much out of Mrs. Brodeur for a while,' Dan said. 'Adil, can you stay here until Stella turns up? Make sure that nobody goes into Rhiannon's bedroom until forensics arrive. In the meantime, I want to go and have a word with this Mr. Lewin.'

Before they drove off Dan called Jean and told her that the photo had been identified as Rhiannon by her mother. He asked her to get her colleagues to immediately start knocking doors on the Drymanshouse

---

[2] The Blackness – The fourth Mac Maguire detective mystery

Estate. He wanted every single house on the estate covered by the end of the day.

'Once they start doing that, we'll have the press descending on us,' Dan said with a scowl, 'but it can't be helped.'

They stopped off by Radley Meadows on the way and Dan gave Rhiannon's phone to Bob Yeardley.

'Once you've had a look at it, can you get it straight to Martin Selby? I'm hoping that he can get something useful from it. Have you found anything yet?' Dan asked hopefully.

Bob shrugged, 'Nothing too exciting. We'll need to get it confirmed but we reckon that she died around midnight give or take a couple of hours.'

'So, she's been lying there all night?' Dan asked.

'That's what we think,' Bob replied.

'Any idea what killed her?'

'The autopsy will tell us for sure but it's my guess that it was some sort of blunt force trauma, probably a hammer. However, don't quote me on that.'

Bob was about to turn away when he stopped.

'Oh, we also found a plastic bag in a rubbish bin nearby that contained half a dozen or so empty beer cans. We've bagged them up and sent them off to the lab. It might be nothing but the bag was the last thing in the rubbish bin so you never know.'

'I always hate this part of the investigation,' Dan said with another scowl as they climbed back into the car. 'Nobody seems to know anything for sure.'

Mac knew exactly what he meant.

Chapter Five

Mr. Lewin's house was as unlike the Brodeurs' chateau as was possible. It was small and unpretentious, being a simple country cottage, and it belonged precisely where it was. Indeed, it looked as if it had been occupying that particular space for some centuries. The house had weathered and warped so that it now looked as natural as the trees and fields around it.

The door was opened by a uniformed policeman who ushered them inside. He led them into a tiny cluttered living room. A high bookshelf that was crammed with books lined one wall and books and papers lay in piles on the floor. A fire was lit in the grate and it gave out a cheerful warmth.

The room was inhabited by a man in his late sixties. He was quite thin and his back was stooped. His hair was grey as was his neatly trimmed moustache. He had a white checked shirt on over which he wore an ancient tweed jacket with shiny leather elbow patches. This was all topped off by a mustard-coloured bow tie.

If Mac had to guess, he'd put his money on him being a retired academic.

Dan introduced himself and Mac before quickly cutting to the chase.

'How did you come to know Rhiannon Brodeur?' he asked.

'She came to my door one day a few months ago,' the old man replied in a firm and resonant voice. 'She had a question for me.'

'What was that?'

'She asked me why her street was called 'The Bastards',' he said.

Dan and Mac looked at each other in confusion.

'Let me explain. I'm a retired university professor and Anglo-Saxon studies was, and still is, my speciality. I wasn't especially pleased when I heard about the estate being built. Somewhere on that site there's an old seventh-century settlement but the developers weren't interested in that. I'd been trying to get one of the local archaeologists to have look at it for a while but I needn't have bothered. As soon as the developers bought it, they ploughed the whole lot up just so that they could make a killing from people who had more money than sense. Anyway, they heard from someone that I knew a lot about the history of the area and so they came to see me. They were looking for a theme, they said. They wanted a brand that would sound good to potential buyers. I mentioned that, according to some ancient Anglo-Saxon chronicles, there was a *drymanshus* somewhere in the area.'

'What's that?' Dan asked.

'In Old English it means 'the Magician's House'. Whoever lived there must have been quite well-known for the time as it's mentioned more than once in the few documents that have made it down through the years. Now, while a 'magician' might have indicated that the person who lived there was a wizard, or indeed even a necromancer, it's more likely that they were a healer of some sort. Anyway, that was just what they wanted. They called it the 'Drymanshouse Estate' and started using words like 'magical' and 'spell-binding' in their promotions.'

The old man stopped and a smile briefly crossed his face.

'They came back to me with a list of words that they wanted me to translate into Old English for the street names. They were all based around magic. So, I gave them some exotic sounding Anglo-Saxon words and they seemed pleased enough with them.'

'I take it that the words that you gave them weren't quite what they ordered,' Mac said.

'No, indeed they were not,' the old man replied with a shake of his head. 'They still think that 'Cifeborene' means 'The Magic Wand'.'

'And it really means 'The Bastards',' Dan said.

'That's right,' the old man said. 'It was petty of me perhaps but they were so annoying and so sure of themselves.'

'So, what does 'Swmhagan' mean then?' Mac asked. He then turned to Dan and explained. 'It's where the woman who found Rhiannon lives.'

'The pig-pens,' the old man replied with a slight shrug of his shoulders.

'How did Rhiannon find out about this?' Dan asked.

'She's a really clever girl. She somehow found an Old English translator on the internet and discovered what the street names really meant. She asked around and found that I had supplied the words and so she came to see me.'

'Was she upset about it?' Dan asked.

'Upset? Oh no, exactly the opposite really. She thought that it was all a wonderful joke. Indeed, I think that's why she warmed to me right from the start. However, she got really interested in the *drymanshus* when I told her about it and so I let her have access to some of my materials.'

'How often did she visit you?' Dan asked.

'Oh, I'd guess about once a week or so. I must admit that I always looked forward to her visits. She was very intelligent and she'd have made a good historian if...'

The old man stopped and wiped an eye before gathering himself.

Dan gave him a moment before asking, 'How would you describe your relationship with Rhiannon?'

'I'd like to think that we were friends, friends with shared interests, I suppose.'

'Did you know that Rhiannon was interested in Wicca?' Mac asked.

'Oh, yes,' the old man replied. 'She explained it to me one day and I told her that it didn't sound too much different to what the *dryman* might have believed in. I think that her interest in magic was just a teenaged thing but I was really hoping that her interest in history might have been a bit longer lived. Anyway, she told me that she was looking forward to this month's full moon especially.'

'Why this full moon?' Mac asked.

'Because it was a Blood Moon, of course, and we're also coming up to the *Blodmonath*, or Blood Month, the Anglo-Saxon festival where they killed and feasted on the animals that they wouldn't be able to feed over the winter. Rhiannon thought that it was a very magical time as just about everyone did in years gone by. I mean, we know nowadays that it's simply a lunar eclipse, the Earth blocking the sun's rays from reaching the moon, and we know that it's red because of the little bit of light that gets reflected back from the Earth. However, the ancients saw it as an omen and not always a good one at that. It's even in the Bible. In the Book of Joel it says, 'The sun will turn into darkness, and the moon into blood, before the great and terrible day of the Lord comes.' Something like that. Anyway, Rhiannon thought that it was a time for some very special magic.'

'Have you any idea what she meant by that?' Mac asked.

'No, I'm sorry. She was quite closed-lipped about her magic and the coven...'

'She had a coven?' Dan asked.

'Oh yes, every half-decent witch needs a coven,' the professor said. 'All I can remember is that she said something about thanking the Goddess for something but she never said exactly what for.'

Dan looked at the old man for a moment before asking his next question.

'Did you ever find Rhiannon sexually attractive?'

The old man shook his head again.

'I was waiting for you to ask that one. No, I didn't and I hope that I wouldn't have even when I had a sex drive. She was just a child and nearly the same age as my own granddaughter. Unfortunately, she lives in America now and so I don't get to see much of her.'

'What do you mean by 'even when you had a sex drive'?' Dan asked.

'Well, a couple of years ago I was diagnosed with cancer of the prostate. My oncologist recommended that I should have it removed. He warned me that it might also remove my sex drive but that was fine with me. My wife had died a few years before and she was the only woman that I had ever felt passionate about anyway. I've found that not having a sex drive, and the constant thoughts that go with it, to be incredibly liberating. Plato had it right when he said that the male libido was like being chained to a madman. I've found that having no sex drive can be very restful.'

Dan and Mac exchanged looks. It certainly made him less of a suspect, in Mac's mind at least.

They left the old man to his thoughts. Mac looked back as he left the room and he saw a look of deep sadness pass over the old man's face.

'Your friend Tim had that operation not long ago, didn't he? Is the professor right about having no sex drive afterwards?' Dan asked.

'Well, it was certainly one of the possible side effects that they told Tim about before he had his operation.'

'Well, I'll get someone to ask his consultant anyway, just to make sure.'

They were about to get into the car when Dan's phone rang.

He listened and then said, 'I'll be right there.'

'That was Adil,' Dan said as he put his phone away. 'Stella's turned up so I'd better go and pick him up.'

'As it's on the way, can you drop me back to the incident room?' Mac asked. 'It's about time I started work.'

'Sure thing,' Dan replied.

The barn was empty except for Martin. Even the workmen had gone. Mac guessed that the rest of the team were still busy hunting down Rhiannon's teachers and schoolmates. It would have been easier for them if it had been a school day and not the weekend.

'Where's Jean?' Mac asked.

'She's gone to the estate to have a word with the uniforms who'll be doing the door-to-door enquiries,' Martin replied. 'She wanted to make sure that they're all aware that everything should come through here and that they all knew how the system works. She should be back soon.'

'Has anything interesting come in yet?' Mac asked as he sat down at his desk.

'Not much,' Martin replied. 'I've sent you a link and a password by email. You should be able to see everything that's been logged onto the timeline to date.'

Mac found the email. There were just two links. One was to a linear timeline that contained a brief description of each item that had logged in plus a link to see the item in full. The other was to a search form where a keyword could be used to filter information.

'That's really clever,' Mac said in admiration.

'It's something that I discussed with Dan a while ago, after Leigh got shot,' Martin said. 'It should allow everyone on the team to access all the information, all of the time.'

'I'll give it a test drive then,' Mac said.

The first item contained the initial photos of the crime scene taken by the forensics team. Even though he'd seen it for himself, he still studied every photo carefully. He looked closely at one that showed the black waterproof blanket. It looked as if Rhiannon must have been sitting on it when she was killed but only half of the blanket lay underneath her body.

Had someone else been sitting there with her? Mac thought. The way it was positioned it looked like there would certainly be room for two on the blanket.

The next item was a photo of the plastic bag that they'd found in a rubbish bin near the body. Although the bag's handles had been tied, the plastic was thin enough for him to make out its contents. The bag contained at least five large cans of Sapporo lager, perhaps more.

Sapporo was a premium Japanese beer and it was quite expensive. It would be well beyond the pocket of the average street drinker but, he supposed, not beyond someone who lived on the Drymanshouse Estate. He'd be interested to see what forensics got from the cans.

The next items were around the initial identification of the dead girl by Mr. Lewin and the confirmation from Mrs. Brodeur. While he was looking, a new item popped into view. Mac opened it.

It was a note from Andy Reid. He had managed to interview the headmistress of St. Hilda's and she had confirmed to him that Rhiannon was a pupil there. Unfortunately, she hadn't known Rhiannon that well and so there was little else that she could add. While he was looking another note popped up. This listed all of Rhiannon's teachers and classmates. Andy wasn't hanging around.

'I take it that we'll be getting all the witness statements on the timeline too?' Mac asked.

'Yes, we should do but that may take a little time,' Martin replied. 'Most statements are still written down on paper and signed so we might have to wait for someone to scan them in first. If they're interviewing a lot of witnesses then I'd guess that we might get them in batches.'

This made sense to Mac.

'Getting a bit bored already?' Martin asked with a smile. 'Don't worry this is just the lull before the storm. You'll have plenty to do before long. Anyway, there was one thing that I wanted to show you as it's a little different to how we did it before. I've already taken Jean through it.'

Martin showed him once again how to attach keywords to an item using the new format. He said that, as before, when Mac reviewed each document or photo it would help immensely if he also reviewed the keywords and added more if required.

'When one of the team is looking for something in the case file, the keywords are a large part of how they'll find it by using search,' Martin said. 'So, just think of what words the rest of the team might naturally use when looking for something and make sure that they're all there.'

'What about witness statements?' Mac asked.

'Although the signed copies will be scanned, I've asked that they be saved as searchable PDFs. That means that you'll be able to search for any words contained in the PDF. I'll be checking them as they come in but feel free to add any keywords that you think might be useful.'

Mac practised by going back to the start and looking at the keywords and descriptions attached to each of the photos. After a few more questions and even more explaining from Martin, Mac felt that he was getting the hang of it again.

While he was waiting Mac went on to the Amazon website and had a look at the books that had been on Rhiannon's dressing table. He bought e-book versions of all of them. He had no idea if Rhiannon's interest in the occult had anything to do with her death but it intrigued him and he wanted to know more.

Another item popped up on the timeline. It was a note from Dan. Stella had told him that Mrs. Brodeur had now recovered enough to give them a statement. She was now taking her to Letchworth Police Station along with her assistant who Mac discovered was called Terri Ocampo. Dan was going to meet her there.

Mac guessed that this might have also saved the bereaved mother the sight of the white-suited forensics team crawling all over her house. For some reason that usually brought the reality of the situation all too forcefully home for the victim's relatives.

Over the next hour and a half, notes popped up from the team giving brief outlines of the interviews they were carrying out but there was nothing of substance as yet.

'Here you go, Mac,' Martin said.

A new item had popped up. It was the statements given by Rhiannon's mother and her assistant. Mac smiled. He opened them up and started reading them avidly. He'd just finished reading them for the second time when Jean arrived. She looked a little flustered.

'I'm sorry about that,' she said. 'It took a little longer than I thought it would to get the message home to the units doing the door to doors. Not only that but I had to go and speak to one of our technical people too. Anyway, they've assured me that you'll get duplicates of everything that goes into our system. They warned me that there's going to be a lot of information coming in once they start the door to doors off.'

'Yes, that could be a problem,' Martin said. 'Mac, I think it might be a good idea if Jean reviews everything that the uniforms come up with and you review everything else. You might never get through it all otherwise.'

'That sounds like it could work,' Mac replied. 'What do you think, Jean?'

'That sounds great,' she replied. 'It will keep me busy too. I was a bit worried about what I'd be doing.'

She did indeed look relieved at having something concrete to do.

'Martin, can you set a shared folder up for us within the system?' Mac asked. 'It would be good if we could quickly place information somewhere that we might want to share with each other or read up on later.'

'No problem,' Martin said. 'By the way, was there anything exciting in Mrs. Brodeur's statement?'

'I don't know about exciting but it was interesting,' Mac replied. 'However, the strange thing is that neither statement really shed much light on Rhiannon herself, you know, what type of person she was. According to her mother she was an independent girl who got herself up for school every day. She said that Rhiannon was doing well at school and had lots of friends there. However, she admitted that's she hadn't actually seen a school report or talked to a teacher since Rhiannon had joined the school. She also didn't know the names of any of her friends. I get the feeling that she didn't really know her own daughter all that well. She was also sure that Rhiannon didn't know anyone else on the estate.'

Mac was thoughtful for a moment.

'That last one was a bit surprising or so I thought,' Mac said. 'Rhiannon took a taxi back from school every day and then seemed to spend every evening in her bedroom. However, they have apps for everything these days so it's quite possible that she could have contacted other teenagers on the estate that way. Martin, can you bear that in mind when you have a look at her phone?'

'Sure thing,' Martin replied.

'Anyway, it seems that her husband, Marc Brodeur, is a film director and he seems to be the flavour of the month in Hollywood at the moment after having had a string of hit movies in France. She said that he paid cash for the house with what he'd earned for just one film.'

'I thought that the name sounded familiar,' Martin said with a smile. 'He directed the last Marvel superhero movie. It was absolutely excellent.'

Mac continued, 'Anyway, he apparently spent ages designing the house with an architect so it would look exactly like a chateau that had once existed in his home town in Picardy. Then, only a year or so later, he fell in love with the leading lady from his latest film and moved back to Paris to be with her. He met his wife on a film set too, he was just a camera operator back then and she was a script consultant. She's a producer now, TV dramas mostly. She said that she works away quite a lot.'

'It sounds as if poor Rhiannon might have been a bit neglected,' Jean said. 'Dad in Paris and mum working away.'

'Yes, I'd guess that she was probably lonely but there was someone else who she might have talked to,' Mac said. 'They employed a woman called Monique Ashton who worked from Monday to Friday as a cook and housekeeper. She originally worked for Mr. Brodeur's family in France and she came over with him when he married. She's now married herself and she lives near Welwyn somewhere. Dan left a note saying that he was on his way to see her.'

Mac stood up and stretched. He saw some movement outside and went to the window for a look. A small group of pressmen were waiting outside the gate, cameras in hand.

'It didn't take them long,' Mac said.

'Who?' Jean asked.

'The press. If her father's as famous as Martin says he is then they're going to be very interested in this case. That will certainly make Dan happy.' Seeing Jean's puzzled look Mac explained, 'I'm sorry, I was being a little ironic there. Dan hates it when the press gets too interested in a case.'

'You can say that again,' Martin said with feeling. 'We had a case a while back that involved a star from a TV soap opera and a famous rock musician. The press were all over the place. He got so paranoid about them that he said he used to look under his bed each night just in case one of them was hiding there.'

'Well, the press definitely have their uses but they can be really annoying at times too,' Mac said. 'Anyway, I'm wondering what Dan's going to tell them. Rhiannon's not been formally identified as yet and won't be until the autopsy's been completed but I'd guess that he won't wait for that. If we can get some DNA confirmation from forensics then that would definitely help.'

At least fifteen more items had appeared in the few minutes that he'd been away from his screen.

He smiled at Jean and said, 'It's begun.'

Chapter Six

The next few hours flew by as they all tried to keep up with the deluge of information that was constantly being uploaded onto the timeline. Between the three of them, they eventually agreed a way of working that helped a little.

Time flew by and Mac was quite surprised when Dan started calling the team to the white board for the briefing. He looked at his watch. It was nearly six o'clock and far later than he'd thought.

'We're having this briefing now because I'll be giving a press conference outside in about half an hour or so and I want to make sure that I'm as up to date with everything as I can be,' Dan said. 'Andy, what did you find out at the school?'

'It would appear that Rhiannon was a bit of an outsider to say the least,' Andy replied. 'As far as we know, there were just two girls that she was friendly with at school. They were both Goths like her but, even so, it seems that she never really told them that much about herself. For instance, they didn't know that she was into Wicca or that her father was a well-known film director. One of them was quite curious about her and she said that she'd been wanting to visit Rhiannon's house for a while but, although she dropped some heavy hints, it never happened. According to her teachers, she was a quiet girl who was in the top quarter of her class in most subjects but she did especially well in History. She'd recently completed a project around Anglo-Saxon religious practices which her teacher thought very highly of. She wasn't into sports though and generally did the minimum necessary to get by.'

'What about any boys?' Dan asked. 'Or girls come to that?'

'She was definitely into boys or so the friend who had wanted to visit her house said,' Andy replied. 'I got the feeling that she was a bit disappointed about that. She told us that Rhiannon once mentioned that she quite liked a boy called Wolf but, as it's an all-girls school, then he must have been someone that she knew from outside.'

'Wolf? That sounds like a German name, doesn't it?' Dan said. 'Jean, has that name cropped up yet in the door to doors? I'm thinking that it's more likely that this Wolf might be from the estate than anywhere else.'

'I've not heard the name mentioned yet,' Jean replied, 'but we've still got a lot of reports to go through.'

'Let me know straight away if it does,' Dan said. 'Andy, was there anything else?'

'Not really,' Andy shrugged, 'but we've still got quite a few interviews to carry out.'

'Okay, Mac's team,' Dan said.

Mac hadn't been aware that he had a team. He looked over at Jean and Martin who just shrugged and smiled back. It looked as if he was in charge after all.

'We've not come across anything as yet but we've set up a way of working which will hopefully ensure that we don't miss anything,' Mac replied. 'We've been deluged with information and this is likely to carry on for quite a while. So, while Martin is managing the initial loading up and tagging of each item, Jean and I will quickly scan each item and put anything of interest into a shared folder that we can look at later. That way we should be able to keep pace while picking up on anything obvious straight away. We're taking a break every couple of hours or so and during that we brief each other about anything interesting that we've come across. We're hoping that nothing will slip down the cracks that way.'

'That sounds good,' Dan said. 'For us, we've visited Monique Ashby and we tried to interview her but, unfortunately, she was too upset to talk to us. If I'm honest, I think that she was even more upset than Rhiannon's mother was. Anyway, we'll try her again tomorrow. We've also heard from forensics that they've got a sample of hair from a brush found in Rhiannon's bedroom and they're checking it against the DNA of the dead girl. As Mrs. Brodeur won't be able to identify the body formally until tomorrow afternoon at the earliest then that should give us a definitive ident-ification a little sooner.'

'I take it that you're not going to give out Rhiannon's name at the press conference?' Mac asked.

'No, not until we're absolutely sure,' Dan replied. 'Forensics have said that they should have the initial DNA results early tomorrow morning. If they can confirm the girl's identity then I'll hold a press conference tomorrow and give them Rhiannon's name. I'll have to visit Mrs. Brodeur first though and formally give her the news.'

'Giving the press her name should help us,' Andy said. 'It might at least get a few more people to come forward with information.'

'That's what I'm hoping,' Dan said, 'and, while we can interview everyone who lives on the estate and all the teachers and pupils at her school, there might be other people who knew her. People like Edward Lewin who, as far as we can tell, Rhiannon never told anyone else about. It seems that she might have been good at keeping secrets which isn't particularly good news for us.'

'So, what are you going to tell the press then?' Adil asked.

Dan gave this some thought.

'I can only tell them that we found the body of a young girl in Radley Meadows and that we suspect that a murder has been committed,' Dan replied. 'I can't really say more than that although, knowing the press, they'll already have her name after all the interviews we've carried out. Oh, by the way, the father's flying in as we speak. What's the betting that he gets a press reception at the airport? Anyway, I'm hoping to have a word with him in a couple of hours. I doubt that he'll know anything but you never can tell.'

Dan looked around at his team.

'I'm hoping that you'll give this investigation as many hours as you can during the first few days,' Dan said. 'We need to make sure that we leave no stone unturned. There's always the chance that...'

Dan's phone rang. The team never did get to hear what he was about to say.

He listened for a moment and then simply said, 'Okay, we'll be right there.'

They all knew from the look on his face that something serious had happened.

'The uniforms have been carrying out a detailed search around Radley Meadows and they've found the body of another young girl,' Dan said. 'It looks as if she too has died from a head injury.'

It was the worst possible news, Mac thought. Two dead girls made this a most unusual case. But why stop at two?

The thought occurred to him that they might now be looking for a serial killer.

Chapter Seven

Dan had to postpone the press conference until just after nine o'clock. Mac kept himself busy trying to keep up with the rising tide of items that were flooding in. Nothing really stood out though until the first photos of the second murder came through. Mac spent some time studying them.

The girl's body was surrounded by young trees and a light knee-high undergrowth. She lay on her face so that he couldn't see what she looked like. She'd fallen to her knees and then collapsed face down with her hands on either side of her head. Her long hair was black as were her flared jeans and her hooded leather jacket. She also wore black laced-up boots similar to the ones that Rhiannon had worn.

Another Goth, Mac thought.

Another photo, taken from the side, showed the injuries that had killed her. There was also a note from Bob Yeardley. He said that one of the wounds looked quite similar to Rhiannon's first wound in that it was a glancing blow. This had landed on the lower part of her left ear and had partly torn off her ear lobe. This would have then bled profusely. They had found two blood types at the first crime scene, Rhiannon's and someone else's. They were hoping that the second blood trail came from the killer but it now looked as if it might belong to the second victim.

Bob guessed that it was the second blow to her head, around her left temple, that had caused some inter-cranial bleeding but it hadn't killed her instantly. She'd managed to get herself well away from the scene of the attack before collapsing and finally dying. They hadn't found any trace yet that she'd been followed by anyone. Of course, Bob gave the usual caveats about the information not being complete until all the DNA and other tests had been carried out, but Mac knew from experience that Bob's guesses usually weren't too far off the mark.

He sat back and ran the murders through his head. He pictured the two girls sitting on the black waterproof blanket together and then someone coming at them from behind. As the second girl had had been hit on the side of her head, he guessed that Rhiannon was probably the first to be attacked.

Was Rhiannon the real target then? Mac thought. If so, then it could be that the other girl, in being attacked afterwards, was just collateral damage.

The first blow on the back of her head didn't quite connect but the next blow, probably only a split-second later, shattered her skull and Rhiannon died more or less instantly. The second girl was hit twice on the left-hand side of her head.

Had she turned to look at the murderer? Was she already getting to her feet? If she was then that might explain why the blows were a little less severe and why she was able to get away without being followed. Of course, it was late at night too and the blood moon might not have provided that much light.

Was that why the killer hadn't followed the second girl? Even in full moonlight the path under the trees would be dark…

He stopped and chided himself. He'd only seen a few photos and he was already making bricks without straw. He promised himself that he'd try not to think about it too deeply until more information came through.

'Mac, we might have something,' Jean said. 'One of our men on the Drymanshouse Estate has just interviewed a woman. She told him that she'd just gotten back from London and that her daughter's missing.'

'Can you get him on your radio?' Mac asked.

'Sure,' Jean replied.

She contacted the officer and then handed the radio over to Mac.

'PC Drysdale?' Mac asked.

'Yes, sir?' a young and rather nervous voice replied.

'The woman who reported her daughter missing, what's her name and address?'

'Her name is Mrs. Monica Hashley and she lives on Wedehundas.' The constable spelt the street name out letter by letter. 'The house is the third one along and it's called 'JXH House' for some reason.'

'Did she give you a full description of her missing daughter?'

'Oh, yes sir,' Constable Drysdale replied. 'The lady said that her daughter's name was Alicia and that she was fourteen. She had long black hair and she was probably dressed in a black leather jacket and boots as they were missing from her room. I've also got a photo of her.'

Mac and Jean exchanged glances.

'Can you send a copy of the photo here straight away?' Mac asked. 'I take it that you've been told how to send information to the detective team?'

'Yes, sir. No problem, I'll do that right now. Is there anything else that I should be doing, sir?' the constable asked.

'No, you can carry on with your interviews,' Mac said. 'Oh, and very good work, PC Drysdale.'

'Thank you, sir,' the constable said with a glow in his voice.

'Martin, a photo will be coming in and it might just be that of our second victim,' Mac said. 'Can you get a copy to Bob Yeardley's team right away and see if they can confirm that it's her?'

'Sure,' Martin said. 'The photo's just been loaded up.'

Mac took a quick look before he alerted Dan. The girl looked quite a bit younger than Rhiannon but, where

Rhiannon looked confident, this girl somehow looked brittle to Mac. Brittle and sad. Her eyes were blue but he could see that there was a darkness hidden there.

He tore his eyes away and rang Dan.

'I'm with Bob Yeardley now,' Dan said. 'He's told me that you've sent him the photo of a missing girl.'

'Yes, she was reported missing just a short while ago. She looks as if she could be a good fit for the second murder victim.'

'Bob's team are going to move the body now so we'll soon find out,' Dan said.

There was a silence. Mac looked up to see that Jean and Martin had stopped working and they were both looking at him. The silence seemed to last forever but, in reality, it was only three or four minutes before he heard Dan's voice again.

'It's definitely her,' Dan eventually said. 'I see that she was from the Drymanshouse Estate as well. We were going over to interview Rhiannon's father anyway but we'll drop in and see Mrs. Hashley first. Good work everyone.'

Mac told Jean and Martin what Dan had said.

'I'll bet that Dan wasn't too happy about having to tell yet another mother that her daughter was dead,' Martin said. 'That's one part of the job that he's always hated.'

'From the way he sounded, I'd guess that you might well be right there,' Mac replied.

It was a part of the job that Mac had hated too. He decided to change the subject.

'Anyone fancy a coffee?' he asked as he stood up and stretched his back.

They all stopped and chatted about the case for a while before returning to work. Not long afterwards the new photos taken of the second girl had arrived. There could be little doubt that the dead girl was Alicia Hashley. He could see that her eyes were still blue but there was no darkness there. In fact, there was nothing at all.

Mac had trouble getting those eyes out of his head. He threw himself back into his work and became immersed in some of the statements from Rhiannon's schoolfriends. She had been at the school for nearly two years but it was clear that she was still something of a mystery to most of her fellow pupils. The two girls who knew her best said that they used to talk about all the usual things; music, gossip and clothes but, while her two friends talked about their families and relationships, Rhiannon rarely did. All they really knew about her was that her mum worked in TV, although she never said exactly what at, and that she liked a boy called Wolf. Just that after knowing her for two years.

Once again, he thought that Dan had been spot on when he said that Rhiannon was good at keeping secrets. However, everyone needs a real friend, some-one who can be confided in, someone you can tell your deepest secrets to. For a teenager, Mac guessed that the need for such a confidante would be even greater. Did Rhiannon have such a friend?

He had a thought. He went back to one of the state-ments and read through it carefully. He found what he was looking for. It appeared that Rhiannon and her two schoolfriends communicated through having their own 'WhatsApp' group. He had a question for Martin.

'Are there any phone apps out there that can tell you if there are other people using the app in the area around you?'

'There are lots of them,' Martin replied. 'I suppose the most famous one is Grindr but there are loads of others out there. Why do you ask?'

'Rhiannon had a couple of friends at school but she wasn't exactly close to them,' Mac replied. 'I'm just wondering if she might have had friends on the estate where she lived but, the way it's designed, each house is separate and in its own grounds. I doubt that there's anywhere for young people to get together, so how else might they meet up?'

'It's my experience that teenagers will always find a way,' Jean said. 'My daughter's nearly Rhiannon's age and I've noticed that she has her schoolfriends and she also has the friends she grew up with who live nearby but she keeps the two quite separate.'

Mac tried to think back to how his daughter Bridget was at that age but his memories were a little hazy. He had a sharp pang of sadness as his first thought was to ask her mother. Even though his Nora had been gone for some time, the fact that she wasn't around still came as a shock to him at times.

'I did exactly the same,' Martin said. 'Being a bit of a nerd, I was a gift to the bullies so I used to keep up a fiction when I went to secondary school. When I first went there, I told them that my elder brother was a karate champion. I got some pictures from the internet and pretended that they were of my brother. Of course, if any of my schoolmates had met any of my real friends then they would have discovered that my brother wasn't a martial arts expert because I didn't have one.'

'And did they ever find that out?' Mac asked getting interested in Martin's story.

'Eventually, yes,' Martin replied.

'And what happened?'

'Well, this big guy who hated my guts trapped me in a corner. He said that he'd found out that I had no brother and that he was going to kill me. He started hitting me and so I dislocated his shoulder.'

'How on earth did you do that?' Mac said looking puzzled.

'Well, in order to back up my big lie, I'd started doing some research into karate and other martial arts and I became so interested in them that I started going to classes,' Martin explained. 'I was a brown belt when it happened. I got a bit of a telling-off for that but there were plenty of witnesses and I think that the head-mistress was quite sympathetic really. Anyway, after that I was left pretty much alone.'

'And do you still keep it up, the karate?' Mac asked.

'Oh, yes. It's a great antidote to all the sitting around I do here at work. I'm a black belt now, second dan,' Martin said with a hint of pride.

Mac smiled and shook his head. The old adage about still waters running deep came into his head.

'Anyway, that's a good thought that you had,' Martin said. 'I should be getting Rhiannon's phone before too long and I'll have a look to see what apps she's been using.'

Mac had just started reading a statement from Rhiannon's history teacher when Dan and Adil came in. While Dan's default expression might be described as being somewhat on the grumpy side, he looked quite thunderous as he sat down heavily at his desk.

'Well, that was fun,' he said.

'We spoke to Mrs. Hashley first and then to Rhiannon's father,' Adil explained. 'Neither went too well.'

'You can say that again,' Dan said. 'Mrs. Hashley, on hearing that her daughter was dead, sat without moving or saying anything for at least five minutes. She then got up and left the room. She didn't come back. I went up and looked for her but she'd gone to bed. I've left a couple of uniforms to keep her company. They'll let me know when she's ready to talk. And as for Marc Brodeur...'

'We had to restrain him,' Adil said. 'He went totally crazy when we confirmed that his daughter was dead.

He started shouting at his ex-wife and then he tried to hit her. Dan here had to hold him back. He and his wife had a right slanging match.'

'What were they saying?' Mac asked.

'God knows,' Dan replied. 'Unfortunately, it was all in French but it didn't sound good. We'll be going back there again tomorrow and hopefully he'll have calmed down a bit by then. I'm going to bring Kate along too just in case they start having a go at each other in French again. At least she'll be able to tell us what they're shouting about.'

Dan looked at his watch.

'Fifteen minutes to go,' he said.

Mac checked the time on his computer. Dan was right. It was now eight-forty-five.

'Are we going to have a debrief tonight?' Mac asked.

'Yes, I've called one for nine thirty,' Dan replied. 'I'm just hoping that someone's got a lead.'

'It's early days yet,' Mac said realising that he was saying it as much to himself as to Dan. 'What are you going to tell the press?'

'Just that we found the bodies of two young girls in Radley Meadows and that we suspect murder. I can also tell them that we should be absolutely sure of the identities of both girls by tomorrow. Beyond that I can't really say anything, mostly because we don't bloody know anything,' Dan said as he gave Mac a frustrated look.

He calmed down almost immediately.

'Anyway, tomorrow's another day. Now, while I've got a minute, I want to run something past the three of you.'

Dan explained what his idea was and they all thought it was excellent. Mac followed him when he went outside. A barrage of flashes went off as they emerged from the barn. Dan looked at his watch again. He still had a couple of minutes.

'Anyway, thanks for putting in the time,' Dan said. 'I know that it's been a long day and it's probably the first of quite a few.'

'I wouldn't want to be anywhere else,' Mac said with complete sincerity.

If his back allowed it, he was going to give this case everything he had. He could do nothing about it now anyway. The case had gotten completely under his skin.

Chapter Eight

Mac shivered. It was freezing cold outside and he'd had to go back in and put his coat on. Comparatively, the barn now felt quite warm inside. It was obviously better insulated that he'd thought for which he was more than thankful.

He stood on the side and watched as Dan gave his statement to the assembled press and TV cameras. The murder of two young girls would ensure that this would be the top news story for days, if not weeks, to come.

Dan told the crowd of reporters what he could, which was next to nothing, but it looked as if the press had been working hard too. They already had the names of both girls and they knew that a hammer was the likely murder weapon. However, there were still things that they didn't know. None of them asked any questions about Rhiannon's interest in Wicca. Mac was fairly sure that they'd be making quite a lot out of that when they did find out.

Dan managed to brush off most of the reporters' questions before retreating back into the incident room.

'I'm glad that's over,' Dan said with some sincerity as he took his coat off. 'Just time for a coffee before the briefing.'

He and Martin handed out the coffees. Dan had insisted that the kettles, coffee, tea and hot chocolate were in one of the first boxes to arrive at the barn. Mac agreed that an overdose of caffeine was a necessary ingredient in any investigation.

As the team drifted in, Mac noticed that there was another new face. She was in uniform and she'd come in with Jo and Leigh. Once they were all there, Dan started the briefing.

'Any suspects yet?' he asked hopefully.

When everyone in the team just looked at each other he frowned and carried on.

'Okay, there's every chance that this is going to be a long investigation but, for the first week or so, I'd like you all to give it as many hours as you can. After that we'll review the situation and, in all likelihood, we'll go back to normal shifts.'

Dan looked around the team and was glad to see that everyone looked up for it.

'Okay, before we go any further, I'd like to introduce someone new. You'll see Sergeant Mahshid Shamshiri standing next to Jo. I want to keep the incident room running twenty-four hours a day so we needed someone to do the night shift. Mahshid's volunteered to do just that. She normally works at the comms room at Stevenage and she comes highly recommended.'

From the smile on Jo's face, Mac was fairly sure who the recommendation had come from. And, of course, Stevenage was where Jo used to work before she joined the team.

'And also, skulking at the back somewhere, is PC Amanda Lingard from Hitchin who's going to be helping Mahshid,' Dan said. 'Most of you will remember the good work she did for us during the Natasha Barker kidnapping[3].'

Mac turned and spotted her at the back of the room. She gave the team an embarrassed smile.

Amanda had manned the incident room in Hitchin when they'd been looking for Natasha Barker, a young girl who had gone missing one Saturday night the year before. She had also dressed up as Natasha when they had carried out a recreation of her last known

---

[3] The Blackness – The fourth Mac Maguire mystery

movements. She'd done a good job and Mac could see why Dan would want her onboard.

'Mac, Jean and Martin have volunteered to show Mahshid and Amanda the ropes before they go home,' Dan continued. 'This means that we'll have someone reviewing everything that's coming in twenty-four hours a day and, as I said before, everything must come through Mac's team.'

Dan looked around. It looked as if everyone had gotten the message.

'Unless something major breaks, we'll be holding a briefing at this time every evening. I know that you'll all be busy so, if you want just one of you to attend, then that's fine with me. Has everyone gotten their teams sorted out?'

Everyone gave a little nod to this.

'And I take it that you're happy with how you're going to divide the work amongst the detectives and uniforms who'll be working for you?'

Another little nod.

'Good,' Dan said. 'If you do have any problems let me know immediately. We need to be as efficient as possible, especially in these first few days. Okay then, I'll start...'

He updated the team on what they knew so far about the second girl.

'I know it's precious little so far,' Dan said, 'but hopefully we'll know a lot more by this time tomorrow. One thing we have just learned about Alicia is that she went to a school near Hitchin. It's called the Queenswood Academy. So, Andy, as you've been leading the investigation at Rhiannon's school perhaps you could take this one on too. Is that alright?'

Andy gave it some thought.

'Yes, it should be. I'll take some of the team and start at Alicia's school and perhaps Jo can lead the team for the rest of the investigation at Rhiannon's school?'

Jo nodded.

'Okay, at least most of you now know what you need to be doing tomorrow,' Dan said. 'I know it's a Sunday and that means lots of leg work visiting the teachers' and pupils' homes but it is what it is. Adil and I will visit Rhiannon's and Alicia's parents again and we'll hopefully be able to get some sense from them this time. Keep an eye on your phones. Martin will be sending out updates throughout the day via text. Make sure that you read them as they might have a direct bearing on your part of the case. There will be another briefing tomorrow at the same time. As I said, make sure that someone from your team attends, unless you have a hot lead, of course. Best of luck.'

As the team started leaving the barn, Jo came over with the new recruits.

'This is Mahshid,' Jo said with a smile. 'She's one of the hot shots from the Stevenage communications team.'

Mahshid's face reddened a little at this. Mac looked at her closely. She was in her early thirties and she had jet-black hair and eyebrows. Her face was oval-shaped and her skin was a light brown. Her embarrassed smile made her face come to life and her eyes twinkle.

'And hiding behind Mahshid is Amanda,' Jo said.

Amanda gave them all a little wave. She had looked so impossibly young the last time that Mac had met her but he could see that she was looking a little different these days. She had her hair cut in a sort of bob that really suited her and, while she still looked a little nervous, there was also some confidence there.

Mac turned to see that Martin was looking at Amanda too. He had a slightly puzzled look on his face which Mac found interesting.

'Mahshid, now that's an unusual name. Where is it from?' Mac asked.

'It's an Iranian name. It means moonlight,' she replied.

Mac was intrigued. He was looking forward to finding out a little more about her as the investigation went on.

The two new recruits picked up what they had to do fairly quickly and so, by ten thirty, Mac was making his way home. As late as it was, he knew that he owed his dog Terry a walk. When Mac shook the dog lead, Terry went in a split second from being comatose to jumping up and down on springs.

As they walked, he let the case percolate through his mind. He found it difficult to believe that Rhiannon's body had only been found that morning. It seemed like days ago now. Except that they now had two bodies. He found the fact that a hammer was used to be more than interesting.

He'd had to deal with quite a few murders where a hammer had been involved but, for most of them, it had only been used because it happened to be what was at hand. The killer here, however, had brought the hammer with them and so the murders were premeditated. Mac had found that when murderers choose weapons such as baseball bats, axes and hammers a large amount of anger was usually involved. It wasn't just about killing someone. It was also about the visceral pleasure of feeling the blows destroy a hated object and the release that this might give to the killer.

What could two teenaged girls have done to cause such deadly anger?

Mac looked up at the almost full-moon. It was quite low on the horizon and it looked much bigger than usual. A movement at the end of the street caught his attention. A figure was standing there, silhouetted against the silver light. Mac couldn't quite make it out but it looked as if it could be a girl with long hair and a dress that nearly reached the ground. She had her back to him. She turned and the long dress whirled at her ankles.

Although he couldn't see her face, he could sense that she was looking right at him and he felt a sudden thrill of fear go up his spine. He had the sudden feeling that he'd somehow slipped into a strange alternate reality and he felt the hairs on the back of his neck rise up. The figure started coming towards him and he found that he couldn't move. His feet might as well have been encased in concrete. The figure then stopped before turning into a driveway. Mac knew where the driveway led.

Into the cemetery.

Terry gave a little whine and Mac looked down. He was pulling hard on the lead and wanting to go in the direction of home which was unlike him. When Mac looked up the moon had disappeared behind a black cloud and the figure could no longer be seen. The spell, or whatever it was, had been broken.

It was probably just someone going for a walk, Mac said to himself but without much conviction.

An icy rain started to fall and Terry just about pulled him home. Once back, Mac dried Terry with an old towel and gave him an extra dog treat for getting him wet. Terry then went straight to his bed and fell instantly asleep. Mac felt tired too and thought that his dog had the right idea.

As he tried to get to sleep, he couldn't get the strange figure out of his thoughts. Perhaps that's why he had the dream again...

Once again it was night time and once again he was lost. Something invisible lay ahead in the darkness, something that filled him with dread. Crippled trees bent over the path and, between the branches, he caught glimpses of a blood red moon high in the sky.

Something screamed in the near distance, a high-pitched note that made him shiver with fear.

He walked on down the path as the blood moon got bloodier. He was aware of rustlings and whisperings in the darkness on both sides and he wanted to run, run away but his feet stayed anchored to the path. Then he saw her.

The red rays of the blood moon illuminated her broken body like a spotlight. He moved towards her. She was dead, he knew this to be true. She was so young, too young to be lying there dead in the night. Despite his gnawing fear he moved closer.

Her face was made up and she wore blood red lipstick on her full lips. Her eyes were closed and she there lay unmoving. A thin stream of blood dripped from one ear. There was something written on her forehead in blood, a word perhaps, but he couldn't quite make it out. He moved closer and bent down.

He was only inches away and he could now see that the word was 'Mordor'. Then she opened her eyes...

Chapter Nine

Sunday

Mac sat up and fearfully looked around. A thin silver light bled in through the crack between the curtains giving some faint illumination. He realised with some relief that he was home and in his own bed. Even with knowing this, his heart was still beating wildly. For some reason this re-run of the dream had been the worst. Perhaps because he knew it was all too real.

Mordor.

That had been the word written on her forehead. He waited until his head had cleared a little before giving this some thought. It took him a few seconds to realise that the word was familiar. When she'd been young, his daughter Bridget had been desperate to watch the 'Lord of the Rings' movies and so he'd bought all three for her. He remembered that 'Mordor' was a place name from the film and it wasn't a nice place either.

With some relief he realised that, after all, it was just a dream and nothing else.

He looked over at the clock. It was only two-forty-five. He thought about going back to sleep but he felt wide awake. From experience he knew that it would be useless going back to bed until he got tired enough to guarantee sleep. He went into the kitchen and poured himself a glass of water. Terry didn't move a muscle as he went by. He stared out at the night and the nearly full moon that was suspended on the horizon. He decided that he needed to work.

He pulled out his laptop and clicked on the link that Martin had sent him. All he got was an error message. He guessed that, for security reasons, only police computers or phones would be able to access the data timeline. He could understand why that should be but he still felt frustrated. He closed his laptop and put it away. He sat there wondering what to do next. Then he had an idea.

He went into the spare room and started removing stuff from a cupboard. As he did this, he wondered why he'd been hanging on to so much junk and vowed that he'd have a proper clear out when the case was over. Then he found what he was looking for and smiled. It had been wrapped up well and so it should be in good condition. He stuffed a couple of items into a large plastic bag and then made for the front door.

Before he left, he sent a text to his neighbour Amanda and asked if she could take Terry in for a few days. He'd call her later and explain why. Mac had decided to give this case his full and undivided attention.

All the items fitted snugly into the boot. It was the middle of the night and bitingly cold. His breath hung white on the still air as he looked up the road towards where he had seen the apparition. There was nothing there.

The streets were silent and empty as he drove towards Radley Meadows. The press had disappeared from outside the incident room leaving just the two policemen who were guarding the gate. They had been sitting in a car to keep themselves warm but they both got out as Mac pulled up. One of the policemen helped him by carrying in one of the items from the boot of his car into the barn.

Mahshid and Amanda looked up with some surprise as he walked in.

'I couldn't sleep,' Mac explained as the policeman placed his item in the corner of the room. Mac thanked him before continuing. 'So, I thought I might as well come in and do some work.'

'Is that a camp bed?' Amanda asked.

'Yes, it's an old ex-army one,' Mac replied. 'It used to stand in the corner of my office when I worked in London.'

'Is that a duvet in the plastic bag?' Mahshid asked.

'Yes, I picked one with quite a high tog rating. It should be warm enough. I brought a pillow too.'

'You're really going to sleep here then?' Amanda asked looking astonished.

'That's the plan. It may sound a bit daft perhaps but it's what I've tended to do over the years when cases like this were kicking off,' Mac replied. 'The first few days of any investigation can be so vital and so I've always found that giving it some extra time can help.'

'I know that you've got a bad back,' Amanda said. 'Do you find sleeping in that comfortable?'

'It shouldn't be too bad. It's quite comfortable really and I think that, over the years, it's sort of adapted to my body or something. Anyway, I slept on one recently when...'

Mac stopped in mid-sentence. The last time he'd slept on a camp bed had been just after Leigh had been shot.

'Anyway, anyone fancy a coffee?' he asked changing the subject.

They did. While they drank their coffee, Mahshid and Amanda brought him up to date with what had come in while he'd been away. The initial findings of the autopsy report on Rhiannon Brodeur had arrived. Mac dove straight in.

As Bob Yeardley had predicted the cause of death was a hammer blow to the back of the skull. The first blow had caused some damage and had probably stunned Rhiannon. The second one had been the killer blow. It had cracked the skull open and had caused massive inter-cranial bleeding. She would have died almost instantly.

The imprint of the hammer head was circular and was twenty-seven millimetres, or just over one inch, across. The report stated that size of the hammer head and the impact crater on the skull was consistent with that of a standard claw hammer being used as the murder weapon.

Oh great, Mac thought. Just about everyone will have one of those.

He liked cases where something exotic had been used to kill the victim. They were usually easier to solve. He read on.

There were also traces of white High-Density Polyethylene in the wound. This had most likely come from a plastic carrier bag. He found this a little more interesting. Rhiannon had obviously been hit by the hammer while it was still wrapped in the plastic bag and Mac briefly wondered why before reading on.

Rhiannon had eaten some pasta around three hours before she died, probably a microwave meal, and had also drunk some beer not long before she was killed. The report concluded with the fact that Rhiannon had most likely showered a few hours before she died and that she had been in good health. She had also been a virgin.

For some reason this last fact had surprised Mac although he wasn't exactly sure why.

The only other items of interest in the report were that she wore just one piece of jewellery, a pendant necklace, and she also had a sort of tattoo. The tattoo had been done with some skill on her upper arm with a black semi-permanent marker. Mac had seen the design before. He took his phone out and got up one of the photos that he'd taken of the posters on Rhiannon's bedroom wall. This particular poster was based on the phases of the moon and it was virtually the same as the tattoo except that the full-moon on her arm had been coloured in with a silver marker pen and

71

contained a five-pointed star. He wasn't surprised to discover that the necklace also had a similar design. It was made of silver.

He found a very similar necklace by looking through Google images. It consisted of a circle in the middle with a crescent on either side. The text below said that it was a 'Wiccan Moon Amulet portraying the Triple Goddess'.

Could Rhiannon's interest in Wicca and magic really have contributed to her murder? Mac found this hard to believe. After all, wasn't it just teenagers playing around with the occult? He remembered that, when he'd been about Rhiannon's age, there had been a craze for Ouija boards and seances. Although he and his friends had scared themselves silly at times, he couldn't remember the 'messages' that they got from the board ever making much sense.

Nonetheless, he was intrigued by the whole notion of Moon Magic in this day and age and he wanted to find out more about this 'Triple Goddess'. He opened one of the books he'd bought on his tablet and found a reference straight away.

The waxing crescent represented the Maiden, the full-moon the Mother and the waning moon the Crone or Old Woman. The Mother Goddess was the most powerful and, due to this, magic carried out under the full-moon was said to be the most effective. Although he couldn't help feeling that such beliefs were, at best, wishful thinking, he couldn't shake the feeling that it was important that he understood why Rhiannon was so fascinated with Wicca.

In his mind, he once again saw the figure that had been silhouetted by the moon and a shiver ran down his spine.

He drove the thought out of his head and went back to work. He dove into the backlog of items on the data timeline. Mahshid and Amanda had made a dent but he resigned himself to playing catch up with the data for some days to come. However, what really mattered was that everything would be looked at and would probably be looked at again when there was more time.

Around six o'clock he felt himself start to wilt. He said his goodbyes to Mahshid and Amanda and curled up in the corner in his camp bed. He'd brought a duvet for a double bed along so he could sleep with it under and over him. He was unconscious in a matter of seconds.

He thankfully had no dreams.

He awoke to the welcome smell of coffee. He opened his eyes and then sat up. Jean and Martin were already hard at work while Dan and Adil were looking at him with amused expressions.

'Sleeping on the job again, Mac?' Dan asked trying to keep a smile from his face.

Mac stood up carefully. Not just because of his back pain this time but because the camp bed was quite light and easy to tip over. There was a particular technique that had to be used to stand up and Mac was quite surprised that it still came naturally to him after all this time.

'Something like that,' Mac replied as he stretched his arms. 'I found that I couldn't sleep last night and I couldn't work from home either so I thought that I'd dig out my trusty old camp bed. I used it a lot when I was with the murder squad in London.'

'Well, you won't find me complaining. The more time you can put into the case the better as far as I'm concerned. Just don't push it too far though, Mac,' Dan said.

'I won't.'

'Coffee?' Adil asked.

'Oh, yes please,' Mac said with deep gratitude.

'So, how are you going to manage it?' Dan said his eyes flicking back to the camp bed.

'Well, there's a sink in the toilets that I can use for shaving and freshening up,' Mac replied. 'I've brought some toiletries and clothes along but I guess that I'll have to pop home every couple of days to have a shower and get more fresh clothes.'

'Well, I can only say that it's above and beyond the call of duty but thanks,' Dan said.

'Oh, it's not that,' Mac hastily replied. 'It's this case. I'm afraid that it's really gotten to me. I couldn't leave it alone now if you paid me to.'

'I know exactly how you feel. Did you manage to get a look at the autopsy report?' Dan asked.

'Yes, but I'll have another look at it again today,' Mac said as he accepted a cup of coffee from Adil.

He stopped and took a sip before continuing.

'It was obvious from the tattoo and necklace that Rhiannon took Wiccan magic fairly seriously and I found the confirmation of a hammer being used to be interesting.'

'I'd have sooner it had been something a little more unusual though,' Dan said echoing Mac's earlier thoughts. 'Why did you find it interesting though?'

'Well, most of the murders that I've been involved with where hammers have been used tended to be spur-of-the-moment things,' Mac said. 'They mostly involved drink or drugs which, often coupled with a long-standing sense of grievance, might cause someone to reach boiling point. Then they simply reached for the first thing that they could find. Just about everyone has a hammer. This time though, the murderer brought the hammer with them. It was the weapon of choice. I think that these murders were personal and that someone was very angry indeed.'

'That makes sense,' Dan said, 'but what on earth could two young girls have done to cause someone to be angry enough to kill?'

'If we can discover that then we might just have found our killer,' Mac replied.

'Well, I'm hoping that Alicia wasn't quite as good at keeping secrets as Rhiannon appears to have been. I'll be interested to see what Andy comes up with.'

'I take it that you're going to try and talk to the parents again?' Mac asked.

Dan looked at his watch.

'Yes, we're supposed to be seeing Marc Brodeur at nine thirty so we'd better get going. Kate's meeting us there. Then after that, I'm hoping that we can prise a few words out of Alicia's mother. I'll be glad to get it all over with.'

Dan did indeed look a little more gloomy than normal as he and Adil left the barn. Mac didn't envy him.

He had a wash and shave and felt a little more alert afterwards.

'There are some pastries over there by the kettle,' Martin said without looking up.

'Oh, thanks,' Mac replied.

He went and had a look. He picked a vanilla crown and refilled his coffee cup.

'Are you really moving in?' Martin asked as he actually looked up from his laptop.

'Yes, sort of. I couldn't sleep last night so I thought that I might as well do some work. When I couldn't get on the system from home, I figured that I might as well come here.'

'Sorry, I forgot to tell you that you can only access the system from inside the police firewall. Anyway, it seems that you found a solution to that problem.' Martin said with a big smile.

Mac couldn't help smiling too.

'Did anything interesting happen while I was asleep?' he asked.

'No, not really. Apart from the fact that we've had an initial forensics report in,' Martin said. 'You might find it interesting reading though.'

Mac found the report and dove in. It was indeed interesting, so interesting that the next hour or so flew by.

Chapter Ten

There was a short note from Bob Yeardley attached apologising for the time it had taken to produce the report. Finding the second body seemed to have thrown something of a spanner in the works.

Mac quickly scanned the report and then read through it again detail. When he'd finished, he sat back and gave it some thought.

'Coffee?' Martin asked.

Neither Mac or Jean refused.

'So, what did you make of it?' Martin asked as he handed Mac his drink.

'Although there's no evidence of sex having taken place, it still looks as if the murder could have some sort of sexual component to it as Rhiannon had no panties on. Unless she made a habit of going without them then I guess that the murderer must have taken them.'

'For a trophy, perhaps?'

'Yes, it could be that. Anyway, the disappointing thing is that the killer appears to have been very careful,' Mac replied. 'They found nothing at the crime scene that might be useful, although we've still got the results of the detailed inspection of Rhiannon's clothing to come, so you never know. Footprints and tyre marks haven't proved very useful so far although they're still looking. However, they noted that it hadn't rained for some days and the ground was quite hard so I wouldn't hold out much hope there. The plastic bag with the empty beer cans in was the only really interesting part of the report.'

'I thought that you'd like that,' Martin said.

'Yes, I did,' Mac replied somewhat dreamily.

There had been seven beer cans in the bag with seven different sets of fingerprints on them. Six of the cans had at least two sets of fingerprints and one set of prints appeared on every can including the seventh. There were three sets of fingerprints on the plastic bag, one of which didn't appear on any of the cans.

He ran the scene through his head. Seven young people meeting at night to do what? As it was at full-moon Mac guessed that it must be some sort of Wiccan ritual. Someone had brought along a bag containing seven beer cans and handed one can to each person there. Then, when they'd finished drinking, another person held open the bag so that everyone could place their empty cans inside. That person then ties the bag up and places it into the bin.

That might well explain it.

Mac wondered if the person who had handed out the beer cans might have been older but, for some reason, he didn't think that would be the case. Perhaps that was because they'd left the cans behind. He knew that most young people were quite keen on recycling these days but, in this instance, it might have been safer not to. They might not have wanted to take the empty cans home in case their parents noticed.

He stopped as he knew that he was surmising again. Still, it gave him a thought.

'Jean, are your colleagues who are carrying out the door to doors noting down exactly who lives in each house on the estate?'

'Yes, they're making a note of everyone currently staying in each house, even if they're just visiting, and they've noted their ages too,' she replied.

'That should make it a bit easier then,' Mac said. 'Can you get the teams to ask everyone who has a child in the house of between say, twelve and eighteen, if they ever buy Sapporo beer?'

'Do you want them to revisit people that they've already interviewed?' Jean asked.

'Yes, please. It could be important.'

'I'll get onto it,' Jean replied as she took her radio out and went into the far corner to make her call.

'So, you think that they were having a drinks party with some stolen beer?' Martin said with a smile. 'I've heard that it happens a lot although, of course, I never did anything like that myself.'

Martin's smile, having gotten even larger, belied his words.

'I think that there might have been a bit more to it than that but, yes, I think that could have been drinking beer taken from one of their parents' houses,' Mac said.

'What makes you think that?'

'Well, years ago there were shops that would sell alcohol to kids who were under age but I'd guess that they're quite rare these days. I'd also guess that type of shop wouldn't stock such an up-market beer as Sapporo anyway,' Mac replied.

Martin thought for a moment before saying, 'Yes, I'd guess that you're right there. We always used to bribe one of our friend's older brothers to get us some beer but it was always the cheapest brand we could get.'

'They're getting right on it,' Jean said as she returned to her desk.

'Thanks,' Mac replied.

His back felt a bit stiff so he stood up and had a stretch. He went over to the window and looked out.

The day was overcast with even darker clouds approaching from the horizon. Although it was still morning, the low light levels made it look more like late evening. Something moved on a small hill to his left. Someone was standing there. They were dressed in black and looking straight at him. A frisson of fear

79

went up his spine as he remembered the events of the previous evening.

The word 'Mordor' went through his head. He strained to see the figure more clearly. The figure stood quite still before finally raising a camera and then taking some shots of the barn.

Just someone from the press, Mac thought with some relief. He wondered for a moment why last night's encounter and the ensuing dream had affected him so badly. He had a thought but he put it on the back burner for now.

He returned to work. Some information was coming in from Alicia's school and Mac gladly immersed himself in it.

Some two hours later Mac came to when Jean asked him if he'd like a coffee.

'Have you had a look at what Andy's been sending us from Alicia's school?' Martin asked.

'Yes, and I must say that she seems to have been a very different person to Rhiannon,' Mac replied.

'In what way?' Martin asked. 'Sorry, I haven't had time to read it all myself.'

'Well, Rhiannon seems to have been quite a self-contained and self-confident young lady. She doesn't appear to have been someone who needed the approval of others and I don't think that she suffered fools gladly either,' Mac replied. 'Alicia was different. There was something that one of her teachers said along the lines of her being a 'bully magnet'. In fact, Alicia had been beaten up quite badly about six months ago and it led to one of the girls who did it getting expelled. This didn't make things any easier for Alicia as the expelled girl's friends were still there and making life difficult for her.'

'Unfortunately, I've known kids like her,' Martin said as he shook his head. 'It's like they carry an invisible target on their back.'

'Well, that was the case up until around three months ago. Apparently, all the bullying seemed to have suddenly stopped although the teacher had no idea why. Andy attached a note saying that he'd be interviewing some of the girls who had bullied Alicia later today.'

Mac went and looked out of the window. There was nothing to see for which he was grateful. However, the dream came back into his mind. It was like an itch he couldn't scratch and, if he didn't do anything about it, he knew that it would only get worse. He sat down and had a think. He found that there was another question he could ask first and it might be quite an important one at that. He found Edward Lewin's phone number and called him.

'Hello, Edward Lewin here,' a voice said.

Mac introduced himself. Thankfully, the professor remembered him.

'You mentioned that Rhiannon was part of a coven. Did she ever say anything about the other members?'

'Not as far as I recall,' Mr. Lewin replied.

'Do you even know how many there were in the coven?'

'Again, I don't think she ever mentioned it. I take it that no-one else has come forward as yet?'

'Unfortunately, no and that has me puzzled,' Mac replied. 'Where did Rhiannon get her knowledge of Wicca from, do you know?'

'Yes, I might be able to help you there,' the professor replied. 'She read quite a bit but the book that she talked about the most was the one about the Wondreth Coven. I'm sorry but I can't remember the exact name.'

Was it 'Wicca – The Deep Magic of the Wondreth Coven' by any chance?' Mac asked.

'Yes, that's the one.'

'Why was that book so important to her?'

'I'm not really sure,' the professor replied. 'I remember her saying that it had resonated with her straight away. I know that she read it many times as she had passages of the book off by heart. Once, she even went to the site where the original Wondreth Coven met over sixty years ago.'

'And where's that?' Mac asked.

'Oh, it's in Cambridgeshire, not too far from here. I remember Rhiannon said that she caught the train to Shepreth and walked from there.'

'Did you ever read the book yourself?'

'No, not really but I dipped into a few times just to try and figure out what Rhiannon saw in it,' the professor replied. 'I must say that, although there was a lot of fluff and nonsense in it, at least some of it was quite similar to Anglo-Saxon practices. For instance, they believed in wights.'

'Wights?'

'Yes, a wight was a sort of animistic spirit. They're fairly vague about it in the Wondreth book saying that spirits are in everything but, besides gods like Woden, Tiw and Thunor, the Anglo-Saxons believed in elves, dwarves, giants and dragons and the like. They also believed that one of the best places to hold a religious ritual was in a wooded area.'

'Is that why Rhiannon held her ritual in Radley Meadows?' Mac asked.

'She never said anything about that but I'd guess that it might be case. The clue is in the name really. A 'leah' or ley is a small wood or, more importantly, a clearing in a wood. Such a clearing might well have been used for religious practices. So, the name Radley goes back to Anglo-Saxon times. Rhiannon knew that.'

Mac found all of this very interesting. Now it was the time for the embarrassing question.

'Before I go, I've got what's probably a silly question for you. What does the word 'Mordor' mean to you?' Mac asked.

There was silence for a moment.

'Well, it's a place name in Middle Earth, isn't it?'

'The Lord of the Rings, you mean?'

'Yes, that's right,' the professor replied. 'Professor Tolkien, who wrote the book, got the word from Old English. I have to admit that he really knew his stuff though. He did a wonderful translation of Beowulf and, apparently, he even used to speak lines from it in the original Anglo-Saxon when he gave lectures.'

This time it was Mac's turn to be silent for a moment. He had to ask the question and he hoped that he'd like the answer.

'So, what does the word mean then?'

'What? Mordor?' the professor replied.

'Yes.'

'Oh, isn't it obvious? It's Old English for 'Murder'.'

The Maiden *...represents the waxing Moon. During this time, we should prepare for the coming of the Mother-Goddess at the full moon. It should be a time of excitement but also of introspection for all Wiccans. As the Maiden starts her cycle, what we wish to achieve with our magic when the Mother comes should now be becoming clearer. Be quiet and do not search too hard for, as she grows, the Goddess will grant us the knowledge that we seek. If our hearts are true, that is...*

Diana L. Selene, Wicca – The Deep Magic of the Wondreth Coven

Chapter Eleven

Mac hadn't been expecting that. He'd been happier when he'd thought that the word was just a place name from a fantasy movie. That would have proved that it was just one in a long line of lucid, but meaningless, dreams that he'd had since he'd started taking fentanyl as a painkiller. But now?

Had he ever heard that Mordor was old Anglo-Saxon for 'murder' before? He was fairly sure that he hadn't but, if that was the case, then why should it appear in his dream?

He looked up and saw Martin and Jean hard at work and he started feeling a little guilty. So, he went back to work too. A few minutes later a large middle-aged woman brought in a large tray of sandwiches, smiled at them all and then left. Mac suddenly felt ravenously hungry.

'I've been waiting for those,' Jean said as she stood up. 'I'm starving.'

They all took a break and were silent for a while as they ate. The sandwiches were really good.

'Where are these from?' Mac asked when he'd eaten his last crust.

'The farmer's wife,' Martin replied. 'Andy asked her if there was somewhere nearby that we could get food from and she volunteered to do a tray of sandwiches for us at lunchtime.'

'They're really good,' Mac replied. 'Home-made bread too from the look of it.'

The door opened and a voice, 'Ah, the sandwiches have arrived. It's nice to know that my timing is as good as ever.'

Dan was followed in a few seconds later by Adil. They both tucked in.

'Any luck with the parents?' Mac asked.

Dan shook his head.

'Rhiannon's dad said that he'd seen her just twice over the last six months or so and, from what I could gather, they didn't talk all that much. He did a lot of shouting at his ex-wife but, thanks to Kate, we know what he said. It was mostly swearing, I'm afraid. We asked him where he was when his daughter was killed and he told us that he was doing a night scene for his latest movie in one of the Paris suburbs. We'll check it out but, as he was directing the movie, I'd guess that it's a pretty good alibi. All in all, he wasn't of much help. As for Alicia's mother, she knew less than nothing. She had no idea that Alicia knew Rhiannon or anyone else on the estate come to that. She also said that she had no clue as to what her daughter might have been doing in Radley Meadows on the night she was killed. She said that Alicia was supposed to be revising for something but she couldn't remember what exactly.'

'You said that she was in London on the night that her daughter died?' Mac asked.

'Yes, she regretted that, or so she said,' Dan replied. 'She told us that she'd asked Alicia to go with her but she wouldn't. She said that she'd wanted to do some revision and that she'd be alright being by herself for just one night.'

Mac guessed that the real reason Alicia didn't want to go with her mother was because she was meeting with Rhiannon and the rest in Radley Meadows.

'Why did she have to go to London?' Mac asked.

'She just said that she needed to see her priest about something related to her husband. Apparently, he died just over three weeks ago. She wasn't very specific about that or anything else really. To be honest she seemed a little confused but, given the circumstances, I suppose that's only to be expected.'

Mac didn't have to say anything. The look of surprise on his face said it all.

'That's probably why she reacted as she did when we told her that Alicia had died,' Adil said. 'The news must have been too much for her.'

'Yes, losing both your husband and your child in less than a month would do that all right,' Mac said. 'How did her husband die?'

'In a car crash. He ran off the A1 motorway near Hatfield and went straight into a bridge support.'

Dan said this with a shrug and Mac got the message. As the crash happened in Hertfordshire, he should be easily able to access all the details.

'And she has no other children?'

'No, just Alicia,' Dan replied. 'She doesn't appear to have any close family either. She's gone back to stay with her priest for a few days while forensics crawl all over her house. Apparently, he's in some sort of religious organisation'

'Religious organisation?'

'Yes, now what was it called?' Dan asked.

'The SS, wasn't it?' Adil said with a smile.

Mac thought for a moment.

'Sanguine Salvatoris,' he said.

'Yes, that's it,' Dan said. 'I take it that you've heard of them before.'

'Just in passing,' Mac said. 'They're a sort of separate sect that exists within the Catholic Church, although some have gone as far as to call it a cult. They've been around for quite a while and they've got a bit of a reputation too.'

'In what way?' Dan asked.

'Well, I don't know all that much about them but I was reading somewhere that the current Pope doesn't think too kindly of them,' Mac explained. 'They're very secretive and pretty much govern themselves. I believe that they've also had a habit in the past of snuggling up to right-wing dictators and the ultra-rich. All I really know is that they bang on about 'family values' all the time but a lot of people think that this is just a fig leaf for the fact that they see homosexuals as being deviants and the spawn of the devil or something.'

'I'm not sure that it's of any relevance but can you look into it for me, Mac?' Dan asked. 'You never know.'

'Yes, of course. I'd be glad to,' Mac replied. 'I'll ring my parish priest and have a word with him. He should be able to tell me something about them.'

'Thanks,' Dan said. 'Oh well, best get back to it then.'

'Where are you going next?'

'To see Monique Ashton in the hope that she can tell us more than her employers could about Rhiannon. We'll be helping out Andy's team at Alicia's school after that. They still have a mountain of interviews to do.'

'Before you go Dan, we've just had something come in from forensics,' Martin said. 'The DNA analysis has confirmed that the first dead girl was Rhiannon Brodeur.'

'Better late than never I suppose,' Dan said glumly. 'I'll arrange another press conference for just after six and give them her name but I'll have a word with all of you first just in case anything else has come in. See you later.' Dan went to go but then he turned and said, 'By the way I've ordered pizzas for the debrief tonight if anyone's interested.'

Although he'd just eaten, Mac thought that by nine he'd be very interested indeed.

Mac rang Father Pat Curran. He said that he'd be free in a couple of hours or so and that he could meet him in the church. He realised that he now had time to have a quick look at the case file on Alicia's father. It made interesting reading.

An inquest was due to be held in a couple of weeks to look into the death of John Alexander Hashley but, from the evidence contained in the case file, there was only going to be one verdict. Suicide.

Mr. Hashley had been seen that evening in a bar in London not far from where he worked. He was alone and he had been drinking heavily. The level of alcohol in his bloodstream confirmed this. Although he hadn't been a regular for some time, the barman knew who Mr. Hashley was and said that he seemed agitated and that he had drank far more than he had used to. The barman offered to call Mr. Hashley a taxi but he was told to mind his own business. He left just before the pub closed and the barman said that he was clearly very drunk.

The crash happened about an hour or so later. It was late at night and traffic was minimal. No other vehicle was involved. John Hashley's BMW hit a bridge support on the motorway near Welwyn Garden City at around one hundred miles per hour. The only witness was another driver who was around three hundred yards behind Mr. Hashley's car when it veered off the road.

The driver, a Mr. John Keenan, stated that he had moved into the middle lane of the motorway after a black BMW had driven to within a couple of inches of the rear of his car and had then started flashing its lights and honking its horn. Once he had moved out of the way the BMW had sped past him. About a half a mile further on he saw the BMW swerve suddenly to the left and then cross all three lanes of the motorway heading straight for the bridge support. He saw no brake lights and the BMW made no attempt to slow down before it impacted the bridge.

Mr. Keenan could see no reason why Mr. Hashley should have veered like that other than having a wish to kill himself. It looked to him as if he aimed his car directly at the bridge and that no attempt was made to swerve in either direction. The investigator asked if perhaps an animal, such as a deer, might have been the cause of the car veering to the left.

Mac thought that this was a good question as Knebworth's deer park ran alongside that stretch of the motorway.

However, Mr. Keenan was adamant that there was nothing there. As soon as the BMW crossed his lane he slowed right down and looked down the road in front of him expecting something to be there but there was nothing. There had been an abnormally bright moon out that evening and he would have clearly seen anything on the road ahead, especially something as large as a deer.

There was a note from one of the investigators. In trying to find a reason for his death, they had started looking into Mr. Hashley's business dealings. He owned a company called 'JXH Sports' but it didn't seem to have had anything to do with his death as it was in really good financial health.

The name sounded familiar to Mac. He was sure that he had recently seen one of Mr. Hashley's shops in the shopping centre in Welwyn Garden City. From what he could remember they sold sports shoes, football shirts and casual wear. The shop was loud in every way. The colours were primary and the music deafening. He had never felt tempted to set foot inside.

Was it just a coincidence that Alicia's father died shortly before his daughter? he thought. While Mac knew that coincidences do happen, he didn't always trust them.

He stood up, stretched and wandered over to the window. He looked out and let the murder roll once again through his head like a movie. It gave him a thought.

'I'm going out for a bit,' Mac said as he put on his coat. 'Does anyone want anything?'

He memorised the order. An orange juice and bar of chocolate for Martin with a sparkling water and two packets of chewy mints for Jean.

As he was leaving the barn, a uniformed officer was coming in.

'Martin Selby?' he asked.

Mac pointed him out. The officer handed Martin a small package. Rhiannon's phone, Mac surmised. He'd be very interested in seeing what Martin might learn from it.

He walked the short distance up the road to the entrance to Radley Meadows. Two uniformed police-men let him in. He walked through the car park towards the little wooded lane. An anaemic sun shone briefly through the thick clouds before disappearing once again. The day became darker than ever. Then, just as he entered the shadow of the overhanging trees, a gust of wind blasted at him. Sharp and icy-cold, it made him shiver and the hairs on the back of his neck rise up. He looked down the path, half-expecting to see a figure in the distance. There was nothing.

The crime scene was still taped off and he was careful not to set foot inside the perimeter. He got as close as he could and just stood there looking. Mac decided that the little clearing was quite strange. It was perfectly circular and, while everywhere around about had knee-high undergrowth, the circle had none. A light feathering of grass covered the area and, around the edges of the circle, there was a ring of large smooth pebbles.

He looked upwards and could see the sky. Although the overlapping branches of trees formed a sort of threadbare canopy everywhere else, the tree branches seemed to have avoided this area. He ran through the murder once again.

With no overhead canopy, the two girls would have been bathed in moonlight and so would have been clearly visible to their killer. He envisaged them sitting on the blanket facing the little path that led to the clearing. They would have been oblivious to anyone coming at them from behind them.

For some reason Mac closed his eyes. With his eyes shut, he found that he could see.

He was sitting crossed-legged and holding hands with Alicia. They were both seated on the ground, facing the way they had come in. They did this so that they could see the whole of the full-moon which was regally sailing by high in the sky above. The moon's rays bathed him with its reddish light. He could feel the rays nourishing, cleansing and healing him. Along with Alicia he was chanting a prayer to the Mother-Goddess, a prayer of thanks for a prayer answered. Even with eyes closed, he could feel the magical energy of the silver-red light tingle on his face. Then he felt a fierce jolting pain on the side of his head and then another at the back. For a split second his eyes opened and he saw the blood moon.

Then there was blackness.

Mac found himself doubled over with pain. Except that the pain was no longer there.

He looked around but he was alone. His heart was beating frantically and his head was reeling from the intensity of the experience. He picked up his crutch, leaned against a tree and tried to collect himself. He felt giddy and slightly nauseous as though he'd just stepped off a fairground ride that had gone far too quickly.

It had felt so real but, as the memory of it started to fade away, he told himself that he was just letting his imagination run away with him. Yet, he knew deep down that there more to it than that. After years of suffering, he was an expert on pain. The blinding pain that he'd felt in his head had been all too real.

He touched the side and back of his head but there was no blood, no pain, nothing. His vision was clear and his stomach had now settled. He decided that he'd mention it to his neurologist anyway.

When he had some time, that is.

As he touched the back of his head again, he thought about the position of the wounds on Rhiannon's skull. The blow that had killed her had impacted the lower back of her head in the occipital region. Forensics had suggested that, from the angle of the blow, it was most likely that the victim was seated and that the blow was delivered under-arm from a standing position while the hammer was still inside a plastic carrier bag.

Why had the killer done that? Mac thought. Why hit Rhiannon underarm and not on the top of her head? Surely the more natural way of using a hammer would have been to have swung it downward, as if banging in a nail. That way the target, being the whole of the top of the skull, would have been larger and the blow could have been delivered with the maximum force.

Perhaps the reason for the manner in which the blows were dealt might simply be because the killer didn't know how to use a hammer correctly, Mac thought.

And what about the plastic bag? Had the hammer been kept in the bag to disguise its shape or just to make it easier to carry? Why not take the hammer out of the bag before using it? Was it perhaps an attempt to keep the hammer clean of any forensic traces?

Mac thought that an answer to any of these questions might be important and so he filed them all away in a mental folder marked 'Important'.

He waited for a moment to clear his head before seeing if he could figure out how the killer might have approached the two girls. He walked around to the back of the circle and found that he was stopped by a line of tape. A yard or so further around the circle, another line of tape followed the same line as the first.

The two tapes ran alongside a faint trail that led back through the trees to another path. Obviously, forensics thought that the killer might have used this path to creep up on his victims. The killer must have seen, or more probably heard, the girls in the little clearing.

Mac walked on a few steps and, try as hard as he might, the undergrowth still made a slight crunching sound.

Perhaps his imaginings weren't so far off the mark, Mac thought. If the two girls were chanting a prayer out loud then they might not have heard anyone approaching them.

He looked down at the spot that they must have been sitting on and wondered why they were there in the first place. If there had been seven of them here earlier then why had the other five gone leaving Rhiannon and Alicia by themselves? Come to that, why hadn't even one of the other five come forward yet? Two of their friends had been killed yet not one of those that were present in the meadows on the night that Rhiannon and Alicia were killed had tried to help the police. So, were they scared of something? That they might be next, perhaps?

He looked at his watch and he found that he'd spent more time in the meadows that he'd thought. It was well past time to find out what Father Pat had to tell him.

Chapter Twelve

Father Pat turned as he heard Mac coming up the aisle. The altar was illuminated by a single electric light but the rest of the church was in darkness. The fluttering flames of the votive candles shone brightly like stars in the night sky.

'Enjoying a little peace and quiet, Father?' Mac asked as he sat down on the pew next to the priest.

Father Pat smiled. He was a gentle man in his forties and Mac liked him a lot. He'd been there for Mac when he'd needed him, during the dark times after his wife had died.

'Something like that,' the priest replied in a thick Cork accent. 'It gets dark so early these days and I was about to put on the lights when I thought that I'd just take a moment.'

'It's nice as it is,' Mac said as he felt the peace infuse through him.

'Well, it's a lot nicer now I know that the building won't be falling down on us. That friend of yours, Liam Flahavan, did a great job on the church repairs and all for nothing too. Did you know that he came from a village just down the road from mine?'

Mac wasn't at all surprised by this as Father Pat had told him that fact several times before. He still looked on the church repairs as some sort of miracle. Perhaps it was.

They sat there for a moment in silence before Father Pat finally said, 'You said that you were interested in Sanguine Salvatoris. What do you want to know?'

'Anything that you can tell me really.'

'Do you mind me asking why?'

'I take it that you've heard about the murder of the two girls in Radley Meadows?' Mac said.

'Yes, and a terrible thing it was too,' the priest replied as he crossed himself.

'Well, the mother of one of the dead girls has some sort of connection with Sanguine Salvatoris. She's gone to stay with them in London while our forensics team goes over her house. It's probably got nothing to do with the murders but...'

Mac shrugged.

'I see. Well, I've not had too many dealings with them myself, for which I thank God.'

'Why is that?' Mac asked.

'They're a funny lot and so I've done my best to steer clear of them,' Father Pat replied. 'Someone once described them as being a cross between the Moonies and the Jesuits and, from what little I've seen, they weren't too far off the mark. They've been accused of using some of the same aggressive recruitment practices as some of the cults while at the same time trying to be more Catholic than the Pope. They even encourage their lay members to practice celibacy and forbid them from reading certain books.'

'It sounds as if they want to return to the Middle Ages or something,' Mac said.

'Yes, I'd guess that wouldn't be too far off the mark either. Did you know that they still believe in the 'mortification of the flesh'?'

Mac had to think for a moment.

'What do you mean? Whipping yourself and wearing hair shirts and the like?'

'Yes, all that plus some of them wear a cilice chain too,' the priest said with a sad shake of his head.

'What's that?'

'It's a sort of spiked chain that they wear around the upper thigh. It's supposed to cause quite a lot of pain and that's supposed to constantly remind them that the flesh is sinful or something like that.'

'Now, that sounds really mediaeval to me,' Mac said with a grimace.

He didn't need a cilice, or whatever it was called, to feel pain. It was a permanent part of his life now. However, the fact that someone might choose to be in pain certainly felt sinful to him.

'What does Sanguine Salvatoris think about Wicca?' Mac asked.

Father Pat shook his head.

'I've no idea but I'd guess that they wouldn't like it much. But, then again, I don't think that they like anything much really. Why did you want to know?'

'I'll have to ask that you keep this to yourself but it would appear that the dead girls may have been into Wicca.'

'Wicca? Yes, it's a bit of a thing these days, isn't it?' the priest said. 'I've heard some Christians condemn it, mostly the Evangelical lot, but I dare say that it's just a fad like a lot of other things.'

'Is there anything else you can tell me?' Mac asked.

'I'm sorry but, as I said, I try to keep my distance from that crowd. Is it important that you find out more about them?'

'I've absolutely no idea,' Mac said with a shrug. 'But I am interested.'

Father Pat gave it some thought.

'There's a priest called Father Donal Farrell and I used to know him quite well some years ago. I've heard that he worked at Sanguine Salvatoris' headquarters in London for a time. I can't promise anything but I could ask him to speak to you, if you like?'

'I'd be grateful if you could,' Mac replied. 'It's probably a wild goose chase yet...'

Mac didn't finish the sentence. Yet what? He had no idea.

It was more or less dark by the time he stepped outside yet it wasn't even five o'clock. He stopped by the supermarket before heading back to the incident room. He had to drive through the press scrum before parking outside the barn. He didn't make any move to leave the car for a while.

He sat there thinking about Sanguine Salvatoris and why he was so interested in them. It was most probably incidental to the investigation yet he couldn't help wanting to know more. He decided that he was going to indulge himself.

He gave Martin and Jean their drinks and sweets.

'Was that Rhiannon's phone that came in just as I was leaving?' he asked.

'Yes, I'm still working on it but I don't think it's going to help us much,' Martin replied with a frown.

This surprised Mac. He was hoping that, with Martin's undoubted skills, the phone might be able to tell them something about who she might have known on the estate.

'Why is that?'

'Well, she didn't use the phone all that much to actually call people,' Martin replied. 'In fact, she only called six numbers in total in the last three months or so. Her mother, her father just the once, her mother's assistant Miss Ocampo, Monique Ashton, her school and the taxi firm that she used to get to and from school,' Martin replied.

'I don't think my daughter uses her phone to make traditional calls all that much either,' Jean said. 'It's all apps with her.'

'Unfortunately, it was pretty much the same for Rhiannon,' Martin said. 'However, I can tell what apps she used most. She used WhatsApp a fair bit and I can get into that...'

'That's the one she used for her friends at school, isn't it?' Mac asked.

'That's right,' Martin replied. 'I'll have a good look at it but it seems from what we've heard so far that she didn't confide all that much in her schoolfriends. I can track what she's been looking at on the internet and any documents or photos that she might have downloaded but I doubt that I'll get very much beyond that.'

Mac gave Martin a puzzled look.

'I was hoping that you might have been able to discover who she might have known on the estate and how they got to know each other.'

'If she was talking to someone on the estate then I think I know how she did it,' Martin said. 'Much good it will do us though. She used a messaging app that's about as secure as they come and I can tell that she used it a lot, mostly evenings and weekends. While most people would store their friends' user names for convenience, you can also select a user by location. I've been able to get into the app and most people would have a list of friends that they can select from. She had none. It also looks as if she's set it up so that all conversations were deleted as they went along.'

'So, even if we could get a court order, the data might not be there anyway?' Mac asked.

'That's about it,' Martin replied. 'I'll keep digging but, as I said, don't hold your breath.'

'Why do you think she was so obsessed with her privacy?' Jean asked. 'I've told my daughter again and again to be careful with her details online but I might as well be talking to the wall.'

Mac thought that this was a very good question.

'I don't know,' Martin replied, 'but it's a question that I'd certainly like the answer to.'

Mac hadn't long settled down to work when Dan and Adil strode in. He looked at his watch. It was coming up to six. He was nearly forgetting about the press conference.

'Is there anything new that I should know about?' Dan asked.

'There are a few things that I'll mention at the debrief later but there's nothing earth-shattering,' Mac replied.

Dan looked disappointed.

'Did you learn anything from Monique Ashton?' Mac asked.

'Not really but she certainly seemed to know Rhiannon a little better than her mother did,' Dan replied. 'She used to live in the house until she got married just over a year ago and moved out.'

'Did she tell you anything that we didn't already know?' Mac asked.

'Well, it seems that Rhiannon mentioned her interest in Wicca about eighteen months ago and Monique warned her that it could be dangerous. Rhiannon never mentioned it to her again.'

'Why did she think it was dangerous?' Mac asked.

'She didn't say exactly,' Dan replied. 'She just said that getting what you wish for is not always a good thing.'

Mac thought on this for a moment before asking, 'Did she say anything about Rhiannon having friends on the estate?'

'She was fairly certain that Rhiannon was seeing someone as she used to go out in the evening every now and then for an hour or two,' Dan replied. 'She told Monique that she was just going for a walk but she couldn't help noticing that, at times, Rhiannon used to change her clothes and she'd wear make-up too.'

'So, no names?' Mac said.

Dan shrugged by way of an answer.

'Why hasn't one of these friends come forward then?' Mac asked.

'That's been puzzling us too,' Dan said. 'Adil and I reached the conclusion that they must be scared of something or someone.'

Dan looked at his watch.

'Time to face the mob outside, I guess. All I can give them is Rhiannon's name and some guff about how the investigation's progressing,' Dan said somewhat despondently.

Before he went outside, he looked towards Martin in the hope that something else might have come in at the last minute. Martin's reply was just a brief shake of the head.

Chapter Thirteen

As before, Mac put his coat on and watched the press conference from the side lines. No-one in the crowd looked surprised when Dan gave them Rhiannon's name. After he'd finished his short statement, Dan took a few questions. He'd done well to hide his frustration but Mac could see it momentarily surface as almost all of the questions were around why the investigation hadn't gotten any further than it had.

Even though it looked painful, Dan could only grit his teeth and reply that things were 'progressing'. As he turned to leave a young woman shouted a question that Mac found more than interesting. He guessed that Dan hadn't heard it amongst all the other questions that were shouted out by the reporters. He had a word with the uniformed officers guarding the gate and, to the bemusement of the other reporters, they escorted the young woman inside the perimeter.

Mac gestured at her to come over. He could see that, close up, she looked even younger than he'd thought. Her long brown hair was tied up in an efficient bun and the black-rimmed glasses showed that she meant business.

'Who are you?' he asked.

'Chris James from the Comet,' she replied.

Mac wasn't surprised that she was from one of the local papers. She was still young and learning the trade, he guessed.

'And you are?' she asked with a defiant expression.

'I'm Mac Maguire,' he replied with a smile.

He found that he was beginning to like Miss James.

'Mac Maguire? Really? I know who you are, well, your reputation anyway,' she said looking a little flustered. 'Why did you call me over? Did I do something wrong?'

'No, no. I was just wondering why you asked the question that you did.'

'A lot of good it did me,' she replied with a scowl. 'He totally ignored me.'

'You and the other thirty or so reporters who were all shouting questions at the same time,' Mac pointed out. 'Tell me, why did you ask about the hammer?'

'Well, it's obvious, isn't it?' she replied. 'Witches and hammers.'

Mac looked at her in some surprise before thinking about what she had said. He felt a tickle of recognition at the back of his mind but it stubbornly refused to show itself.

'Assume that I'm stupid and tell me exactly what you mean.'

'Well, I opted to do Gender Studies at university, mostly around how women have been treated through the centuries. Shockingly, of course, and one of the first things I looked at was the Malleus Maleficarum.'

Seeing no look of recognition on Mac's face she continued.

'It's a book from the fifteenth century by some German priest and it basically gave people the justification to torture and burn anyone who they thought might be a witch. Of course, ninety-nine percent of those accused at the time of being witches were women. It's basically the biggest load of misogynistic crap ever published.'

'And the hammer bit?' Mac asked still somewhat mystified.

'It's right there in the title,' Chris replied. ''Malleus Maleficarum'. It's Latin and it can be translated as 'The Hammer of Witches'. It was certainly used to hammer down women all over the world for centuries.'

'Come with me,' Mac said and walked towards the barn.

She hesitated for a moment before following him inside. He sat her down in one of the new interview rooms and had a quick word with Dan.

'Miss James, firstly I must apologise. I genuinely didn't hear your question,' Dan said as he and Mac took their seats. 'However, before I give you an answer, I'd like you to answer one of mine. How did you know that witchcraft was a factor in this case?'

She looked anxiously from one to the other before saying, 'Well, you must have mentioned it at one of your press conferences.'

'No, I didn't,' Dan replied. 'We haven't released that information yet. So, tell me, how did you know?'

She looked from Dan to Mac and back again and her shoulders slumped.

'My younger sister Amy goes to the Queenswood Academy. She told me that Alicia was a witch.'

'What exactly did she tell you?' Dan said.

'Although she's in the same year as Alicia Hashley, she didn't know her that well. No-one really knew her, she said, and that was mostly because they didn't want to get on the wrong side of Megan Harding and her little band of morons.'

'Was she one of the girls who had bullied Alicia?' Dan asked.

'That's right,' Chris replied. 'Megan's best friend had gotten herself expelled for beating up Alicia and being stupid enough to get herself caught on camera doing it. Megan vowed that she'd get even. Poor Alicia had been getting harassed daily by Megan and her gang but about three months ago it all stopped.'

'What happened?'

'Amy saw it all. She said that there was something different about Alicia that day, there was a sort of confidence about her that she'd never seen before. Megan had gotten hold of Alicia and was about to tear her hair out when Alicia looked Megan right in the eye and told her to let her go. Everyone was surprised when Megan did just that. Even Megan seemed surprised. Then Alicia drew a circle on the floor with a piece of red chalk and stepped inside it. She then pulled a piece of paper from her pocket and set fire to it. It was spooky, Amy said, as no-one saw how she managed to set it alight. As it burned, she chanted something in a foreign language of some sort, all the time looking Megan straight in the eye and smiling as she did so.'

'What happened then?' Dan asked.

'Nothing really but Megan left Alicia alone for the rest of the day. That happened on a Friday. Megan didn't turn up for school on the following Monday. No-one knew why until the day after. One of Megan's friends had gone to see her and she said that Megan had come down with the worst case of acne that she'd ever seen. She said that there were more spots than skin on her face and that's why she wouldn't come into school.'

Chris paused for effect.

'Everyone looked at Alicia differently after that, especially when she said that, the next time that someone upset her, she'd make them fat. My sister said that no-one bothered her again after that.'

'Did she actually ever say that she was a witch or that she was into Wicca?' Dan asked.

'According to Amy, one of the girls asked her if she was a wizard like Harry Potter,' Chris replied. 'Alicia said that she wasn't a wizard, they were just in books. She was a witch. She said that she was part of a magical coven and that she was now learning how to turn nosy people into frogs. They didn't ask again.'

Dan looked at his watch.

'Would we be able to speak to your sister now?' he asked.

'Well, I suppose so...'

'It's just in case she can tell us anything more,' Dan said.

'I'll give mum a ring,' Chris said as she took her phone out.

Dan and Mac waited outside the interview room while Chris made her call.

'Do you think that there's anything in it?' Dan asked.

'Who knows? The killer choosing a hammer might be just a coincidence,' Mac shrugged, 'but, in this case, it might be well worth looking into.'

Chris emerged and said, 'Mum said that if you want to speak to Amy, you'd better come now as she'll be in bed in an hour or so.'

Dan and Adil went out with Chris and Mac returned to his work. He started by looking up *Malleus Maleficarum* on Google. Even a quick read-through of the results showed that Chris hadn't been wrong when she'd said that it had been used 'to hammer down women all over the world'. The book declared witch-craft as the worst of heresies and also that anyone accused of being a witch, historically almost always a woman, should be tried by a local magistrate and not by a church court. It also recommended that torture and lies be used to obtain confessions.

So, anyone could accuse anyone else of being a witch and the cards were then massively stacked against the accused who would then be held and tortured until they inevitably confessed.

No wonder they called it the Dark Ages, Mac thought. He thought again about the coven and remembered Edward Lewin's remarks. He picked up his tablet and opened the book. It opened at the title page.

Wicca – The Deep Magic of the Wondreth Coven
by Diana Luna Selene

He looked at the contents and found a chapter called 'The Coven'. He skimmed through it until he came to the part he was looking for.

'While a Coven may consist of any number from two upwards there are certain magical numbers that will ensure that the energy of the Coven is maintained at its maximum. The greatest of these is thirteen and consists of the priestess and the twelve disciples. However, another magical number, and one that may be far more practical for many Covens, is seven. This was considered by ancient religions to be not just a lucky number but a powerful one too...

There were seven beer cans and so, in all likelihood, seven members of the Coven, Mac thought. Where are the other five then?

His thoughts were interrupted by Martin.

'The initial autopsy report for Alicia is in.'

He got coffees for everyone before diving into the report's details. As grisly as it was it still made better reading than the witch book.

Alicia had been hit twice. The first blow had damaged her left ear but the blow that had killed her was the one to her left temple. That blow was consistent with that of a hammer and the impact had cracked her skull and caused some major inter-cranial bleeding. They estimated that she died some five to ten minutes after receiving the injury.

She had the same semi-permanent tattoo on her arm as Rhiannon and she wore a similar necklace. She'd eaten a pizza a couple of hours before she died and, like Rhiannon, she had been drinking beer not long before she was killed. Unlike Rhiannon, Alicia had not been a virgin. He read that section again. He then called up the author of the report.

'Have you found something interesting?' Martin asked after Mac had finished his call.

'You could say that,' Mac replied. 'The autopsy states that, while they cannot be absolutely certain, there is a chance that Alicia might have been sexually active. Given her age, I was wondering if she might have been sexually abused but, while the doctor couldn't rule it out, he felt that it just as likely to be normal consensual sex. Interestingly, the doctor also said that he was waiting for a mobile X-ray unit to arrive.'

'They're going to X-ray the body? That's hardly normal procedure for them. Did they say why?' Martin asked.

'No, I asked but he just said that he wanted to check something out. We'll just have to wait for the report, I suppose.' He turned to Jean. 'Has anyone come forward yet about having any Sapporo beer missing?'

She shook her head.

'How many people do you think they've asked so far?'

'I'd guess that they must have asked just about everyone on the estate by now,' Jean replied.

Mac frowned and returned to his work. However, he couldn't help thinking about the missing five members of the coven and why they weren't coming forward. Was it because they were scared? Scared that they might be next perhaps? Although it seemed unlikely, maybe they had good reason for keeping silent. Whatever was going on, he found it very frustrating.

He had a sudden thought and pulled his phone out. He found what he was looking for and it immediately cheered him up.

'Have you found something?' Martin asked.

'Only that Aston Villa won a few hours ago.'

'Oh yes, they were playing United, weren't they?'

'That's right and it's not often that we get a win there,' Mac said as he returned to work a little happier.

They worked non-stop but the number of items coming in kept growing too. Martin said that it should start tailing off in a couple of days and Mac prayed that he was right. His big fear was that a vital piece of information might get passed over so he tried to give every item the attention it warranted. He gave one of the items his especial attention.

Just in case it was relevant, the investigating officer had also included the initial findings of the person who had been reported missing on Friday, the day that the murders had been committed. Mac printed the report off and took an early coffee break.

The missing person was called Cameron Aitken. He was twenty-two years old and he lived by himself in a flat on the Grange Estate in Letchworth. Then a name caught his eye and he sat up in surprise. The person who had called him in as missing was a Ms. Eileen Ryan. Mac checked her address. It was definitely his favourite taxi driver.

Mac wouldn't have been able to count the number of times that Eileen had driven him to and from the Magnets. She knew all the local gossip so, for the price of a taxi ride, he could catch up on all the latest news as well.

He quickly read through the report. It seemed that Mr. Aitken was still at large. He got his phone out and called Eileen.

'Mac!' she exclaimed with surprise. 'Have they found him yet?'

'I take it that you're talking about Cameron Aitken?'

'Yes, Cam. He went missing the day before last and no-one's seen him since. He's done it before but never for this long.'

'Tell me about Cam,' Mac asked.

'His mum, Iona, was a good friend to me and Sam, a really good friend. Cam never knew who his father was and, as far as I know, she never told anyone. It was always just Iona and Cam. He's a lovely lad,' Eileen said with some emotion,' and he was heartbroken when his mum died. He'd been doing so well until then...'

'What do you mean by 'doing well'?' Mac asked.

'Well, Cam was always a bit different, I suppose. His mum told us that he was bullied a lot at school and he sort of went into himself. He tried to get a job but none of them seemed to stick and he eventually had some sort of breakdown. He was diagnosed as having severe depression with psychosis. He spent some weeks in a hospital and they tried some drugs on him. They seemed to work too, until his mum got ill that is. She died two years ago now and he's been up and down ever since. Probably, more down that up though, if I'm being honest.'

'Why exactly did you report him missing?' Mac asked.

'It was his medication,' Eileen explained. 'He takes half of it in the morning and the other half at night. Sam and I have a key and we pop in every day to make sure that he's okay. I popped in that afternoon and he wasn't there. I checked his pill box and he hadn't taken his medication that morning. We were told by his doctors that, without his medication, he can go downhill pretty quickly, so we were worried. When he hadn't turned up by eight o'clock that evening, we called the police.'

'Has this happened before?'

'Unfortunately, yes and we had to call the police out that time too,' Eileen replied. 'They found him a day and a half later on the other side of Biggleswade.'

'That's a fair distance away. How did he get there?'

'He walked. Walking helps him sometimes when he's not feeling so good but, when he hits rock bottom, it becomes a compulsion. On that occasion, he'd apparently walked through the night. It had been raining and he was absolutely soaked.'

'So, he could be anywhere then,' Mac said. 'If I hear anything, I'll let you know.'

'Thanks, Mac,' Eileen said. 'I'll be saying a prayer for him.'

Mac sat back and thought for a moment before going over to Martin.

'Can you do me a favour? Cameron Aitken, the young man that was reported missing, can you pass me his case file and let me know if anything new comes up?'

'Do you think he might have had something to do with the murders?' Martin asked.

'No, I doubt it. It's just that the woman who reported him missing is a friend of mine and she's really worried.'

As he walked back to his desk Mac wondered if he might have been a bit too quick in dismissing the missing boy's possible involvement. It was something he'd need keep in mind.

Chapter Fourteen

Mac was quite surprised when Amanda turned up. She was closely followed in by Mahshid. He looked at his watch. It was now nearly eight o'clock. He got up and stretched. He felt a momentary panic as he felt his back click but no extra pain followed. He said a silent prayer of thanks and then decided that he needed some fresh air.

As he put his coat on Mahshid stopped him.

'I've brought you something,' she said as she pulled two plastic tubs from a plastic bag. 'I thought that you might need some proper food.'

'What is it?' Mac asked.

'It's an Iranian dish called Khoresh-e Bamieh. It's a lamb and okra stew. My mum made a load of it yesterday so I saved some for you. I've brought you some rice too.'

'That's really kind of you,' Mac said with a huge smile. 'Dan's ordering some pizzas for the briefing but you're right. Some real food would be very welcome.'

'I'll put it in the fridge for you then,' Mahshid said.

It was really cold outside and he wondered at the hardiness of the small group of pressmen that were still hanging about at the gate. A few took photos of him. He didn't really mind as he guessed that they were bored out of their skulls and it was something for them to do.

He looked up at the cloudless night sky. The stars were bright sparkling points of light and he could even make out a few of the constellations. It was the moon that really caught his attention though. It was nearly full but he could see a thin shadow creeping in from one side. The moon was waning now and, in time, the shadow would grow until it covered the entire disc and the cycle would start again.

He stared at its soft grey surface mottled with darker grey splotches. He knew that these were called 'seas' but, in reality, they were areas where ancient volcanic eruptions had covered the surface of the moon. He wondered at how he knew this and a memory came back to him.

It was July 1969. Mac had been called Denny back then and he was just six years old. He had been allowed to stay up a little later than normal to watch the lunar module land on the surface of the moon. He and his sisters had sat on the floor on cushions as the adults had taken up all available seats. While everyone waited breathlessly for the big moment, one of the presenters was explaining what the lunar 'seas' were and he described the area around the Sea of Tranquillity where the module was due to land. The landing itself had been a heart-stopping moment and the silence before Neil Armstrong finally said 'The Eagle has landed' was excruciating.

Everyone in the room had smiled in relief at this including his mother. She was also crying and he had wondered at that as, until then, he'd always associated crying with sad things.

Mac wondered at the clarity and freshness of the memory. He could even smell the fish and chips that they had all shared that night as mum hadn't wanted to cook just in case she missed something. He felt sad. It was a memory from a lost world. Apart from his sisters, everyone who had been in that room was now dead.

He looked up as the moon made its stately procession across the sky. He could well understand why people might think that there was something magical about it. After all, it had magicked up a memory from long, long ago.

Thinking of his mother also brought another memory to mind. She had been a quiet woman who wouldn't even hurt a fly but she used to love reading magazines that featured true crime stories. As a child Mac would sometimes get to see the cover, usually featuring a lurid drawing of a woman being either attacked or tied up or both, but that would be about it. His mother was careful not to leave them lying around but one day she did and Mac couldn't help but look inside.

The image that had struck him was that of a young woman lying dead. The photograph had been touched up and her lips were a bright red. He remembered that it had scared him. Death was a frightening concept to an eight-year-old and, for a while, he had started worrying about his mum and whether she'd end up as a photo in a magazine too.

This made him think.

He wondered if this long-forgotten memory might have been behind the dreams he'd been having. He must have also heard about the blood moon as it would have been mentioned on the news at some point. However, why the dreams had started when they did was still a mystery to him.

He was jolted out of his reverie by a car arriving at the gate. The policemen guarding the gate let it inside. Dan and Adil climbed out. Dan looked grumpy, which was his default setting, but he looked tired too. He nodded to Mac as he went inside. Mac took one last lingering glance at the moon before following him inside. He knew the rest of the team would be arriving soon for the evening briefing.

Martin and Jean were drinking coffee and talking to Mahshid and Amanda, handing over to the new shift. Dan and Adil were making coffee. Mac joined them.

'Any luck?' Mac asked.

Dan looked thoughtful for a moment.

'I'm not sure that Amy James told us anything we didn't already know from her sister but she had a friend from school for a sleepover and what she said was quite interesting. They agreed to let us record the interviews and I've sent them to Martin so you can have a listen for yourself, if you like. By the way, how's Martin's new system working?'

'It's working fine but we're still lagging behind a bit. I'll keep going for a few more hours and, hopefully, Mahshid and Amanda should help us catch up a bit overnight.'

'Is there anything that I should know about?' Dan asked.

'Not really, apart from the fact that Alicia Hashley may have been sexually active.'

'Was it abuse of some sort perhaps?' Dan asked.

'Possibly but they couldn't say for sure,' Mac replied.

Dan gave this some thought.

'If it was abuse then I suppose that it would most likely have been her father. Of course, there could have been other relatives or friends of the family who might have had access to Alicia too. I think that I'll have to have another word with Mrs. Hashley tomorrow.'

'Oh, and they're going to X-ray Alicia's body for some reason,' Mac added.

'Did they say why?' Dan asked his surprise evident.

Mac shrugged by way of an answer.

The rest of the team arrived over the next half an hour or so. The pizzas arrived right on time so that everyone could get a few slices before the briefing began. Mac only had the one slice as he didn't want to fill himself up too much. He was really looking forward to trying the food that Mahshid had brought in.

Dan called the team together and started the briefing. Mac listened to each of the team as they summarised what they had found but, unfortunately, he didn't hear much that he didn't already know. Finally, Dan called on Mac.

He first talked about the autopsy reports and what they had learned from those before going on to what was really worrying him.

'Although it looks as if we've probably asked just about everyone on the estate, I find it puzzling that no-one's admitted yet to buying Sapporo beer. With regard to that, I spoke to Edward Lewin earlier today and he told me about Rhiannon's favourite book on Wicca. In the book, they say that a coven consisting of thirteen people is the best but seven is also good too. As seven beer cans were found at the murder site, I think we can safely assume that there are five young people out there who know what was going on in Radley Meadows last Friday night but have yet to come forward. Why? This worries me. Are they in danger too? I think we need to find them sooner rather than later.'

Dan was thoughtful for a moment.

'It shouldn't be too hard to find them if they all live on the estate. Jean, do you have a list of all families with teenaged children living with them?'

'I can put that together for you,' Jean replied.

'Good,' Dan replied. 'Can you prime your people to speak to everyone on that list first thing tomorrow morning?'

'Sure thing,' Jean said. 'I'll do it before I leave tonight.'

'Thanks. I'll be on the estate first thing myself. It's my guess that they might be unwilling to speak to us for some reason so tell your people that, if they suspect anyone, to not push it any further but to contact me straight away. It's my guess that they'll be around the same age as the dead girls so I'll arrange to have someone from Youth Services to be available to act as an Appropriate Adult just in case.'

Dan handed out the tasks for the next day and the team drifted away to their beds. A half an hour later Jean said her goodbyes after sending out the list of teenaged children on the estate to both Dan and her uniformed colleagues. Martin followed soon afterwards.

Mac, Mahshid and Amanda worked in silence for a while. Mac stood up and stretched in an effort to get the kinks out of his back just as Amanda picked up the phone.

'There's someone outside who wants to speak to us,' Amanda said, 'but they say that they don't want the press to see them.'

'Who is it?' Mac asked.

'He wouldn't give a name but he sounded quite young to me,' Amanda replied.

'Tell him to hang on.'

Mac went to the fire exit which was at the other end of the barn from the main entrance and pushed the bar down to open the door. He hoped that it wouldn't set off some sort of alarm and, thankfully, it didn't. He looked out over a field illuminated by the moon. He smiled and went back inside. He took the phone from Amanda.

He introduced himself to the mystery caller and then asked, 'Where are you?'

'I'm standing just up the road from the barn,' the young man replied.

'Is that in the direction of the Drymanshouse Estate?'

'Yes, that's right.'

'Good,' Mac said. 'About sixty or seventy yards from the barn there's a long metal gate. Can you see it?'

'Yes, I can see it.'

'Okay, climb over the gate and you should see me waving from the back entrance to the barn,' Mac said.

Mac opened the back door and the bitterly cold air made him shiver. A few seconds later he saw a dark figure awkwardly clamber over the gate and then walk across the field towards him. The figure turned out to be a tall slim young man with jet-black hair. He was dressed in blue jeans, a black hoodie and scuffed trainers. Mac guessed that he could be no more than fifteen.

Mac ushered him inside. He stood just inside the door looking at Mac with a mixture of uncertainty, fear and something like despair. Had one of the five missing members of Rhiannon's coven finally come forward?

'Hello,' Mac said. 'Have you come to tell us something?'

The young man nodded. Mac gestured towards a chair and the young man sat down.

'My name's Mac Maguire. What's yours?'

'Rubaih, Rubaih Alzahrani.'

'How old are you?' Mac asked.

'I'm fifteen. Sixteen next month,' he said.

'I'm afraid that, due to your age, we can't interview you without having a responsible adult present. Can I call your parents?'

'No, no please don't!' the young man said with some urgency. 'They can't know, please.'

'Is there anyone else we can call?' Mac asked.

'My uncle Ahmad. You can call him but tell him not to tell my dad,' Rubaih replied. 'He owns a restaurant in Hitchin so he'll be at work right now.'

The restaurant was grandly called 'The Middle Eastern Food Emporium' and Mac had to ask for the owner. When he finally picked up the phone Ahmad Alzahrani seemed more than a little puzzled at Mac's request.

'Rubaih's with the police? He's a good boy. What's he supposed to have done?'

'Nothing, he's done nothing as far as we know. He wants to tell us something but we can't interview him without having an adult present. As he doesn't want his parents to know anything about this, he suggested

118

that I call you. Can you come? It's really important that you do.'

'Yes, of course. I'll leave right now.'

Mac explained about the gate and coming in the back way in order to avoid the press. Ahmad said that he'd drive down from the direction of the estate and park well up the road. He'd call when he found the gate.

Rubaih looked relieved to hear that his uncle was coming.

'Can I get you anything while we wait?' Mac asked. 'We've got coffee but we've got some hot chocolate too.'

'Hot chocolate would be nice,' the young man replied.

Mac went and got him a chocolate and a coffee for everyone else.

'Have you eaten recently?' Mac asked.

Rubaih shook his head.

'Are you hungry?'

Rubaih nodded his head.

Mac hoped that Mahshid's mother had given her a large portion of stew. He heated up the stew and rice in the microwave and then divided it onto two plates. There was just about enough for each of them. He gave one plate to the young man who started tucking in straight away.

The stew was utterly delicious, the lamb soft and melting in the mouth but there was a taste there that he hadn't expected.

'Brown sauce,' Mahshid said on seeing Mac's puzzled look. 'My mother uses tamarind paste in just about everything she cooks, it's also one of the ingredients used in brown sauce.'

'It's delicious,' Rubaih said. 'My mother makes something like this too but it's nowhere near as good.'

Mac thought it was delicious too but he didn't say so until every morsel of food was eaten.

'Give your mother my sincerest thanks. I can't remember when I've tasted anything better.'

'I will and it will make her day,' Mahshid said with a smile. 'She loves being complimented on her cooking.'

A few minutes later Mac's phone pinged. Ahmad was at the gate. Mac opened the back door and watched as he put one hand on the gate and jumped effortlessly over. He jogged across the field towards Mac.

'Is Rubaih okay?' he immediately asked.

'Come in and see,' Mac replied holding the door open for him.

Mac looked closely at him as he stepped inside. He was a handsome man with the same jet-black hair and features as Rubaih. However, while Rubaih still had the spindly body of a boy, the man's athletic build showed how he might fill out when he got older. He had a light stubble on his chin and he had thrown a jacket over his chef's uniform. He was younger than Mac had expected and his handsomeness was confirmed by the slightly dreamy looks on Mahshid's and Amanda's faces.

'Are you okay?' the man asked Rubaih.

'I'm okay, Uncle Ahmad. Thanks so much for coming.'

'Are you sure that you still want to tell us something?' Mac asked. 'If you've changed your mind that's okay. We can't keep you here.'

'No, I need to talk to you. If I don't then I think I might well go mad.'

It was clear from the expression on Rubaih's face that he wasn't joking when he said this. Mac led them both into an interview room and asked Mahshid to join them.

'When they were all seated Mac said, 'Rubaih, I'd like to record our conversation, if that's okay?'

Rubaih looked at his uncle and then nodded.

Mac turned the recorder on. He asked everyone to state their names and, in Rubaih's case, his address. Mac wasn't surprised to learn that he lived at Wedehundas on the Drymanshouse Estate.

Mac found that he couldn't wait to hear what the young man had to say. However, he reminded himself to take it slowly and to make as easy on Rubaih as he could.

Chapter Fifteen

Mac surprised himself by superstitiously crossing his fingers as he started the interview off.

'Rubaih has come to the incident room this evening of his own free will as he wishes to tell us something,' he said for the benefit of the record. 'Rubaih?'

Again, he looked up at his uncle before he spoke.

'I was with them on the night they were killed,' he blurted out. 'Arian and Sunni.'

'Arian and Sunni?' Mac asked looking puzzled.

'I'm sorry, I meant Rhiannon and Alicia. We all had our own special names, our magical names Rhiannon called them. Whenever we met up those were the only names we used. It was fun having another name. It felt as if you could be a different person if you wanted to be.'

'And what was your name?'

'It was Wolf, short for Wolfgar. We all picked our new names from a list of old Anglo-Saxon names that Arian had written down for us.'

Wolf. So, Rubaih was the boy that Rhiannon had liked.

'Who were the others?' Mac asked.

'I'd rather not say, if that's alright. They could all be in real trouble if I tell you who they are,' Rubaih said.

'Would you be able to give me their magical names?'

'I'd sooner not if that's okay,' Rubaih said looking once again at his uncle.

'I take it that he doesn't have to tell you anything that he doesn't want to?' Ahmad asked.

'No, he doesn't,' Mac confirmed. 'What can you tell us then?'

'My dad loves living on the estate. He thinks that he's made it because he's rubbing shoulders with other rich people but I hate it,' Rubaih said with real feeling. 'We're locked in behind a gate and there's nothing to do. We all met up on the estate through using an app. It was Arian, sorry, Rhiannon who first used the app to contact us all. We started meeting up at a place at the back of the estate. There's a sort of shed there, which no-one uses, and so it became our meeting place.'

'Who suggested starting up a Wicca coven?'

'That was Rhiannon too. It took a while but she finally managed to convince us all. She always came up with the best ideas. She'd be amazed by stuff and then she'd make you feel amazed too. It was never boring when she was around.'

'Why did you use Radley Meadows?' Mac asked.

'Rhiannon was mad about history and she'd really gotten into all this old Anglo-Saxon stuff. She said that she'd read about a magician that used to live near here and she said that they used to hold their religious ceremonies in sacred groves and clearings in the woods. She was convinced that the little clearing in Radley Meadows was one of these sacred sites.'

'And what did you think?'

Rubaih shrugged, 'At first, I just thought it was a bit of fun, something different and exciting to do but later, I don't know. If I'm being honest, I think that I began to believe in it just like the rest.'

'How long had the coven been meeting in Radley meadows?' Mac asked.

'Just over eight months, eight full moons ago.'

'What did you do there?'

'Rhiannon had this book and she took some of the rituals out of that. It always started off with 'The Magical Silence' as Rhiannon called it. We would enter the circle, hold hands and stand still in the moonlight preparing ourselves for the prayers. Rhiannon, being the priestess, led the prayers but we all had our part to play. Once one of us had said a prayer, we'd all take a step to the left and then the next one would speak. The way Rhiannon had put it together, it was almost like a dance and at the end we would all speak the lines together. Then we would thank the Goddess for prayers answered, for friendship and a load of other stuff. After another silence, the priestess would declare the ritual over and she'd break the magical circle.'

'What happened after that?' Mac asked.

'We'd break out the beers and have a chat. Rhiannon said that us all being together and enjoying each other's company was as much a part of the ritual as anything,' Rubaih replied. 'It was definitely the bit I liked best.'

'Is that what happened last Friday evening?'

Rubaih nodded.

'Was it you who brought the beer along?' Mac asked.

'Yes, my dad has this fancy shed in the back garden where he and his friends go to watch football and get drunk. He has cases of the stuff in there.'

'Didn't the police ask him if he'd bought any Sapporo beer?'

'If they did, it's my guess that my brother lied,' Ahmad interrupted. 'He still does most of his business with Saudi Arabia and the surrounding states and being seen to be a good Muslim is really important to him.'

'He's a hypocrite,' Rubaih said with some anger.

'Yes, that I can't deny,' Ahmad said with a shrug.

'Why were Rhiannon and Alicia in Radley Meadows by themselves?'

'I don't know. We normally all went back together but they stayed behind. Rhiannon said that she had a special prayer of thanks to say.'

'Had she ever stayed behind before?'

'Yes, just the once, a month ago. She and Alicia stayed behind then too.'

'And you've no idea why?' Mac asked.

Rubaih shook his head.

'So, last Friday the rest of you all walked back together and only Rhiannon and Alicia stayed behind?' Mac asked.

'That's right.'

'How long did it take you to walk back?'

'Well, we weren't rushing so about forty-five minutes, I'd guess,' Rubaih replied.

'How did you get off the estate in the first place? I take it that you didn't go through the front gate,' Mac asked.

'No, ages ago we made a rope ladder and attached it to the wall just behind the shed,' Rubaih explained. 'The wall's only about six feet high there so we'd just climb to the top and then let ourselves down on the other side. We had a rope attached to the ladder so that we could pull it over the wall and then use it to get back in. We used that ladder a lot. Getting off of the estate for a while felt like getting out of prison.'

'Did you see anyone else around while you were in Radley Meadows?'

Rubaih thought about this for a while.

'No, there was no-one else around. There never is after it goes dark. I guess that's why we liked it so much. Whenever we went there it felt quite special, as though the whole place belonged just to us.'

'Were there any cars in the car park?' Mac asked.

Rubaih had to think for a while.

'I don't remember but I'm sure that I would have noticed if there had been any.'

'So, apart from Rhiannon and Alicia staying behind, everything was as usual?'

Rubaih nodded.

'What did you do after you went back to the estate?' Mac asked.

'We talked for a while. Wilda was wondering why Rhiannon and Alicia were staying behind and so we talked about that for a while.'

Mac had another name, Wilda, but he didn't let on to Rubaih.

'How long did you talk for?'

'Around half an hour, I'd guess.'

Mac had been wondering if it might have been possible for someone from the coven to have doubled back and killed the two girls. However, because of the time it would have taken, that now seemed unlikely. He looked at the young boy and felt some pity for him. He knew that he had to ask the question again.

'Rubaih, two young girls have been brutally murdered and, if we're going to catch their murderer, we need every scrap of information we can get. I'm asking you again for the names of the other members of the coven.'

'I...I don't know,' he looked at his uncle for some sort of answer.

'If you liked your friend then I think you should tell them,' Ahmad said to his nephew.

'I did like her,' Rubaih replied. 'I really liked her.'

'She liked you too,' Mac said.

Rubaih looked at him in wonder.

'She told some of her friends in school that she liked a boy called Wolf,' Mac explained.

'She did?' He was silent for a moment. 'I wanted to tell her how I felt about her but I thought we'd have time. I thought we'd have...'

At that moment Rubaih totally fell apart. He started sobbing and his whole body started shaking. His uncle put a protective arm around him. Mac formally ended the interview and signalled for Mahshid to follow him out of the interview room.

'Poor kid,' Mahshid said. 'That was very kind of you.'

'What?'

'To tell him that Rhiannon liked him.'

'Well, while it may have been kind, it means that we'll probably learn nothing more tonight,' Mac said.

In truth, he was somewhat annoyed with himself. They waited for a few minutes until Ahmad appeared.

'If it's okay, I'll take Rubaih back home with me for a while. I've never seen him so upset. I think he needs to be quiet for a while and he definitely won't get that at home. I'll talk to him and, if he's willing to tell you what you want to know, we'll drop by first thing in the morning.'

'Thank you, Ahmad. Are you going to call his father?' Mac asked.

'I suppose I'll have to but I've got no idea what I'm going to tell him.' Ahmad glanced over at the open door to the interview room. 'He's a good boy, Mr. Maguire. Thanks for going easy on him.'

'He's going to be in for a rough ride. In fact, your whole family are. Due to his age, we should be able to keep Rubaih's name secret and hopefully out of the press. However, sooner or later, they're going to get hold of this and you can probably guess what some of them will make of it when they discover that magic and a coven are involved.'

'Well, his father's going to love that alright. Anyway, Rubaih can always come and live with me if it comes to it.'

Mac watched as the man and the boy walked back across the field. Mac thought that Rubaih was truly lucky in at least one thing, having an uncle who loved him.

'So, it looks as if we may have to wait until tomorrow then,' Mahshid said.

Mac sat down and was about to call Dan when he heard a tapping on the back door. He wondered if

Rubaih or Ahmad had left something behind. He opened the door.

A young girl stood in front of him. She was almost as tall as Mac and she wore a light green parka that had seen some use, ripped jeans and high black lace-up boots. Her hair was cut quite short and she had a tomboyish look about her. She looked at Mac with some trepidation before she spoke.

'I saw Wolf coming in and, well, I've decided that I need to speak to you as well.'

Perhaps we won't have to wait for tomorrow after all, Mac thought.

Chapter Sixteen

Mac ushered her inside. The night had turned bitterly cold and, as she had been waiting outside for some time, it was no surprise when she started shivering. Mac gave her a hot chocolate and let her warm up a little before he spoke to her.

'My name's Mac Maguire. What's yours?' Mac gently asked.

'It's Roz, Roz Spaak,' she replied looking into her hot chocolate. 'I suppose that Wolf has told you all about me and the rest of the coven.'

'No, he didn't tell us anything. He was afraid that you all might get into some sort of trouble and then he got quite upset.'

'I can understand that. He really liked Arian and I think that she really liked him too.'

'When you say Arian, I take it that you're referring to Rhiannon Brodeur?' Mac asked.

'That's right. I'm sorry but we're so used to using our magical names all the time. I hate my real name but I loved the name Rhiannon found for me.'

'And what was that?'

'Wilda. It means 'the wild one'. When I'm eighteen and I finally get out of the prison of an estate where I live and go to university, I'm going to change my name to Wilda.'

'How old are you Roz?'

'I'm sixteen.'

'In that case we can interview you without having an appropriate adult present but if you'd like one...'

'No thanks,' she replied looking up at Mac. 'I don't think I know any 'appropriate adults' anyway.'

She said this with a scowl.

'What about your parents?' Mac asked.

'Well, the last I heard, my dad was somewhere in the Caribbean screwing one of his barbie-doll girlfriends and as for my mum...' she stopped and sighed. 'Well, my mum could never be described as being either appropriate or an adult.'

'Okay, shall we get started then?' Mac said.

He led Roz to an interview room and gestured for Mahshid to follow them. He started the tape running and Mac and Mahshid stated their names.

'Can you state your full name, please?' Mac asked.

'Do I have to?' Roz asked.

'I'm afraid you do.'

She gave a big sigh and said, 'My name is Rosalinda Daisybell Spaak.'

Mac could well understand why she might have wanted to change her name.

'I'll need to ask you what happened on Friday evening but first I have to ask for the names of the other three members of the coven,' Mac said. 'While it's likely that either Rhiannon or Alicia or both were the targets of the attack, it's also possible that the murderer might be after the other members of the coven too. In either case, it's entirely possible that the killer will kill again so we need to speak to, and possibly protect, everyone in the coven.'

She thought about this for a while. Mac let her think.

'The other three are Modig, his real name is Noam Klein and he lives in the house next to mine. He's really nice and he was my first friend on the estate. Then there's Cwen and Circe. They're twins but they're not identical. They live in the street next to Rhiannon.'

'And what are Cwen and Circe's real names?'

Roz was quiet for a moment and looked down at the table.

'It's going to spoil everything, isn't it?' she said in a small sad voice. 'Anyway, their names are Bimpe and

Ibukun Ladipo. They live in Hellegrut, about two streets away from where Wolf lives.'

Mac excused himself, turned off the recorder and left the room. He looked at his watch. It was now ten fifteen. He hoped that he wouldn't be waking Dan up but this was news that he needed to hear. Luckily, he was still up.

'So, you've got the names and addresses of all five of them?' Dan asked. 'That's great. I know it's a bit late but I'll get Adil and probably Jo and Gerry out and we'll speak to them tonight.'

'I think that you'd better tread carefully when you speak to the Ladipo family,' Mac said.

He then told him why.

'Yes, we had one of those cases in Luton when I was a sergeant,' Dan replied. 'Don't worry, I'll watch my step. See you later.'

Mac returned to the interview room and started the tape running again. He went through most of the questions he'd asked Rubaih and he got more or less the same answers. She'd seen nothing out of the ordinary in Radley Meadows. There was no-one about and she was definite that there were no cars parked nearby.

'Roz, just before I stopped the interview you said something about 'it spoiling everything'. I'm interested in knowing why you said that.'

She thought for a moment before she spoke.

'It's all going to come out now and, once Bimpe's dad hears about it, I probably won't get to see her for quite a while.'

Mac looked at Roz. He had an idea why but he asked anyway.

'Why is Bimpe so important to you?'

'It's all down to Rhiannon really. For years now, I've felt as if I've been living in the bottom of a deep dark hole. Everything just seemed so pointless. The thought

131

of killing myself was becoming more and more attractive when Rhiannon finally got it out of me. She's good at that, persuading people.'

'What did you tell Rhiannon?' Mac asked.

'That I was gay,' she said giving Mac a defiant look. 'I'd never told anyone before, not anyone. After what my mum has been saying about gay people, I thought that Rhiannon wouldn't want to know me afterwards but she was great.'

'Your mum?'

'Yes, unfortunately you might know her better as K. T. Sparks,' Roz replied.

Mac had to think for a moment. The name was familiar but why?

'She knows who my mum is,' Roz said as she nodded towards Mahshid.

'I do,' Mahshid said. 'She's just got thrown off Twitter again, hasn't she?'

'That's right. This time it was for suggesting that a way to solve the 'gay problem' was to put us all in boats and sink them in the middle of the Atlantic,' Roz said.

Seeing Mac's puzzled expression Mahshid explained, 'She writes some columns in the right-wing press and she pops up on radio and TV usually spouting some really nasty anti-immigration stuff.'

'That's my mum,' Roz said who looked on the point of tears. 'If you're white, straight and think that Hitler had some really good ideas then you'll get on with her just fine.'

Mac didn't want her getting upset too so he steered the conversation away from her mother.

'You said that Rhiannon was okay when you told her you were gay. What happened then?'

'She was better than okay,' Roz said with a little smile. 'She said that the only point in living is to be true to yourself and that you should never have to hide who you really are. So, at the full-moon ritual just after my sixteenth birthday, on Rhiannon's advice, I came out to the whole coven. It was such a relief. Of course, most of them had already guessed but being able to say those words out loud was the second-best thing that ever happened to me.'

'And what was the first?' Mac asked getting truly interested.

'That came just afterwards,' she said with a smile that lit up her face. 'It was my suggestion that Bimpe take the name Circe. It's also the name of a great enchantress in Greek mythology and Bimpe had certainly enchanted me. I never for a moment thought that she'd be interested but, after the ritual, I was so elated about coming out that I was in a dream and I found myself walking behind everyone else. Then Circe appeared walking beside me. She said something about me being brave and then she stopped and kissed me. It was just a peck on the lips but afterwards we just stood and looked at each other. Then she really kissed me. It was my first proper kiss and the best thing that has ever happened to me.'

'And now you're afraid that you might not be able to see her?'

Roz nodded.

'Although her mum and dad were born here, their family are Nigerian and she told me that a lot of them don't hold either witchcraft or being gay in much regard.'

Mac knew that all too well. He had once been involved in a case where the self-proclaimed pastor of a Nigerian Pentecostal church had been involved in the torture and murder of a twelve-year-old boy who had been accused of being a witch. They had found parts of his body all over London. Yet, the people involved, some of which were from the boy's own family, were totally convinced that they were right in carrying out such a gruesome murder.

Roz continued, 'We've been seeing each other as often as we could and we were both hoping that we might be able to go to the same university and try having a life together. Now, I just don't know.'

'My boss will be interviewing Bimpe and her family as we speak. He's aware of the situation with her family and he'll go as carefully as he can. Also, as you're all under eighteen, we'll be asking the court to keep your identities secret but it's not something we can guarantee. I think it's going to be difficult for all of you for quite some time to come.'

She looked up at him and nodded. She looked so young and so vulnerable that his heart went out to her. Whatever happened, the dark days that lay ahead of all of them would never be forgotten.

'Rubaih told me that, when you got back to the estate, you all talked for a while together before you went home. Is that right?' Mac asked.

'Yes, we talked about Rhiannon and Alicia and tried to figure out why they had stayed behind,' Roz replied.

'And did you come to any conclusion about that?'

Roz shook her head.

'Not really but we were fairly sure that it was something to do with Alicia though.'

'Why did you think that?'

'Alicia was the last the join the coven,' Roz said. 'Rhiannon said that we needed her so that there would be seven of us. She had problems though, that was obvious enough to us all, but I guess that Rhiannon couldn't resist trying to help her.'

'And did she help her?' Mac asked.

'Yes, she did. At first, Alicia would hardly say a word and she'd flinch at the slightest sound. She mentioned something about being bullied at school but I think that there was more to it than that. Anyway, Rhiannon loved a challenge and so she worked on her and Alicia gradually became more talkative and more confident in herself. In the end, she was confident enough that she was able to cast a spell on the head bully at her school and it worked too! I'd never seen her so happy. She was like a different person.'

'How was she after her father died?' Mac asked.

Roz gave him a puzzled look.

'I didn't know that her father had died. When did that happen?'

'Just over three weeks ago.'

'Really? We didn't see her for a couple of days but she didn't say why. Anyway, I don't think that Alicia could have been all that upset about it. In fact, I think that these last few weeks she's looked as happy as I've ever seen her.'

This interested Mac immensely. For some reason he felt that it might be important.

'It would appear that Alicia wasn't a virgin. Do you know if she was seeing someone?'

Roz smiled, 'I know that she and Modig, sorry Noam, were seeing each other but I didn't think that it had gone that far. They kept quiet about it but I saw them once walking hand-in-hand and they looked good, you know, as if they belonged together.'

'How has Noam been since he heard the news?' Mac asked.

'I honestly don't know. We all met up when we heard what had happened. Ibukun said that we should keep it to ourselves for now and we were all so confused, and scared I suppose, that we went along with it. Noam never said a single word the whole time we were together.'

'Would you like another hot chocolate?' Mac asked.
Roz nodded.

Mac suspended the interview and left her with Mahshid. He needed to talk with Jo who should right now be talking to Noam and his father.

'Mac, I was just about to call you,' Jo answered somewhat breathlessly.

'What's happened?' Mac asked.

'We got here just before the ambulance. Noam Klein has taken an overdose of his father's anti-depressants. He's on his way to hospital right now.'

Chapter Seventeen

Monday

Ten minutes later Mac found himself on the motorway heading towards the Lister Hospital in Stevenage with Roz Spaak sitting beside him. She'd insisted on going to see Noam straight away and she'd told Mac that she'd walk there if she had to. Mac had believed her.

However, he had first made Roz call her mother and tell her what she was planning to do. Mac spoke to her himself just to make sure that she was okay with him taking Roz to the hospital. She was quite short with Mac and seemed more interested in getting back to bed than hearing about what was happening to her daughter.

He'd also called Jo back and told her that she and Gerry might as well go home and get some sleep and that he'd hold the fort at the hospital for now. He glanced at the car's clock as they turned off the motorway. It had just gone midnight. He realised that he might be at the hospital for some time and that it would catch up with him eventually. So, he decided that he'd go straight home when he finally got tired and sleep until he woke up.

He showed the reception nurse at A&E his warrant card and asked for Noam Klein. He and Roz were shown a seat and told to wait while they found out what was happening. They waited for over fifteen minutes. Mac noticed that, somewhere in that time, Roz's hand had found its way into Mac's. Eventually a man pushed open one of the double doors behind which lay the treatment bays.

'Roz!' he said with some surprise and more than a little relief. 'I was told that there was a policeman out here who wanted to see me.'

The man was tall and thin and he had a slightly stooped back. He was dressed in a checked shirt and a pullover that had seen better days. He had thick black-rimmed spectacles and a look of confusion on his face. Mac reckoned that he was probably in his late forties but, at that moment, he looked much older.

'That would be me,' Mac said as he stood up.

'How is he?' Roz asked. 'Is he...is he alright?'

'They're still trying to get the drugs out of his system so they can't say anything definite just yet. But tell me, why are you here and why are the police involved?'

Mac didn't answer. He went and had a word with the nurse at reception.

'If you follow the nurse, she'll take us to somewhere where we can talk privately. She'll tell the doctor who is treating your son where you are in case there's any news.'

Mr. Klein said nothing. He just nodded and followed Mac into the treatment area. The nurse showed them into a little room containing four chairs, all different, and a coffee-ringed table. Mac guessed that this is where the relatives waited until they were told the bad news.

'Mr. Maguire, what's going on?' Mr. Klein asked as soon as Mac shut the door behind him.

Mac told him.

'Is that right?' Mr. Klein asked turning to look at Roz. She nodded.

'A coven? He was really into this magic thing?' Mr. Klein said with a look of disbelief. 'And you say that he really liked this girl, the one who was killed?'

Roz nodded again.

'I thought that the overdose might have been some sort of delayed reaction to his mother's death but what you've told me makes more sense.'

'Mr. Klein, how long...'

'Oh, please call me Micah.'

'Okay Micah, how long has it been since Noam's mother died?' Mac asked.

'Nearly two years now but it seems like yesterday in some ways. Sara had been ill for some time with her heart but it still came as a bit of a shock to us all. And now this girl has died too. I can understand why it might have been too much for the poor kid.'

'I take it that the citalopram pills were yours?' Mac asked.

'They were,' Mr. Klein replied with a frown. 'I was quite depressed after Sara died but I decided that I needed to keep going. So, I continued teaching and I was also a partner in a business at the same time. The pills helped me or, at least, I thought they did but after two years I'm still taking them. I think that all they've really done is to help me to postpone things. I still haven't dealt with my grief, I know that now, but they helped me to keep working. I teach an Advanced Bio-chemistry course at Cambridge University. That's where a few of us started our own company up producing predictive software for drugs trials. We've been very successful but, in achieving that, I think that I may have ignored Noam somewhat. We never really talked about how he felt and if I lose him now...God, he's the last bit of Sara I've got...if I lose him...'

Mr. Klein started shuddering and he wept, the tears rolling down his cheeks in streams. Roz held his hand tightly and spoke to him. Mac felt as though he was intruding, so he left and waited outside in the corridor for a few minutes. While he was waiting, a doctor came towards him. He looked very young to Mac. He looked very tired too.

'Mr. Klein?' the doctor asked.

'He's in there,' Mac said nodding towards the door.

He waited anxiously in the hallway wondering what was being said on the other side of the door. He got an inkling as the door opened and a smiling doctor emerged.

'Mr. Klein said that you can go in now, if you like.'

One glance was enough. There were still tears on Micah's face but both he and Roz were smiling too.

'It's good news, Mr. Maguire,' Micah said as he wiped the tears away. 'Luckily, he must have taken the pills not long before I found him so they've managed to get most of the drugs out of his stomach before they went into his system. They said that he should be alright. He'll be alright, Mr. Maguire.'

'That's excellent news,' Mac said as he slumped into a chair.

'I've been so selfish,' Micah almost to himself.

'No, you haven't,' Mac said. 'We all deal with grief in our own way, as best we can.'

Micah looked up at Mac.

'You say that like someone who knows.'

'I do. My wife died at around the same time that yours did. I would have thrown myself into my work too but I never got the chance. Unfortunately, I had a chronic pain condition which soon became evident to everyone and I had to retire from the police force. The following six months were the worst of my life. It was only when I started working again, acting as a consultant to the local police as I'm doing now, that I started to recover a little. So don't blame yourself and, also, don't blame Noam. He must think that the whole universe is against him.'

'I won't,' Micah said. 'Noam and his mother were very close. I know how deeply her passing affected him. Losing this girl too, someone he really liked, would have been the last straw for most us, I think. No, I won't blame Noam but please catch whoever killed those young girls.'

'We're doing our best,' Mac said. 'Roz, what are you going to do now?'

'I'd like to stay. I want to see Noam before I go home.'

'Okay, I can understand that but I'll need to get going. I'll arrange for a uniformed officer to sit with you and then drive you home when you're ready.'

Mac had to wait for a while until a young police-woman tapped on the door. He said his goodbyes and he was making his way through the waiting area when he saw something that made him stop in his tracks. Two police officers were sitting on either side of a young man. He looked anxious and his right foot was tapping on the floor at quite a speed. He looked familiar. Then Mac remembered that he'd seen his photo recently in a case file.

It was Cameron Aitken.

Mac caught the eye of the policeman sitting nearest to him and beckoned at him to come over. He looked incredibly young to Mac. He glanced over at his partner before standing up. He approached Mac with a puzzled expression on his face. Mac showed him his warrant card.

'That's Cameron Aitken you've got there, isn't it?' Mac said.

'Yes, but how could you know that?'

'He's been reported as missing and I've had a look at his file. I'm one of the team that's investigating the murder of the two girls in Radley Meadows and so we're interested in anything that happened around the same time. Where did you find him?'

'We passed him by as he was walking in the direction of Duxford on the A505,' the young policeman replied.

Mac knew that Duxford was some twenty-five miles or so from Letchworth. Young Cameron had covered some ground.

'We saw him again two hours later when we were on our way back,' the young policeman continued. 'It was nearly dark and he was in the middle of nowhere so we pulled up and had a word. It was clear that he wasn't right, he was quite confused and muttering about hearing voices, so we brought him here to get him checked out. Do you really fancy him for the murders?' the policeman asked as he turned and glanced back at Cameron.

'No, we've got no evidence of his involvement, we're just trying to cover all the angles. I take it that you're waiting for the psychiatrists to section him?'

'Yes, he's just seen someone and they said that he was in a bad way, having psychotic visions and the like. They said that it was most likely that they'd admit him to hospital under Section 2. They also said that it might take some time,' the policeman said with a frown.

Mac knew this all too well from experience. When he had been a uniformed officer, he'd spent countless hours hanging around hospitals waiting for the panel of psychiatrists to turn up to make an assessment. Under Section 2 of the Mental Health Act doctors are allowed to detain a patient in hospital for up to twenty-eight days to assess their condition. He glanced over at young Cameron. He looked both scared and exhausted and he kept looking suddenly around as if he was hearing a noise that no-one else could hear.

Mac was glad that he had never had to make a decision to section someone himself but, from the anxious and exhausted look on Cameron's face and the bedraggled state of his clothing, he reckoned that twenty-eight days of rest and recouperation might not be such a bad thing.

'Did he say anything?' Mac asked.

'I asked him why he had walked so far and he said that it kept the voices away. He said that if he kept walking then they couldn't catch him up. He also kept going on about the moon being full of blood and seeing the devil and angels and so on. Oh, and he asked us to help someone. Yes, he went on about that a bit.'

'Who did he want you to help?'
'A girl he said. A girl with red lips.'

Chapter Eighteen

Mac awoke in several stages. When he could finally summon up the energy to open an eye, he saw that there was no light coming through the chinks in the curtains and he was surprised for some reason. He glanced over at his clock. It was six-thirty.

Morning or night though?

Unrelated thoughts and images swirled around in his head as he struggled to get them into any sort of order. Then he saw Micah Klein's anxious face and everything clicked into place. As he had left the hospital around four in the morning, he guessed that it must now be six-thirty in the evening. He had slept for nearly fourteen hours.

He reckoned that he'd needed it though. He had been running on empty while he'd been waiting for Eileen to arrive. As she was technically his 'nearest relative' then she would be able to sit in when the sectioning panel spoke to Cameron Aitken. Mac had made no attempt to speak to Cameron directly as any interview with the police would have to wait until a doctor sanctioned it.

However, both Eileen and the doctor had agreed to the police taking a DNA swab.

Mac sat up and then steeled himself as he stood up. His back was okay, or as okay as it was likely to get. The rest had obviously done him some good. While he was calling Tim, he noticed that there was a text from Eileen. After reading it he had a shower which succeeded in waking him up a little more. He then drove into town to meet Tim in the Magnets. His stomach rumbled and reminded him that it needed filling.

He was really happy to see his friend and was just as happy to see his steak and chips when it arrived. He talked over the case with Tim as he put his meal away.

'So, do you really think that this Cameron had something to do with the murders?' Tim asked.

'I doubt it but the DNA might tell us something different, I suppose. If he was walking aimlessly around then it's always possible that he might have somehow come across Rhiannon but, then again, it might just have been something he dreamed up.'

'How was Eileen?'

'I think that she was just relieved that someone had finally found him and that he hadn't ended up under a bus or something. Anyway, she sent me a text this morning. They've taken Cameron to a mental hospital called Egret Court for assessment. We should be able to interview him there once the doctors have seen him.'

'What's it like?' Tim asked.

'What? The mental hospital?' Mac asked as he pushed his empty plate away.

Tim nodded, 'Yes, I've never been in one but they always look really creepy when you see them in the movies.'

'I remember years ago that they used to be desperate, dark and uncaring places, but, thankfully, Egret Court is nothing like that. It's near London Colney and it's only a few years old. It looks more like a hotel than a hospital and it's got a good reputation. Cameron should be okay while he's there.'

'Good. Anyway, it's nice to see you, Mac,' Tim said as he held up his pint.

'You too,' Mac replied as he held up his cup of coffee. 'I'm hoping that it won't be too long before I can join you for a proper drink.'

'So, you're still going to camp out in that barn until the case is solved?' Tim asked.

'I am, for now at least. If the case doesn't break in a week or so then...' Mac finished his sentence by shrugging his shoulders.

They spent the rest of their short time together discussing their favourite football club's exploits. For once, Aston Villa wasn't flirting with the relegation places and had started the season reasonably well. For the first time in many years Mac and Tim talked positively about what the rest of the season might bring.

The conversation was finally brought to a halt when Mac's phone went off. From Mac's side of the call, Tim figured out that his friend would soon be meeting someone at the incident room.

'That was Father Donal Farrell,' Mac explained. 'He's a friend of Father Pat and he seems quite anxious to see me.' Seeing Tim's puzzled expression, he continued. 'He used to work at the headquarters of Sanguine Salvatoris in London for a while.'

'And you really think that they might have something to do with the murders?'

'I've no idea but I know next to nothing about them and that's something I find intensely annoying. I'd guess that it's unlikely but, as Monica Hashley seems to be deeply involved with them, then you never know. Anyway, Father Farrell said that he'll meet me at the barn in about an hour or so.'

As Mac drove back towards Radley Meadows, he went over in his mind what he already knew about Sanguine Salvatoris. It wasn't much. It was founded by a young Spanish priest in the 1930s who attached himself to the dictator Franco under which the organisation flourished before spreading to Catholic communities in other countries. Its credo appeared to be the worship of the family as the centre of all things with the father being its unquestioned head. It all sounded quite old-fashioned as they quite publicly excluded anyone who wasn't straight, conservative or

Catholic. Yet he'd read that the sect was growing, not just in numbers but in power. Their targeting of the rich and powerful gave them some influence, even in political circles it seemed. One article he'd read stated that a number of MPs and several ministers in the government were suspected of being members.

However, just about everything he'd read contained those words 'alleged' or 'suspected' as very little of what the sect did ever made it into the public domain. They were a mystery and Mac didn't like mysteries. He was hoping that Father Farrell might throw some light into these dark corners.

Martin and Jean were handing over to Mahshid and Amanda just as he arrived. Martin gave him a bit of ribbing for 'sleeping in' which made Mac laugh.

'Has anything happened?' Mac asked.

'Not much,' Martin replied. 'Rubaih Alzahrani came in this morning with his uncle and they spoke to Dan but it seems that he couldn't add anything new. Dan told Rubaih about Noam Klein and he looked quite upset as he left to visit him in hospital. I felt sorry for him to be honest.'

'From what I've learned about them so far, they weren't a bad bunch of kids. They certainly didn't deserve any of what's happened to them. Was there anything else?'

'Well, Dan held a press conference around three and formally identified the second girl we found as being Alicia Hashley,' Martin replied. 'That's it really.'

'Did anything new come in about Cameron Aitken?' Mac asked.

Martin shook his head.

'Dan tried to arrange an interview with him but his doctor wouldn't hear of it just yet. Forensics have been looking at his flat but we haven't heard anything from them so far.'

It seemed that Mac had picked the right day to sleep in. He sat down at his desk and tried to concentrate on doing some work but his eyes kept straying to the door. He found that he couldn't wait to hear what Father Farrell had to say. He didn't have to wait very long.

Just after Martin and Jean had left, a uniformed officer showed a man inside. He was in his fifties, red-haired and slight of build. He knew that it was Father Farrell by his black clothes and his white Roman collar. He ushered him into one of the interview rooms.

Mac gestured for him to sit down and then said, 'Father Farrell, thanks for coming. This isn't an official interview but I'd like to record it for my own benefit, if you don't mind that is?'

The Father didn't.

'I've just heard on the news that one of the dead girls was Alicia Hashley. Is that why you're so interested in SanSal?'

'SanSal?' Mac asked.

'Sorry, it's how they refer to Sanguine Salvatoris within the church. It's less of a mouthful,' the priest said.

'We've learned that Monica Hashley is involved in the organisation and so we'd like to know more about it. Did you ever get to meet her when you were working there?'

'Yes, I met Monica and her husband a number of times when I was working at SanSal's headquarters in London. John Hashley was the Second Most Humble Luminary at the time. He later became the First Most Humble Luminary.'

'And what is that?' Mac asked.

'The Luminaries officially run Sanguine Salvatoris and so, as they are all members of the laity and not priests, the church has no say in the organisation. The

First Most Humble Luminary is supposed to be the leader of the movement.'

'Supposed to be?'

'In reality it's run by Father Xavier Peverett. Although technically he's just an unattached parish priest, in reality he's at least as powerful within the church as the Cardinal, if not more so. That's why I was sent to work with them.'

'The Cardinal sent you there?' Mac asked.

Father Farrell nodded.

'I don't know why he'd thought I'd make a good spy but I did my best to find out what they were up to.'

'Does the Cardinal know that you're here?'

'He does and he's happy for me to help the investigation in any way I can.'

Mac thought for a moment.

'Tell me about Father Peverett and John Hashley.'

'They worked very closely together but, like all Luminaries, they always allowed Father Peverett to have the last word.'

'Why was that?'

'I suppose it was because it was Father Peverett who founded the British branch of the movement over twenty-five years ago. As a young parish priest working in Salford, he'd gotten himself into some trouble. I heard that he'd had a relationship with a female parishioner and had gotten her pregnant. His Bishop suggested that, if he wanted to stay a priest, then he had better show some contrition and stay well away from the woman. So, he took himself off to Spain to work in a poor parish and there he somehow met Monsignor Etxeberria who was in his late seventies at the time. He had founded the Sanguine Salvatoris movement during the Franco years and, as it basically sucked up to the dictator, it really took off. It took a while longer to spread to other countries though.'

'How popular is the movement now?' Mac asked.

'It's in just about every country where there's a Catholic church and it's still growing. Everything it espouses is in black and white and said with complete certainty and conviction. Its message is simple; family, obedience and avoiding sin. It's simplistic beyond belief but it seems that a lot of people like that approach as it saves them having to think for themselves.'

Mac detected more than a hint of bitterness in that last sentence.

'Anyway,' Father Farrell continued, 'it seems that, as Father Peverett had actually met with the Monsignor and had obtained his direct approval to start a branch in Britain, it now gives him tremendous cachet within the movement. And the church come to that, now that Monsignor Etxeberria has been made a saint.'

'Yes, I remember something about that now,' Mac said. 'It wasn't a universally popular choice, was it?'

'No, it wasn't and the Cardinal didn't take it well either. That was part of the reason why I was despatched to find out what I could about them. Not that I found much.'

'How long were you with them for?'

'Just over nine months. They were all very nice to me while I was there but they made sure that I was never invited to any meetings and everyone watched what they said when I was around. It was quite a frustrating experience and more than a little creepy, if I'm being honest.'

'What did Monica Hashley do within the organisation?' Mac asked.

'Nothing really. Oh, there's a women's wing of the organisation called 'Virgo Maria Servi Dei' which means 'Servants of the Virgin Mary' and she was part of that. However, that was basically just a talking shop, no-one ever took any notice of what they said. All the decisions were made by the male Luminaries and

150

always under the guidance of Father Peverett, of course.'

'What was the relationship like between John Hashley and Father Peverett?'

'They were quite close, I believe,' Father Farrell replied. 'John was a true believer and he took it all very seriously. I heard that, like many Luminaries, he had committed himself to the El Diezmo or Holy Tithe which meant that he handed over at least ten percent of his earnings to the organisation. As John was very rich, this came to quite a sum. He also lent them some eye-watering amounts of money at very favourable rates as did some of the other Luminaries. That's how they could afford to build their grand new headquarters in London.'

'So, what do you think happened to all those loans when John Hashley died?' Mac asked.

'I've honestly no idea.'

Mac was more than interested and he made a mental note to contact someone who might be able to give him the answer.

'Is there anyone else that John or Monica Hashley were close to at Sanguine Salvatoris?'

'Well, I believe that John had known Father Manley for a number of years but I don't think that he was all that friendly with Monica. Her friend and confessor was a young priest who, it was rumoured, Father Peverett was training to one day take over the organisation,' the priest replied. 'His name is Father Julian Renfield. If ever you saw Father Peverett around then you could be sure that Father Renfield was hovering somewhere nearby. I didn't see him that often with John Hashley but they clearly got on alright. I'm still puzzled as to why you're so interested though. You surely don't think that anyone at Sanguine Salvatoris has anything to do with the dreadful murders of those two young girls, do you?'

'I don't think anything at the moment, if I'm being honest, and that's because I know so little about them. They're definitely a piece in the jigsaw though but, with regard to how important they might be, I've honestly got no idea.'

Mac continued asking questions but didn't learn anything new. It seemed that Father Farrell had indeed been kept out of the loop during his time at Sanguine Salvatoris.

'Do you know of anyone else who might be willing to talk to me?' Mac asked with more hope than certainty.

The priest gave this some thought. He then slowly shook his head.

'I'm sorry but no. I spent nine months on the inside trying to find people who might talk to me and got nowhere. I even tried talking to some members who had recently left the organisation but they weren't talking either.'

As he showed Father Farrell to the door, Mac noticed that Mahshid, Jean and Amanda were looking over Martin's shoulder at something on his laptop. They all looked very interested at what was on the screen. Had they found something?

As soon as the door closed behind the priest, Mac scuttled over to Martin's desk as fast as he could.

'What is it?' he asked.

'Have a look,' Martin replied as he set the video to play from the start.

Mac glanced at the time stamp. It was 21:11 on the evening of the murders. The camera showed an empty stretch of driveway beyond which there was a road. A car's headlights flashed by at speed. He knew where this was as he'd been there not long ago. It was the main entrance into the Drymanshouse Estate. A Porsche Cayenne slowed down as it pulled into the driveway. The car came to a halt as the gates slowly opened and the numberplate was clearly visible. As it was dark, it wasn't possible to see who was behind the wheel.

'Do we know whose car it is?' Mac asked.

'We do,' Martin replied. 'It's Monica Hashley's.'

'But wasn't she supposed to have been at the headquarters of Sanguine Salvatoris in London on the night that her daughter was killed?'

'That's what she said in her statement. She said she went to bed early and slept until late the next morning.'

They all looked at each other in anticipation.

'You'll need to look at this too.'

Mac did as Martin said and saw the same car leaving the estate just ten minutes later. The car turned left onto the main road.

'She's heading towards Radley Meadows,' Mac said.

So, it looked as if Monica Hashley had lied to them. She wasn't in London but was back home just before the murders took place.

Was it really possible that Monica Hashley had taken her own daughter's life?

Chapter Nineteen

Just over an hour later and the whole team was assembled in the barn. There was an excited hush as Dan started the briefing.

'I know how hard you've all been working and I also know that all of the vast amounts of interviews we've carried out so far haven't really gotten us much further. However, it looks as if we've had a breakthrough. Martin will tell you all about it.'

Martin cued up the video on the big screen.

'This video shows Monica Hashley arriving at the Drymanshouse Estate at 21:11. She turned the burglar alarm off in her house off at 21:14 and then reset it again at 21:19. It only took her one attempt to correctly enter the code on both occasions.'

That alone was fairly damning, Mac thought.

Martin continued, 'She left the estate again at 21:24 and the car then turned left onto the road which is in the direction of Radley Meadows where, not long afterwards, the two girls were killed.'

'How certain are we that it's actually her though?' Jo asked.

'As certain as we can be,' Martin replied. 'The security company that guards the estate is based in the Netherlands, believe it or not, and that's partly why it took so long for them to get the data across. I had to call them myself and explain the situation but, once I did that, they really got their act together. They told me that it was definitely Monica Hashley's phone that was used to open the gate and they were also able to piece together her journey through the estate. She went straight home and then emerged a short while later carrying something in a white plastic bag. The camera was a fair distance away but the resolution of the video was good enough so that it could be seen that she was wearing a coat with a very distinctive design.'

A photo appeared on the screen. It showed a figure wearing a mid-length padded coat with a design that Mac couldn't quite make out. The hood was up obscuring the face.

'Here's a better photo of the coat,' Martin said. 'It's a Gucci and costs around two thousand pounds if you want to buy one so I'd guess that there aren't that many of them floating around.'

The coat had a floral design of pink and yellow flowers and it was now easy to see that it was definitely the same as the one captured by the CCTV camera.

'If Mrs. Hashley has one of those in her wardrobe then I'd guess that would be conclusive,' Dan said as he pulled his phone out.

Everyone correctly guessed that he was calling the forensics team.

'Yes, I know you've done the house but can you do it again and give her Porsche a thorough going over too,' Dan said before he put his phone away. He then turned to face the team. 'If our murderer was Monica Hashley, does anyone have a clue as to why she might have done it?'

No-one said a word. They all just looked at one another.

'What about you, Mac?' Dan asked.

'I've absolutely no idea why Monica Hashley would want to kill Rhiannon Brodeur and her own daughter but there've been a few cases I've been involved in where it's happened.'

'What was the motive in those?'

'Jealousy mostly, I'd say. The stereotypical aging mother suspecting that her young and more attractive daughter was having an affair with her boyfriend behind her back. Sometimes it was true too. However, I remember one case that might be closer to the mark. In that one a devoutly Christian woman killed her young daughter to 'save her from falling into the sins of the flesh', if you can believe it.'

Dan stood and thought for a moment.

'Okay everyone, go home and get some sleep,' Dan said. 'You too, Adil. You look exhausted.'

Adil did indeed look as if he was ready for bed. He gave Dan a grateful smile.

'Mac, as you've just rolled out of bed, how about coming with me to interview Mrs. Hashley? A car should be picking her up right now.'

'That's fine with me,' Mac replied. 'I have to admit that I can't wait to see what she has to say.'

It only took them ten minutes to drive to Letchworth Police Station but Monica Hashley was already waiting for them when they got there. She was a small and quite attractive woman in her early forties who was very elegantly dressed. The word 'petite' came into Mac's head. She also looked as if she might be the nervous type.

Mac couldn't help noticing that on the back of her chair hung a coat. A coat with a floral design of pink and yellow flowers. It was clear that Dan had seen it too.

'What am I doing here?' she asked as Dan and Mac walked into the interview room. 'I was going to go to bed. I haven't been feeling too well lately.'

As she said this Mac noticed a slight tremor in her right hand which she quickly hid under the table. He glanced over at Dan. He'd noticed it too.

'Some new evidence has come to light. I'd like you to look at this,' Dan said as he pushed a tablet in her direction. 'Just tap the screen and the video will play.'

'What screen?' she said looking mystified.

The tablet was slightly to her left. Mac noticed Dan looking at her quite thoughtfully before he pushed it over to her right.

'Oh that!' she said. 'I'm sorry but I've not been with it for a while.'

She tapped the screen and watched the video intently.

'That's my car,' she said. 'At least I think it is.'

'I can confirm that it's definitely your car,' Dan said. 'Here's another one.'

She tapped the screen again and saw someone in a Gucci coat go inside her house.

'Is that you?' Dan asked.

'It must be as that's my coat,' she said, 'but I don't understand. When was this taken?'

'It was taken the same evening that Alicia died.'

'Alicia's dead? What happened to her? Why didn't anyone tell me?' she said looking quite distraught.

Mac and Dan exchanged puzzled glances.

'Your daughter was murdered last Friday evening. We told you about it as soon as you came back from London.'

'Really? Are you sure?' she said looking totally confused. 'Well, I'll ask Alicia anyway. She's got a good memory and she remembers things for me. I'll just give her a call.'

Mac and Dan exchanged more puzzled looks. It occurred to Mac that she might be putting an act on for their benefit but he quickly dismissed the thought. Whatever was happening to her was very real.

While she was searching in her bag for her phone, Dan got up and stood on her left side. He flashed out a hand at her face as though he was going to slap her. She didn't flinch, in fact, she didn't move a single muscle. Dan sat down again. He suspended the interview and turned off the tape recorder before he left the room.

Once outside, he went straight to the Duty Sergeant and told him to get two officers to take Monica Hashley to the Lister Hospital and get her checked out. He also got a large plastic evidence bag and some gloves.

'And tell them not to let Mrs. Hashley out of their sight. She's a murder suspect.'

The sergeant assured Dan that they wouldn't.

'What do you think it is?' Mac asked.

'I'd guess that it's brain damage of some sort,' Dan replied. 'I've seen it before. My dad had it after he suffered a major stroke. It's called Left-Sided Neglect and, although there's nothing wrong with their vision, people with it just don't seem able to notice anything if it's in their left-hand field of view.'

'Brain damage might explain her confusion too,' Mac said. 'Imagine forgetting that your own daughter had been murdered. She must be in a bad way. From what she said, she might have been in a bad way for some time.'

'What makes you say that?' Dan asked as he put on some latex gloves.

'She said that Alicia had been helping her to remember things.'

'That's right, she did say that. If that's the case then why didn't she go to a doctor?' Dan quickly answered the question himself. 'Of course, it's probably a case of domestic abuse, isn't it?'

'That's certainly the best bet. Some people seem to think that domestic violence only happens in poor working-class families but that's so not true. Rich people can be just as handy with their fists too.'

'Might it have made her more likely to kill though?' Dan asked as he carefully placed Monica Hashley's coat in the evidence bag and sealed it.

'Well, I've heard of some scientific studies which strongly suggest that traumatic brain injury can lead to violent behaviour so who knows?'

'We'll just have to wait then…'

Dan was interrupted by his phone. He listened for a while and then said, 'We'll be there as soon as we can.'

'What is it?' Mac asked as they made their way to the car park.

'It looks like Monica Hashley, brain injury or not, is definitely our killer,' Dan said. 'They've found something in her car. Something quite damning.'

The gates were open when they arrived and they drove straight into the Drymanshouse Estate. The door to the Hashley's house was wide open as was the bonnet and boot of the Porsche Cayenne that was parked in the driveway. A man in a white all-in-one was taking photos of the car from different angles.

'Bob,' Dan said to another white-suited member of the team who had come out of the house to greet them.

Mac recognised Bob Yeardley and was glad that he was still on the case. Dan gave Bob the evidence bag containing Monica Hashley's coat and explained what it was.

'You might find this interesting,' Dan said. 'Okay, what have you got?

'We waited for you to come before we moved them. Have a look for yourself,' Bob said as he walked towards the car.

The lid of the boot was open and the spare tyre holder had been moved to the left.

'We found this in the boot hidden in an old blanket,' Bob said pointing towards a large book.

The book had a six-pointed star on the cover with what looked like Hebrew letters in a circle around it. The title simply said 'Malleus Maleficarum – The Hammer of Witches'.

'However, this is what will really interest you,' Bob said as he pointed towards the spare tyre holder.

There was something wedged between the spokes of the alloy wheel. Mac could see the edge of a white plastic bag but, when he got closer, he could see that the bag was tightly twisted around what looked like the haft of a hammer. Below that he could see some pink material with a floral design and the looped handles of a pair of scissors.

'So, that's what happened to Rhiannon's panties then,' Dan said.

'The scissors must have been used to cut the panties so that the killer could easily remove them,' Mac conjectured.

'Well, you'll know for certain tomorrow once we've put them through the lab,' Bob said being ever cautious. He then frowned and said, 'I'm afraid that I've also got an apology to make.'

Both Mac and Dan were surprised at this. It was unlike Bob and his team to make mistakes.

'We discovered something in Alicia Hashley's room, something that we should have spotted the first time around. It's a school exercise book and it was taped to the underside of one her drawers. Yes, I know it's one of the oldest tricks in the book but it caught us out anyway. We haven't looked inside it yet but, on the outside of the book, she'd written in capital letters 'Sunnivar's Grimoire'. Does that mean anything to you?'

'It certainly does,' Mac said. 'Can you photograph every page and get them to me as quickly as possible?'

Bob promised that he would.

'How soon do you think you can get an initial report on all this to me?' Dan asked hopefully gesturing towards the car.

'We'll do our best but it won't be with you before tomorrow midday,' Bob replied. 'Oh, and I'll send you the report on Cameron Aitken's flat too. I was just finishing it off when we got your call to come here.'

'Did you find anything interesting?' Dan asked.

'Not really apart from the fact that he walked out without his keys, his wallet and his phone. They were all still there.'

'What about his DNA?' Mac asked.

'You'll probably get a report on that first thing tomorrow,' Bob said. 'It looked really interesting.'

Bob said nothing more and pretended to walk away.

'And?' Mac said loudly.

Bob turned and smiled. Mac felt his leg being pulled.

'And we found some of Cameron Aitken's DNA on Rhiannon Brodeur's dress. It looks as if you've gone from having no suspects at all to having at least two.'

Chapter Twenty

Tuesday

Mac awoke to the smell of coffee and the muffled sound of voices. He opened an eye and looked at his watch. It had just gone ten o'clock. He carefully sat up and looked around. Martin and Jean were at their desks pounding away on their keyboards. The voices he'd heard were coming from one of the interview rooms. One was definitely Dan's but the other one was totally unfamiliar to him.

The interview rooms, being only temporary, weren't totally sound-proofed, however, while Mac could make out who was talking, he couldn't hear exactly what was being said. His curiosity was satisfied when the door to the interview room opened and Dan walked out with Rhiannon's father. They shook hands before Marc Brodeur walked out of the door.

Dan turned and saw that Mac was up.

'Did you learn anything from Rhiannon's dad?' Mac asked as he rubbed the sleep from his eyes.

'Not really. He just dropped by to tell us that he's going back to Paris. His girlfriend is due to go into labour any day now.'

'Really? He must be having some very mixed emotions right now,' Mac said.

'Yes, I think it would be fair to say that. He was quite upset just now when he spoke to me. I told him that he might has well go back to Paris and that I'd keep in touch with him if anything new happened. Anyway, what time did you get to sleep last night?' Dan asked.

'Around four, I think,' Mac replied. 'I'm afraid that my sleep is all over the place at the moment.'

'Just don't try and push it too far, Mac,' Dan said. 'Anyway, you might not need to do this for much longer, it looks like we might be nearing the end of the case.'

'You think that it's definitely Monica Hashley then?'

'I do. The evidence is overwhelming. We have her very close to the scene of the murders, the murder weapon was found in her car and forensics told me about an hour ago that the panties definitely belonged to Rhiannon Brodeur. Oh, and they also found traces of Alicia's blood on the coat.'

'What about Cameron Aitken?' Mac asked.

Dan shrugged, 'I'm not totally ruling him out as forensics said that they found a small piece of Cameron's fingernail caught up in the fabric of Rhiannon's dress. Otherwise, there was nothing to tie Cameron Aitken to the scene. They think that it broke off as he tried to pull Rhiannon's dress down.'

'Down?' Mac said.

'That's right. Your friend Eileen called me first thing this morning and she was obviously worried that we might be considering Cameron to be a suspect. She said that she'd spoken to him and he told her that he had come across a girl lying down in a dark wood. Her dress had been pulled up so that she was naked from the waist down. Cameron said that he didn't think it was right to leave her like that and so he pulled her dress down as far as he could.'

'I suppose that fits in with what we know so far,' Mac said.

'Cameron said something else too,' Dan said. 'He said that he saw a dark shadow moving in the woods behind where the girl lay. It felt evil and it scared him. He said that his voices were catching up with him and so he had to leave her there and keep walking. However, it seems that he was scared and was glad to get away in any case. He also said that he wished that he could have helped the girl but he couldn't.'

'Yes, when the police picked him up, he asked them to help the girl with red lips. That shadow, could that have been the murderer, do you think?'

'It's certainly possible. Cameron might have been lucky that he left the scene so quickly. Who knows but he might have been attacked too? Anyway, Eileen said that Cameron's convinced that it was all in his head; the red moon, the evil shadows and the dead girl. No-one's told him yet that it was all real,' Dan said. 'I guess that it might come as a bit of a shock to him.'

'But he's still a suspect though?' Mac asked.

'Absolutely, as his DNA has been found at the murder scene. His doctor said that we can interview him this morning and so I'm going to meet Adil over at the Mental Hospital. It will be interesting to hear what he has to say first hand. However, Monica Hashley is still our number one suspect at the moment. With all the evidence that we've got so far, it won't be hard to make a case stick. Given the current state of her health though, I'd guess that it will be a verdict of 'Manslaughter by reason of diminished responsibility' at the absolute best,' Dan replied.

'What exactly did her medical report say?'

'The report said that she had been a battered wife for quite some time and probably on a regular basis too. She's suffered some quite severe and irreversible brain damage. I spoke to the doctor and she said that she'd seen professional boxers at the end of their careers who were in a better state than Monica Hashley. It seems that her husband dying when he did might have saved her life. The doctor said that even one more beating might have killed her. We won't be able to speak to her for some time as she'll shortly be undergoing an operation to ensure that she doesn't die of a bleed on the brain.' Dan then looked at his watch and said, 'I've just got time for a coffee. Want one?'

Mac didn't turn the offer down.

'I still find it puzzling though,' Mac said as he gratefully sipped at his coffee.

'In what way exactly?' Dan asked.

'Well, while all the evidence points to it being her, I'm just wondering what could have driven Monica Hashley to murder? Even in her quite probably confused state, she must have had some sort of motive for doing it. Also, if we accept what Cameron says, then why would she leave Rhiannon naked from the waist down? The only reason I can think of would be to make it look like a sex crime which might then make her an unlikely suspect. For someone with severe brain damage it all looks a little too well-planned to me.'

'Yes, I can see your point but all we can do for now is follow the evidence. Anyway, Bob Yeardley's sent you the photos of Alicia's book that you were so interested in. Perhaps you'll find the motive there.' Dan drank the last of his coffee. 'Call me if you find anything.'

Mac promised that he would.

He had a wash and a shave before putting on a fresh shirt. He told himself that he would have to go home at some point to have a shower and get some fresh clothes. If he could last the day out then he promised himself a night in his own bed.

'We've got some bacon rolls being delivered in about fifteen minutes,' Martin said without looking away from his screen. 'We got a little fed up of pastries.'

Mac felt his mouth starting to salivate.

'That sounds absolutely wonderful.'

They were just simple buttered rolls that had two rashers of fried bacon inserted into them but to Mac they tasted divine and absolutely hit the spot. He felt re-energised and ready for work as he opened the file that contained the photos of Alicia Hashley's book of spells.

Mac was disappointed at first. The book contained some drawings of five-pointed stars and moon phases and quotes that Alicia had found on the internet. He could be sure of this as she had handily noted down all the web addresses. All in all, there was a lot there but nothing personal apart from one entry. The page was blank apart from a single sentence that was more of a scrawl than Alicia's usual neat writing.

'I saw them. I saw them at it and it was so disgusting. They were like animals. God help me but it can't be true. I can't stand much more of this.'

He wondered what it was that Alicia had seen and who 'they' were. Her father and mother perhaps?

Mac found himself to be somewhat disappointed. He desperately wanted to know what Alicia and Rhiannon had prayed for and he was hoping that he would find it in the Grimoire. He then noticed that there was another file. A note said that, 'We had to turn the book over and upside down.'

Of course! Mac remembered doing that himself when he was in school. His school work would be at the front while the pages at the back would be full of doodles and silly drawings. He opened the file. The first page was entitled 'Prayers and Spells'.

Mac smiled.

The first section, however, was incomprehensible to him. It was about six lines long and he guessed that it was in Old English. Underneath Alicia had written, 'A powerful plea to the Goddess to be said with any prayer or spell if it is to work.'

He guessed that this text had come from Rhiannon. He would have to ask Edward Lewin what it meant.

The first prayer was to be said silently during the Magical Silence part of the ritual. She prayed for sleep and that the Goddess would make the constant sadness go away.

The second prayer was to be written on a sheet of paper and burned during the ritual. Alicia had rewritten the prayer several times and, although she had used some flowery language, it was in essence a simple prayer. She prayed that Modig would love her.

Mac paused. It certainly looked like that one had worked. He wondered if that was why Alicia was so confident when she faced her bully down? He read on.

It seemed that he might have been right because in the next prayer, she asks the Goddess for the strength to face her enemies. Below that the recipe for a spell was written –

'Write down on flash paper that which your enemy most fears. Draw a circle on the ground and step inside the magical barrier. Here you will be safe. Recite the ancient plea to the Goddess loudly as you light the paper. As it burns your prayer will be carried up to the Goddess who will look kindly on your plea if you are good of heart.'

This was written in another hand. Rhiannon's perhaps? He would need to get that checked.

Anyway, Alicia's prayer was answered as Megan Harding broke out into the worst case of acne that any of her friends had ever seen. For a teenaged girl this might indeed be a fate worse than death.

Mac read on.

The next prayer was scribbled out so violently that the pen had gone right through the paper. Below it she had written, 'Make him stop. MAKE HIM STOP NOW!'

He sat back and, in his mind, he could see Alicia writing in her room while the angry sounds of violence played out downstairs. Her father's angry shouts, her mother's pleas and then her mother's screams. She must have known how ill her mother was and that another beating might literally be the death of her.

Did she fear that she would be alone with her father if her mother died? That he might somehow get away with killing his wife and he would then start on her?

He had a thought and made a call. It certainly answered that question.

'Did you find something?' Martin asked as he handed Mac a coffee.

'Yes, yes I think I have,' Mac replied. 'Forensics have confirmed that Alicia had her bones broken on at least four occasions, over a period of around three years. Can you see what you can find out from the local hospitals? It's my guess that they wouldn't have taken her to the same hospital twice. Oh, and can you also check her mother's medical records while you're at it.'

'Yes, sure. I take it that it was her father who was responsible?'

'Yes, that's what we think. It's more than likely that John Hashley's anger was directed at his wife but Alicia loved her mother and I guess that, at times, she may have tried to intervene and help her.'

As Mac read on, he realised that she had tried to intervene once again.

'*Mother, please grant your daughter's fervent wish. She wishes for peace and for an end to anger in her house. She wishes that her mother may recover and that her father finds peace. Most of all, she wishes for an end to anger and she prays to you with all her heart and will pay any price that you might demand.*'

There was just one more prayer. It was entitled 'A Sincere Prayer of Thanks'.

'*Great Mother, we thank you for answering your daughter's prayer. We accept your judgement and your will with all our heart. There is now peace in your daughter's house and the anger has gone. We praise you for your power and wisdom.*'

Mac sat back and let this run around his mind. He couldn't help feeling that he might just have found the motive for the two girls' murders. He then called Professor Lewin.

'Oh yes, that definitely came from me,' Edward Lewin said after Mac had sent him a photo of the mysterious text from Alicia's Grimoire. 'I found it just over six months ago tucked away in a tenth century manuscript. They claimed that it was written word for word from an older manuscript that had been damaged in some way.'

'What does it mean?' Mac asked.

'It's Old English of course, at least eighth century as it's written in the Latin alphabet but it could be older. It's the beginning of a prayer, to Frig I'd guess as it's addressed to a Goddess. It praises the Goddess and then asks her to look kindly on the person praying and to grant them their wish. The find was very exciting as there aren't many religious texts that date from around that time. I'm writing a paper on it,' here the professor paused, 'or at least I was.'

Mac could feel the Professor's sadness in the silence that followed.

'I take it that Rhiannon knew about this?' he asked.

'Oh yes, she was almost as excited as I was. She had me write it down and then teach her how to say all the words. She was a very quick learner. If only...'

The professor stopped again. This time Mac took the opportunity to thank him before saying goodbye.

He sat back and thought some more. He then called forensics. They told him that they had found just three sets of fingerprints on the Grimoire besides Alicia's. They were from Rhiannon, Monica Hashley and an unknown person.

So, Alicia's mother knew about the Grimoire and had presumably read it. The case against Monica Hashley was now more or less irrefutable.

So, why was it that he still had some doubts?

Chapter Twenty-One

Mac worked throughout the day, trying to catch up with all of the information still flowing into the team. Yet his dissatisfaction with the case against Monica Hashley, a case that he had helped put together, only grew. It began to gripe him like a persistent heartburn and he was glad when the time for the team debrief finally arrived.

The evidence against Monica Hashley had grown. Dan had contacted Sanguine Salvatoris in London. Father Renfield had taken the call and he seemed more than happy to help the police. He explained that the only cameras at the organisation's headquarters were in the car park, put there for security purposes. He had quickly arranged for the CCTV footage to be sent to Martin. Martin put it up on the big screen.

The video showed a figure wearing a Gucci coat getting into a Porsche Cayenne and driving it out of the car park. The time fitted in well with the subsequent sighting of the Porsche entering the estate.

Not only that but further footage showed the car pulling up in exactly the same parking place just after one o'clock in the morning. A figure got out carrying a white plastic bag. They then pulled out the spare tyre carrier and could be clearly seen stuffing the bag, and something else that was taken from the pocket of the coat, behind the spare wheel.

'Monica Hashley is our killer,' Dan said, 'there can be no doubt about that. The only thing that's missing is a motive. Mac, I believe that you can help us out there.'

For some reason, Mac found himself strangely reluctant to tell the team what he had discovered. He did it anyway.

'It would appear that Monica Hashley had found her daughter's Grimoire, or book of spells, and it's possible that she may have taken what she read there quite badly. I've been involved in quite a few cases of domestic violence that have ended up with murder. Unfortunately, despite the injuries and broken bones, many of the women involved appeared to have still been deeply in love with their eventual murderers. Of course, that may be down to the controlling behaviour of their partner who sometimes manage to brainwash them into believing that they couldn't exist without them. However, in many other cases, the women seemed to have still genuinely loved their killers. They often blamed themselves for the violence or harboured the hope that it would magically one day stop.' Mac shrugged. 'If Monica Hashley is one of these women, then you may have your motive.'

'Go on,' Dan said.

'In all likelihood, Monica Hashley had read her daughter's book after the death of her husband. In the first prayer, Alicia asks for peace in her house. She doesn't ask for her father to die but, in the prayer of thanks, Alicia not only accepts her father's death but praises the Goddess for her wisdom. One of her friends told me that Alicia wasn't exactly heartbroken after her father died so I'd guess that, if Monica Hashley had been standing in Radley Meadows listening to this, then it might have been enough to send her into a rage. However, as she came out that night with a hammer in her hand anyway then I'd guess that she must have already been considering killing her daughter.'

'And the hammer itself only had her husband's prints on it,' Dan said.

'That's what forensics have told us,' Mac replied. 'Monica Hashley didn't appear to have used it herself which might well explain why the hammer was swung in the way it was. As the hammer hit Rhiannon on the back of the head then it must have been swung underhand. Anyone who has ever used a hammer properly would have automatically swung it overhand and brought it down on the top of the skull thus exerting the maximum possible force.'

'That makes sense to me,' Dan said as he turned to face the team. 'I think that we have a watertight case here. However, keep working on what you're doing for the next few days just in case. Oh, and from tomorrow you can go back to normal shifts for now.'

A sigh of relief ran around the team on hearing this.

Mac stayed on until they had handed over to Mahshid and Amanda and then he went towards home.

He suddenly thought about Emma Dawson and how he had promised to follow her up. Almost without thinking, his car pulled up outside Genny Albrighton's little bungalow. Genny herself opened the door and ushered him inside.

'Have you kept in contact with Emma?' Mac asked as Genny led him into the living room.

'I should say so,' Genny replied with a grin, 'she's living in my son's room at the moment.'

'Why is that?'

'Well, I think she finally realised that her husband was a total shit and that she needed a new start. She's a very nice girl and I told her that she could stay with us while she figured out what she wanted to do.'

'Where is she now?' Mac asked.

'At her Zumba class. She said that she'd always wanted to try it but her husband would never let her.'

'That was very good of you to put her up,' Mac said.

'Oh, it's nothing and anyway, we're getting all of this great free financial advice,' Genny said with a wicked wink.

He had picked up Terry and thanked Amanda for once again stepping into the breach with little or no warning.

'It's really nothing, Mac,' she had replied. 'It was terrible what happened to those poor girls and, if I've helped by even the tiniest bit, then I'm more than happy.'

It was still only nine fifteen when he pulled up outside his house. He guessed that Tim would be up for a few drinks in the Magnets if he called him now. For some reason he didn't. He felt restless and irritable and he knew that he wouldn't be good company. He looked down to see Terry looking up at him with his impossibly soulful eyes.

Perhaps a walk and some fresh air was what he needed too, he said to himself.

He let Terry pull him along from tree to tree as he tried to figure out why he felt as he did. He quickly reviewed the evidence in the case. He had gotten convictions with a lot less. Everything pointed to Monica Hashley as being the killer.

Yet.

But what was it exactly that made him feel it might not be her? The way that Rhiannon had been left exposed was one thing. He had assumed that it had been done to make it look like a sex crime but could it have been something else? A punishment or humiliation after death, perhaps? He had certainly come across that many times before. What else?

Mac thought and thought but he couldn't think of anything else that might support his doubts. They had video evidence that covered pretty much every moment of Monica Hashley's journey from Sanguine Salvatoris in London to the Drymanshouse Estate and back again and they had the murder weapon that she had hidden in her car. They also had a motive. He realised now that this was what had been irritating him so much.

The evidence was just too good.

The moon went behind a dark cloud and a cold breeze went right through him. There was a sudden feeling of electricity in the air and he felt the hairs rising up on the back of his neck. He looked up and he found that he was near the cemetery. He knew that something was going to happen.

Terry started whining and he pulled on the lead so hard that it slipped out of Mac's hand. Mac hardly noticed. His eyes were fixed on the driveway that led to the graveyard. He felt fear and more than a little sick. He wished that he too could run off but he knew that he would be unable to move until whatever was about to happen was over.

A figure appeared in the driveway, darker than the dark shadows that surrounded it. The moon sailed out from behind a cloud and threw the silhouette into stark contrast. She turned around and looked straight at him, straight into his eyes. He felt as though he was paralysed. He could only wait.

He knew who she was. How he knew this he had no idea but he didn't question this new knowledge. The ghost whispered to him. Although the apparition was some twenty-five yards or so away, she whispered and Mac heard every syllable clearly.

'It's not the boy,' she said slowly. 'It's not the mother. It's the father.'

The apparition took a few steps towards him and Mac's fear grew.

'It's the father.'

After she had said this, the moon went behind a cloud and the apparition went with it.

He stood there, dry-mouthed, heart-pounding and totally disoriented. She could have only been there for a moment but it had been one of the most intense moments of his life. He slowly walked home as he tried to re-assemble his brain.

Mac would not need to remember her words. They were seared into his mind. He tried to think of what they might mean but, right then, he found thinking impossible.

Terry was waiting for him at the door. He was shaking and had obviously found the experience a little too intense too. Once inside, Mac sat down on the settee and Terry climbed up beside him. He found that comforting his dog was helping him to calm down too. When Terry finally fell asleep, Mac made no attempt to move. He sat there and tried to figure out what had just happened.

He could only accept what he had just seen and heard. It had been real and he knew this down to his bones. He could not deny that a ghost had spoken to him but what did her words mean? He relaxed and stopped trying to chase his thoughts around, Eventually, he found that he could think rationally again.

He ran her words through his head.

'It's not the boy,' she had said.

He was fairly sure that she might be talking about Cameron Aitken. If that was the case then he agreed.

'It's not the mother.'

Here she was telling him straight out that Monica Hashley wasn't the murderer and he believed her. However, the next two sentences flummoxed him.

'It's the father.'

Which father? Alicia's father had been dead three weeks while Rhiannon's father had been in full view of a film crew in Paris at the time of the murders. How could they have anything to do with it? Was it someone else's father? Someone from the coven perhaps?

He had absolutely no idea what the apparition meant by that. However, he would be back on the case tomorrow, working as hard as ever and looking for the real murderer. He knew that he would have to be careful. After all, if someone asked him where he had gotten his information from, he could hardly say that it was from a ghost.

And the ghost of Rhiannon Brodeur at that.

Chapter Twenty-Two

Wednesday

His alarm clock told him that it was seven o'clock. He turned the beeping off without opening his eyes as he replayed the strange experience of the previous evening in his head. It had been all too real. For once, the thought that it may have just been one of his lucid dreams never even entered his head.

He was still chewing it over as he drove towards the incident room. Mahshid and Amanda were talking to Jean as she was taking her coat off. Jo and Gerry were on their way out but they stopped for a chat. They were obviously in no rush.

No-one was in a rush now. The case was over.

Mac couldn't wait to get to work. However, the case against Monica Hashley was so devastatingly complete he wasn't sure where to begin. He sat back and tried to identify any weak points in the case.

'Taking it easy, Mac?' Martin said as he walked in. 'I can't blame you. I set my alarm as normal but I still slept right through it. Still, I don't suppose it matters all that much now.'

Mac replied with a vague nod.

He said goodbye to Mahshid and Amanda as they left to go home before returning back to his thoughts. The only idea he could come up with was it might not have been Monica Hashley who had been wearing the Gucci coat after all. The only problem with that was, if it wasn't her, then this other person had her car keys, her phone, knew how to get into the estate, knew the burglar alarm code to her house, where the hammer was kept and exactly where Rhiannon and Alicia were going to be and all without leaving any sort of trace.

As much as he was hoping that there might be something to his latest theory, it all seemed a bit far-fetched even to him. He put it all on the back burner and went to work. There was still a lot of information to be reviewed and categorised and Dan had told them that he wanted to get it all squared away before the file officially went to the prosecutor.

Thinking about it he was quite surprised that, with such a strong case, Dan hadn't already gone to the prosecutor with it. He wondered if he had some doubts too.

Sandwiches arrived on the dot at midday and Mac tucked in. The food supplied by the farmer's wife was so good that he was firmly of the opinion that she should start up her own business. After eating he decided to get a little fresh air. He put his coat on and stepped outside. He needed it. The air was fresh indeed and an icy wind was blowing.

The few journalists who had stuck it out seemed to have retreated back to the warmth of their cars. Mac looked up at the sky. A bank of ominous dark-grey clouds seemed to be coming straight at him. His eye caught a dark shadow on the hill opposite. That was all it was, a shadow, but Mac knew that this shadow had eyes and those eyes were looking straight at him.

The world fell silent around him as the dark clouds above turned day into night. Even the wind stopped blowing. The tension built and the hairs on the back of his neck rose in fear. He was frozen to the spot, waiting to see what was going to happen.

Help me, he whispered. Help me to find what I need.

It was a whisper, no more, but Mac heard it clearly.

'If you want to find the truth then look up.'

He looked up.

There were clouds and more clouds. He slowly swivelled around. There were trees, the farm house at the top of a small hill and then the roof of the barn. He stood and stared at it for a minute or so while her words tumbled around his head. This was what she wanted him to find. He knew that now.

But why?

He turned around as the dark clouds scudded by and the wind began to blow again. He looked up at the hillside but the shadow had gone. Mac immediately walked up the driveway to the farmhouse and had a word with the farmer's wife and then, more importantly, with her son.

His heart was thumping as he made his way back to the barn. This was it, of that he was certain. The only problem was that he had no clue exactly what 'it' might be.

He made his way to Martin's desk.

'There's a CCTV camera just outside the barn, over the front door there, and it's permanently switched on. The farmer's son, who's just sixteen, knows how it all works and he's going to send you all the CCTV footage he has.'

'There's a camera outside?' Martin said in surprise. 'I never noticed it.'

'It's well disguised,' Mac replied. 'It's pointing down the driveway towards the road so it's possible it might have caught something.'

'The lighting wouldn't be that all good out there though, would it?' Martin said looking somewhat sceptical.

'That may not be a problem. The son, who seems to be something of a techie like you, told me that it's state of the art, low light sensors and all that. They only had it fitted a few months ago for insurance reasons as they were storing some high-value stuff in here before an auction. They keep it on as extra security for the farm as the driveway is the only way in.'

'Okay, I'll have a look then,' Martin said with a shrug.

It only took thirty minutes for the footage to arrive but it took another hour before Martin found anything that might be relevant. He called for Mac to come over but he didn't seem at all excited by what he had discovered.

'I've gone over and over it and all I've found is this,' Martin said.

The first clip showed a brightening on the left-hand side of the road before it abruptly went dark again. Obviously, someone had pulled up on the road and then turned their headlights off. A figure then quickly walked by carrying something white in one hand. They were only on the screen for a few seconds before disappearing off the right-hand side of the screen. Mac had Martin play it again. And again.

'There's not much there, is there?' Martin said.

'No there isn't, but it does tell us that the killer must have taken a detour from the main road so that they could come in from the other direction.'

'Do you think that was to make sure that they wouldn't be seen by Rhiannon and the rest of the coven who were walking down the road from the other direction?'

'Yes, but, if that is the case, then ask yourself why?' Mac said.

Martin thought for a moment.

'Of course, because Alicia would recognise the car straight away and there would be no element of surprise.'

Mac frowned and shook his head.

'Can you play it again?'

Martin did, twice.

'You look disappointed. Were you hoping for more?'

'I was,' Mac replied but he didn't say why.

'There's another bit,' Martin said.

It looked like the first clip played backwards as the figure walked back towards the car. The headlights came on and then disappeared as the car turned around and went back the way it had come.

'Is there anything at all that we can get from these bits of video?' Mac asked hopefully.

Martin played them again and gave it some thought.

'Not really,' he said with a shrug. 'Apart from the person's height, I suppose.'

'The person's height?'

'Yes, the first video is probably the best for that. You can see that they pass right in front of that road sign there. The triangular sign itself is a foot or so above their head but, if we measure the distance from the ground to that sign then I should be able to calculate the height of the person. Do you think that it might help us?'

For some reason Mac did.

Martin went up to the farm and borrowed a tape measure. Between them they managed to get the exact height of the road sign. Martin looked back at the camera.

'We're lucky, Mac. It's usually quite hard to be accurate about things such as people's heights because the CCTV camera is usually on the top of a very high pole. However, the driveway rises up slightly as it meets the road here and it looks as if the camera is pointing straight at us. That should make things a lot simpler. No angles to work out.'

Back in the incident room, Mac watched Martin as he took a frame from the video and started drawing lines over it and measuring it with some sort of computer program.

'The person wearing the Gucci coat here is one hundred and seventy-eight centimetres tall, give or take a centimetre or so,' Martin announced.

Mac felt his heartrate speed up.

'What's that in feet?' he asked.

'Er...it's five feet ten inches,' Martin replied.

'Look up Monica Hashley's height in the file, will you?' Mac said with the beginning of a smile.

Martin did.

'She's only five foot six inches tall,' he said with a puzzled expression. 'You've met her, is she really that small?'

Mac pictured the woman he had met in Letchworth police station.

'Yes, she really is that small. So, unless she was wearing stilts, it looks as if Monica Hashley isn't our killer after all,' Mac said. 'I need to call Dan.'

'I'll have another look at the rest of the video evidence while you do that,' Martin said.

So, it looks as if the ghost was right, Mac thought as he waited for Dan to turn up. Of course, the new problem was that, if the killer wasn't Monica Hashley, then who was it?

He thought for a moment and then sat bolt upright, cursing himself for a fool. He now had a clue to who the murderer was. She had told him plainly but he had misunderstood. It was only a single letter but he knew from experience that the smallest of things can make a massive difference.

Just over half an hour later, Dan was sitting back in his chair and giving some thought to what he had just seen. Martin had played the short videos for him on the big screen and had then explained how they were able to measure the height of the figure seen walking by.

'And you're totally sure of this?' Dan asked.

'As I can be,' Martin said. 'I'll be doing some more test videos for the record first thing tomorrow, just to make sure, but there's something else that might back this up.' He then replayed the footage taken from the Sanguine Salvatoris car park. 'The videos taken on the estate are mostly long distance but this one is better quality as the camera's much closer. I've taken some stills from the video.'

A photo showed the person as they were walking away from the car not long after stashing the hammer in the spare tyre. The hood of the Gucci coat was up and the head was lowered so that the face couldn't be seen. The coat was unzipped.

'What exactly am I looking for?' Dan asked.

Mac was wondering the exact same thing. Without a word Martin zoomed in on an area of the photo.

'Whoever's in that coat is showing a lot of wrist,' Dan said. 'The coat looks as if it's too small for them. So, any ideas?'

'If it's not Monica Hashley who was driving the Porsche then it has to be someone from Sanguine Salvatoris, doesn't it?' Mac said.

'How many people do they have there?'

'I've no idea but I don't think that really matters. Whoever was driving that Porsche must have been close to Monica Hashley, close enough to slip her a sedative and then make off with her coat and phone. They must have also visited her house and probably more than once.'

'What makes you say that?' Dan asked.

'Well, for a start they must have known the burglar alarm code as well as their way around the house. The security company said that the alarm was switched off and then put back on again some five minutes later. In that time, whoever it was had managed to find a hammer, a pair of scissors and a plastic bag.'

'I see your point,' Dan said. 'I'm not sure that I could go into my own house and find those items in that amount of time.'

'I must say that you don't seem all that disappointed by our news,' Mac said knowing how much Dan loved a win.

'Well, I have to admit that the thought had struck me that the evidence against Monica Hashley was beginning to look a little too good to be true.'

Apparently, Dan had had the same misgivings as Mac.

'Is that why you delayed sending the case to the prosecutor?' Mac asked.

'Something like that and I'm so glad now that I didn't. You've looked into Sanguine Salvatoris, Mac, how do you think we should go about it?' Dan asked.

He had indeed thought of little else since discovering that Monica Hashley was no longer a viable suspect.

'I'd guess that it's quite likely that the press will pick up on the amount of evidence we have against Monica Hashley,' Mac said.

A split second later the front page of a tabloid newspaper filled the screen. The headline blared 'Mother killed own daughter in brutal attack' and then in smaller type 'Police have overwhelming evidence of guilt'.

'Thanks, Martin,' Mac said with a wry smile. 'I think that we should let them keep thinking that. Meanwhile, a couple of us could go to the headquarters of Sanguine Salvatoris and start interviewing people there. We'll go easy and, if anyone asks, we can tell them that the case against Monica Hashley is more or less an open and shut one and that we're just trying to get more background information for the trial.'

'And, with any luck, the real killer won't feel threatened and do a runner. I like it. Okay, let's keep this new evidence to yourselves for now. You too, Jean,' Dan said as he turned around.

'Of course,' she replied looking mildly offended.

Dan called and arranged to see Father Peverett at nine o'clock the next morning and asked Mac to spend whatever time he could in finding out more about Sanguine Salvatoris.

He was looking at an article about the organisation when he had the nagging feeling that there was something he should have done. He sat back and let his mind run free.

Of course! He had made a mental note to have a closer look at the financial situation at Sanguine Salvatoris after speaking to Father Farrell. He knew just the man to ask.

He called DI Colin Furness at the London Fraud Squad. He had helped him before when murky financial dealings had been part of one of his cases. Luckily, Colin was more than willing to see what he could find out about JXH Sports and Sanguine Salvatoris.

Mac carried on with his research. He had managed to find an organisational structure tucked away in a PDF. It was quite basic but it did give Mac an idea of how many priests were involved in the organisation. There were thirteen in all.

The perfect number for a coven, he thought.

They were all listed as 'Spiritual Advisors' but Mac knew from his interview with Father Farrell they these priests were the real power behind the throne. Father Peverett, Father Manley, Father Ryan and Father Renfield were stationed at the London headquarters while nine other priests were stationed at branches of the organisation in Birmingham, Manchester, Bristol, Liverpool, York and Glasgow.

He was only interested in those at the headquarters. If there were still just the four priests to consider then it should make their job a lot easier. Of course, he might find it hard to explain to Dan why they should concentrate on the priests and leave the lay workers and Luminaries to one side. He still kicked himself mentally when he thought of how mistaken he had been. It was such a tiny thing, a change to a single letter, but it was the entire case to Mac.

Rhiannon hadn't said, 'It's the father.'
What she had actually said was, 'It's the Father.'

Chapter Twenty-Three

Thursday

They were caught up in the inevitable traffic jam at Watford Way when Mac got the call. Dan could see from Mac's face that the conversation was more than interesting but he had to patiently wait until the call had ended.

'Anything?' Dan asked.

'I'll say. That was Colin Furness from the Fraud Squad. He's been trying to find out what he could about how Sanguine Salvatoris are financed. Tell me, did we ever get a look at John Hashley's will?' Mac asked.

'I think we sent out a request for a copy to his solicitor but I haven't seen one as yet. To be honest, it didn't seem to be all that important at the time.'

'I think that we should chase it up,' Mac said. 'It might turn out to be crucial.'

'Why? What did Colin tell you?'

'Well, it would seem that Sanguine Salvatoris are very close to being broke or I should say were if what Colin's told me is correct. Father Farrell said that the organisation went into a lot of debt to build its new headquarters and one of its main creditors was John Hashley. Colin's confirmed this. He also had a word with a friend of his who works for the firm that audits the accounts for JXH Sports. He told him that John Hashley's death had probably gotten Sanguine Salvatoris and Father Peverett out of a really tight spot.'

'Let me guess. He mentioned them in his will,' Dan said.

'It was a bit more than a mention. It seems that John Hashley was serious about his devotion to Sanguine Salvatoris as he appears to have left them half his company. Colin's friend said that he didn't mind telling him about the will as it was common knowledge within JXH Sports itself.'

The traffic started to move but Dan didn't. He was deep in thought until he got a few louds beeps from the cars behind.

'What about the other half?' he said moving off again.

'That was left to his daughter, Alicia,' Mac replied. 'Apparently his wife was left next to nothing. Even more interestingly, the will stated that, if his daughter died without issue, then her share in the company would also go to Sanguine Salvatoris.'

'Can you call Martin and get him to get us a copy of the will straight away?' Dan asked.

Mac did just that.

'Are we sure that John Hashley's death was really suicide?' Dan asked as they started moving again.

'From what I've read in the case file, it looks fairly certain.'

'Okay but, if Colin's correct, then it certainly provides a motive for Alicia's murder, doesn't it?'

'It certainly does,' Mac replied.

'JXH Sports, how much is it worth, do you know?' Dan asked.

'Colin said that their revenue last year was over six billion pounds.'

'Six billion? Well worth murdering for, wouldn't you say?'

'I would,' Mac replied.

He couldn't shake the feeling that, the closer they got to Sanguine Salvatoris' headquarters, the closer they were getting to solving the case.

The going was slow, especially once they neared Hyde Park. He could see Hyde Park Corner up ahead and Mac didn't envy Dan being in the driving seat. It was literally chaos on wheels as cars jostled one another to get to their exits or even just to get one car's length ahead. Its only saving grace was that, as the traffic moved so slowly, any collision usually meant no worse than a dent. It didn't seem to bother Dan too much as he was deep in thought all the way around it.

'It's near Westminster Cathedral, isn't it?' Dan eventually said.

'Yes, it's just at the back, on a street called Morpeth Terrace.'

'I always used to get them mixed up, Westminster Cathedral and Westminster Abbey,' Dan said.

'A lot of people still do,' Mac replied. 'Of course, the Abbey is where they marry and crown royalty whereas the Cathedral belongs to the Catholic Diocese of Westminster. I guess that's why Sanguine Salvatoris is situated where it is. The Bishop of Westminster is a Cardinal and so he's the head of the Catholic Church in England.'

'I guess that they wanted to be near the seat of power then,' Dan said.

'I'd be willing to bet on it,' Mac replied.

They got a beautiful view of the Cathedral just before they turned into Morpeth Terrace. Mac had seen it once or twice before but he'd forgotten how huge and imposing the building was. Its red brick and white stone horizontal stripes, Romanesque arches and decorated domes made it look somewhat oriental. It certainly looked out of place when compared to the fussy Victorian mansion flats that lined much of the streets surrounding it.

They had no trouble finding Sanguine Salvatoris, indeed they could see the building at the end of the street. It had a corner all to itself. It had high white-marble Romanesque arches at street level and, above that, a familiar pattern of red bricks and white stone in horizontal bands, regularly interrupted by wide arched windows. It was five storeys high and was topped off with a flat Italianate roof supported by stone lintels that mimicked wood.

It was not as huge as the Cathedral but, amongst all the stuffy architecture around it, it certainly stood out.

The main entrance was through one of the arches. The statue of a man looking off towards a far horizon was suspended above the arch. He had a halo so it was obviously the statue of a saint but, instead of the usual flowing robes, this saint was dressed in modern clerical garb.

Monsignor Etxeberria, Mac guessed.

The door was locked. A woman's voice asked them to identify themselves. They did. The door then clicked and opened for them. Mac expected to be let into the lobby but instead he found himself in a large unadorned room with another door facing him. The room was made smaller by being cut in half by a wooden counter on top of which several glass panels reached right up to the ceiling. The two halves of the room were totally separated from each other.

A woman entered the other half of the room. She was in her forties and she had a long shapeless black dress on. She looked very much like a nun but without the headgear. Her face looked as if a smile might break it.

'Show me your warrant cards,' she ordered.

Her voice came out of speakers on either side of them. They took out their cards.

Another order, 'Press them to the glass.'

She took a photograph of each card and then one of each of their faces. She then disappeared without a word.

'A right little ray of sunshine she is,' Dan said under his breath.

Mac could only agree. She returned just over five minutes later.

'You are who you claim to be,' she said with zero emotion. 'The Father will see you now.'

The Father.

Mac smiled on hearing those words.

The door clicked and a light went from red to green. Beyond, it was like stepping into another world. You could definitely see where all the money had gone.

The lobby was huge and was made to feel even more spacious by a circular well that went right up to the roof. Natural light streamed through and illuminated all five storeys of the building. Walkways ran around the well at every floor and a surprising number of people were coming and going.

The lobby itself was clad in marble. The walls reflected the outside of the building and were striped with wide bands of dark red and pure white marble. The floor was marble too, jet-black pierced with flowing lines of white. The walls were unadorned except for a large cross which hung at an angle at the far end of the room. Mac could see no cables and the effect of it just hovering there was slightly unsettling.

He looked up to see that, around the well, the roof was decorated with four large mosaic panels. The panels were titled 'Domo, Patria, Ecclesia, Dei'. He recognised this as being the organisation's motto. It meant, 'Family, Country, Church, God'. The panels depicted an idealised family of a man, a woman and a young boy and girl all holding hands and looking happily off into the distance; two flags waving in the wind, one being the Union Jack while the other was the Papal flag; what looked like St. Peter's Basilica in Rome transferred to the top of a golden shining hill and, finally, God in the figure of a haloed lamb holding a white flag with a red cross.

They were all beautifully done but Mac realised with some disquiet that the style reminded him of a programme that he'd seen some time ago on his television. It had been called 'The Art of Fascism' and it had featured public art works from the reigns of Hitler and Franco.

Hanging on the wall nearest to them there was a large painting. Mac went to take a closer look.

It showed an old man in clerical garb standing in a field, his arm was outstretched as he gave the Sign of the Cross. A lamb was looking up at him and a dove hovered over his head. Below him a young priest was kneeling and looking up at the old man with something like adoration. Mac recognised the standing figure as being Monsignor Etxeberria, now known to all as Saint Miguel.

'I'm afraid that I've aged a bit since then,' a voice behind him said.

Mac turned and found himself looking at a man in his mid-fifties who, with his iron-grey hair and grey fluffy beard, looked quite patriarchal. He had filled out a bit since the days of his youth and Mac found it quite difficult to see the young man from the painting in him.

'The artist took that from a photo. The Monsignor had just given me his imprimatur to take the Blessed Movement to this country. Well, I take it that you're here about poor Monica?'

'We are, Father Peverett, and thanks to agreeing to talk to us,' Dan replied. 'Is there somewhere private where we can go?'

'Of course. Please follow me.'

They followed Father Peverett across the lobby and into a glass lift. They went up two floors and he then took them along the walkway, stopping to look at the electronic screen outside each room. Mac tried to gauge his height and he came to the disappointing conclusion that he was, at most, around five feet eight inches tall.

'Ah, this one's free for the rest of the day,' he said as he held open the door. 'This is one of our instructional rooms. I hope that you will find it suitable for your needs.'

The room was illuminated by one of the arched windows and it was far bigger than Mac would have guessed. It was a classroom alright but it very high tech. Three of the biggest screens that Mac had ever seen hung around the walls while on every desk there was a large tablet computer. The desks and chairs themselves were of the best quality. All in all, it reminded him of the time he had visited an elite business school.

'It'll do,' Dan said keeping a straight face. 'We'd like to start with you, if that's okay?'

'I guessed that might be the case,' Father Peverett replied as he looked at his watch. 'I can give you twenty minutes right now but I can always come back later if needed.'

'Fair enough,' Dan replied.

They used the teacher's desk at the front of the class and positioned two chairs on either side. Dan took out his phone and started the interview off.

'I hope you don't mind if we record this interview,' Dan asked. 'It's easier than making notes.'

The priest shrugged. Dan started recording.

'How well did you know Monica Hashley?' he asked.

'Not as well as some here did,' Father Peverett replied. 'I knew her husband a little better, I'd guess. We worked quite closely together on a number of things before...'

The priest shrugged again.

'Who would you say was closest to Monica? We've got an idea about her motive but it would really help our case in court if we could flesh things out a bit.'

Mac glanced over at Dan whose face was as innocent as could be. Making it clear that Monica Hashley was the one and only suspect and that they were only fishing for some extra evidence to back their case up would help to put everyone at their ease.

He hoped that this included the real killer.

'Well, Father Manley has probably known her the longest while Father Renfield has been her confessor for the last two years or so. However, I think that she may have been closer to some of the Servants than to anyone else.'

'The servants?' Dan asked looking puzzled.

'Sorry, our women members belong to a group called 'The Servants of the Virgin Mary'. We often call them 'Servants' for short.'

Mac bet he did.

'And who might these 'Servants' be?' Dan asked.

'Well, I guess that Sister Mary Edda and Sister Mary Jane worked closely with Monica so they might be able to tell you something. Otherwise, I know that she spent a lot of time with Servant Amelia who acts as Secretary to the group.'

'Are these 'Sisters' nuns then?' Mac asked.

'No but this is what we have come to call the senior Servants. There can only be three as they are modelled on the 'Three Marys' who were present at Our Saviour's crucifixion.'

Father Peverett automatically crossed himself at this point.

'Where is the other Sister?'

'Oh, Sister Mary Ellen is currently stationed at our Glasgow branch and has been for some years now.'

'Thanks, that gives us an idea of who we should speak to,' Dan said. 'We'd also like to know a little more about her husband, if you have time.'

Father Peverett looked at his watch again.

'I've got just over ten minutes, so what can I tell you about John in that time? He was a devout Catholic who loved this organisation. He helped us out financially at times which was a blessing...'

'Even after he died, I believe,' Dan said.

'That's true and I'll be honest with you, his generosity has helped to keep a roof over our heads. He is remembered in all our prayers.'

'Have you any idea why he might have wanted to kill himself?' Dan asked.

'Is it certain that it was suicide?' the Father asked.

'We haven't had the Coroner's verdict yet but it certainly looks that way.'

Father Peverett held out both hands in a gesture of helplessness.

'If that is the case then I'm truly sorry. John was a, well, complicated man, shall we say. His belief in the Church and our cause was unquestionable as was his skill as a businessman. However, it became clear that, in his latter months at least, he was seriously conflicted over something.'

'What do you mean by 'conflicted'?'

Father Peverett thought about this for a few moments.

'He became quite touchy and self-absorbed which was unlike him. I felt that he was angry about something.'

'Have you any idea what?' Dan asked.

Another shrug.

'I asked him once but he wouldn't even admit that there was a problem.'

'He was very drunk on the night he died. Do you know if he had a problem with drink?' Dan asked.

'No, at least not as far as I know,' Father Peverett replied. 'He admitted that he'd had a problem with alcohol in the past when he had first joined us but he told me that he hadn't touched a drop since. That was some ten years ago.'

'Who was his confessor?' Mac asked.

'Father Renfield.'

'So, he took the confessions of both John and Monica Hashley?'

'That's right,' Father Peverett said. He then gave them both a hard look. 'I hope that you're not planning on asking Father Renfield what was said during any of the confessions he may have taken?'

'No, of course not, Father,' Mac replied. 'We're well aware of the Seal of the Confessional. We would never ask a priest to directly reveal what was said to him in the confessional box.'

'I'm glad to hear it. I'm sure that Father Renfield will tell you everything that he can but I'm surprised that you're asking so many questions about John. I thought that you wanted to know more about Monica.'

Dan glanced quickly over at Mac.

'We do, Father, we do,' Mac said. 'I can't tell you too much at this time but we believe that Monica's motive in killing her daughter and the other girl is because she blamed them for his death. That may sound a bit strange, silly even, but Monica was ill and we think that her husband's death tipped her over the edge.'

'I see,' Father Peverett replied. 'They seemed such a perfect couple, a perfect family even. I still can't quite believe what's happened.'

'What did John's position as a Luminary entail?' Mac asked.

'Well, he was Second Luminary for quite a while but, as Mark Appleby was getting on, he did most of the First Luminary's work. Father Renfield is my deputy and, as I have so much else to do, it seemed logical that they should work together. They were a very good team.'

'How did Father Renfield take John Hashley's death?'

'I think that they became friends but, even so, Father Renfield took the news of John's demise with quiet resignation. It was, after all, God's will.' The Father looked again at his watch. 'I'm afraid that I need to be somewhere else. I'll arrange for the Sisters to come and see you next, if that's okay?'

'That's fine,' Dan said.

The Father left them to it. Dan stood up and had a stretch. He was about to say something when he noticed Mac was writing something in his notebook. He held it up for Dan to read.

Before you say anything look in the corners of the room.

Dan stretched again and quickly glanced from side to side. There was a CCTV camera in each corner so that the room was fully covered. Where there was a camera there was likely to be a microphone too. Dan sat down and got his own notebook out.

We'll only talk outside. BTW wouldn't you say that Father P was a few inches short of being five feet ten inches tall?

Mac glumly nodded his agreement but then started up a conversation about football. Dan was a Luton fan so Mac started talking about what it had been like when his club had been in the same division. The talk became quite animated and anyone watching them could only take it as being real. Mainly because it was.

They were interrupted by the door opening as a tiny woman came in. She was in her late sixties or early seventies and she had the same type of black shapeless dress on as the woman who had let them in. However, unlike her, this lady had a beatific smile on her face.

'I'm Sister Mary Jane,' she said as she sat down opposite Dan and Mac. 'The Father said that you wanted to speak to me.'

Her voice, like the rest of her, was tiny and sounded almost like a child's. Both Dan and Mac couldn't resist a smile.

'We're looking into the murders of Alicia Hashley and another girl,' Dan said. 'I take it that you've heard about this?'

'Unfortunately, I have,' she said as her smile quickly faded away. 'Poor Alicia, she was such a good girl really.'

'In what way?'

'Well, she was a teenager and I think she might have started her rebellion phase, if you know what I mean. All those black clothes and the glum looks. I was a bit like that myself except that it was kaftans and wearing flowers in my hair in those days. I was at the Isle of Wight festival when Dylan played but it was Jimi Hendrix that I really went there for. I liked the bad boys best.'

She smiled as she looked up at Dan and Mac.

'You look surprised,' she continued. 'Well, I wasn't born seventy, you know. I think that Alicia used to find our mass a bit boring and so she used to volunteer to help me out with the creche. She was wonderful with the children. No glum looks when they were around, she was always smiling and playing little games with them.'

She had to stop and force back a tear before she could carry on.

'I've had a full life with more than a few wild moments thrown in but I eventually came back to my God. It was my hope that Alicia would too.'

'We've been told that you know Monica Hashley quite well. We'd like to know as much about her as we can,' Dan said.

'Poor Monica too,' she said with a slow shake of her head. 'Is it true that she might be charged with Alicia's murder?'

'That's why we're here,' Dan replied not quite answering the question.

'I thought that I knew Monica. She's the type of person that this organisation needs; she was hard working, sympathetic and always thinking of others before themselves. Someone told me that the evidence against her is more or less airtight, is that right?'

Dan merely nodded in confirmation.

She sighed and then said, 'I just can't conceive of any way that the woman I knew would hurt a hair on her daughter's head. They were always very close and, for some reason, Alicia had grown very protective of her mother.'

'What was her marriage like?' Mac asked.

'She and John seemed to have the perfect marriage. They were both devoutly attached to their religion and to each other, or so I thought.'

'Have you any idea why John Hashley might have committed suicide?'

Sister Mary Jane looked shocked. Her hand covered her mouth.

'Did he really kill himself?' she asked her voice sounding even more childlike.

'That's what it looks like,' Mac replied.

'And here's me saying that they had the perfect marriage,' she replied. 'Although...'

She paused for thought. Dan and Mac let her think.

'I think that something might have been getting John down in the last few months before he left us.'

'In what way?' Dan asked.

'I'm not sure. As I said both he and Monica kept up appearances as it were but, on the odd occasion when he thought that no-one was looking, I can only say that he looked deeply troubled.'

'Have you any idea what might have been troubling him?'

'I'm sorry but no,' she said with a shrug.

'Who knew John the best, do you think?' Dan asked.

'Father Manley, I'd guess. He was with Father Peverett when he founded the British branch of our organisation. I believe that it was he who brought John into the fold some ten years ago now I think it was.'

'Anyone else?'

'Well Father Peverett, of course, and Father Ryan too. I think that they used to talk a lot about football together,' she replied.

'What about Father Renfield?' Mac asked.

'Well, Father Renfield was John and Monica's confessor but, beyond that...'

Another shrug.

'What about the other Luminaries?' Mac asked.

'I don't think he was that close to anyone other than the Fathers really. John worked with the previous Number One Luminary, Mark Appleton, for some years but I don't think that they were friends or anything like that. Sadly, Mark is no longer with us.'

'He's dead?' Dan asked.

'The next thing to it,' she replied. 'Alzheimer's and quite a severe case too. They kept him on for as long as they could and that meant that John, in reality, did almost all of the work. Poor Mark doesn't even recognise his own wife now.'

Once again, she became thoughtful.

'You don't think that Monica might have Alzheimer's too?' she asked.

Dan and Mac glanced at each other.

'Why do you ask?' Dan said.

'Well, lately she's seemed to be somewhat forgetful and unfocussed, if you know what I mean. I suppose that her husband dying might have played a part in that but she was going that way before he went. I remember that Mark was a little like that before he got diagnosed.'

'No, she hasn't got Alzheimer's,' Dan said.

'Well, one small mercy then. Anyway, I'm sorry, I just wish that I could tell you more,' she said with another shrug.

So did Mac. The next Sister must have been waiting outside the door as she came in just seconds after Sister Mary Jane had left.

Sister Mary Edda looked like an older and somewhat grimmer version of the woman who had admitted them into the building. Mac could tell that her mission was to tell them as little as possible and, in that, she succeeded admirably.

'Fancy a breath of fresh air after the next one?' Dan asked.

'A bit of a walk would do me good,' Mac replied. 'These seats aren't all that comfortable and I'm getting a bit stiff.'

Mac knew that Dan was intimating that they should have a chat out of reach of the cameras and microphones but what he had said was still true. They hadn't got anywhere yet and this made him feel a little on edge.

However, there were three priests still to come and Mac knew that one of them was likely to be the killer. However, as soon as this thought crossed his mind, he questioned himself. How could he be so sure? He was going on what a ghost had said to him and there was a chance that it might have been a dream after all. It had certainly felt like one when it was happening.

Yet deep down he knew. One of the Fathers had blood on his hands.

Chapter Twenty-Four

The next interviewee wasn't quite as prompt as Sister Mary Edda had been. Dan had a look at his emails while they waited. Mac just let his thoughts roam.

'Do you think that these Sisters get to pick their own names?' he asked.

Dan looked up and gave it some thought.

'Well, I guess that if they're like nuns then they very well might. Why do you ask?'

'I suspect that there might still be a little streak of rebelliousness in Sister Mary Jane,' Mac replied. Seeing Dan's puzzled looks he explained. 'Mary Jane, it used to be one of the many slang words in the sixties and seventies for marijuana.'

Dan smiled, 'I think it was just 'weed' and 'ganja' when I was young. Not that I ever partook, of course.'

Dan was still trying to keep a straight face when his phone pinged. He had received a text.

'That was from Father Peverett,' he said. 'He's arranged for the other Fathers to see us this afternoon.'

'It looks like he wants to get this done and dusted as quickly as possible, wouldn't you say?' Mac said.

'I'd guess,' Dan replied. 'Father Manley will be first at around two so we should have a chance to get a breath of fresh air before then.'

Dan quickly glanced up at one of the CCTV cameras. Mac got the message. A tentative knock was followed by a head peeking around the door.

'Er...Servant Amelia?' Dan asked unsure if that was what he was supposed to call her.

A woman in her early fifties came in and sat down. She gave them both a good long look. Mac looked back.

She wore very large glasses that magnified her eyes and she had a hairstyle that piled her dark brown hair on top of her head. Mac couldn't get the image of an owl out of his head. He wouldn't have been totally surprised if she'd been able to turn her head right the way around.

'Ms. Amelia Gambrinus is my name and I'm no-one's servant,' she eventually said with certainty.

'I'm sorry but that was the only name I was given,' Dan said.

'Apology accepted. How can I help you?'

Mac noticed that she blinked when she spoke which only reinforced the image of an owl in his head.

'We'd like to know as much as we can about Monica Hashley. We've been told that you worked with her,' Dan said.

'Yes, Monica used to help me with the accounts when I was getting a bit snowed under,' she replied.

'What accounts were these?'

'Just those of the Servants. They're nothing like the ones on the men's side. There they deal in millions where, for us, it was counting pennies by comparison.'

'So, you just dealt with the monies raised by the 'Servants of the Virgin Mary'. Is that right?' Dan asked.

'That's about it. I shouldn't really knock it though, compared to a lot of religious organisations I suppose that it still amounts to a fair bit of money.'

'What was Monica Hashley like?'

Amelia gave this some thought.

'She was a quiet and unassuming woman, I suppose, that's really all I can tell you.'

They asked more questions but got nowhere. She was clearly stonewalling and Mac could see that Dan was starting to get a little grumpy.

'I take it that you'll want my address?' she asked which puzzled Mac. 'Unlike the Sisters I don't live here.'

Dan took his notebook out, opened it up and pushed it across to her. She scribbled away and then closed the book before pushing it back. She then looked meaningfully at the notebook before getting up and leaving the room.

Dan opened up his notebook. Underneath an address in Clapham, she had written –

Meet me in the pub opposite the Little Ben Clock in half an hour

He closed his notebook and pushed it back into his pocket.

'I think that we should take a breather,' Dan said as he looked at his watch. 'We've got about an hour and a half before we meet with Father Manley.'

It was easier getting out than getting in as they only had to press a button to open the doors. Even so, they were still aware of the steely gaze of the woman who had let then in following them every inch of the way out.

The air was cold outside but Mac gratefully breathed it in. There was something oppressive about the atmosphere inside the building.

They walked around the corner into Carlisle Place and then towards the main road which was just a matter of yards away. Once they had Little Big Ben in their sights Dan took out his notebook and passed it to Mac who wasn't totally surprised.

'I thought that there might have been something else. There aren't many addresses that take that long to write.'

Mac looked ahead and remembered when he had seen it for the first time just a few years before. Although the clock, a miniature of the Big Ben Tower at the Houses of Parliament, was Victorian, it had been taken away in the sixties and only restored to its rightful place recently. It was such a lovely landmark that he wondered why anyone would want to remove it in the first place.

Then his eyes wandered to the pub on the opposite side of the road. He felt a tinge of excitement as he thought that they might finally get some information they could use.

Amelia Gambrinus was sitting in a corner at the back of the pub with a large pink gin in front of her. Mac joined her while Dan ordered coffees and sandwiches at the bar.

'I take it that we're safe to talk here?' Mac asked.

'Safe as houses,' she replied. 'You'll never find any of that sanctimonious lot in here.'

Mac waited until Dan came back with the coffees before asking his next question.

'You don't seem to be anything like the others we've met so far. Why do you volunteer to work there?'

'Well, I'm a Catholic but, if I'm being honest, I'm not all that into it. For instance, I often skip mass for the pub on a Sunday but there is one thing that gets my dander up and that's abortion. I'm fiercely pro-life and Sanguine Salvatoris is just about our best hope of getting something done,' she said with real conviction. 'They have tremendous influence, even in Parliament or so I've been told. That's why I'm happy to lend a hand but I must say that it's all terribly old-fashioned. I mean calling the men 'Luminaries' while us poor wee women are lowly 'Servants' is a bit nauseating. Anyway, I keep my head down and put up with it for the sake of the cause.'

'I take it that you wanted to tell us something?' Dan asked.

'I'm not sure if I can tell you anything you might find useful but at least I can talk freely here. They've got cameras and microphones all over the place, except for the top floor that is.'

205

At least one person has lied to them then, Mac thought.

'What's on the top floor?' Dan asked.

'That's the accommodation floor. It's where the Fathers and Sisters live and also any guests who might want to stay overnight.'

'I take it that was where Monica Hashley stayed on the night of her daughter's murder?' Mac asked.

'That's right,' she replied. 'Anyway, it's my guess that they didn't want the cameras there in case of any bed-hopping.'

She then gave them a naughty smile.

'Does any of that really go on?' Mac asked.

'Well, I've heard some rumours but nothing specific.'

'So, what did you want to tell us?' Dan asked.

'I knew Monica only a little and John hardly at all but I do have eyes in my head,' she replied. 'From what I saw and heard, John Hashley was a real alpha male and he always had to be the boss. Apart from the Fathers, he thought that everyone else was there just for his convenience. As for Monica, she was the perfect little wee wifey. A doormat in other words. She used to counsel other women in the movement who were having marital problems and I used to think that was rich as she was obviously getting beaten black and blue by her husband.'

She stopped and took a big gulp from her drink.

'I used to have a friend who went through that and I know all the signs. You know, wearing long-sleeved blouses and turtle necks in the middle of summer and the constant excuses for the bruises that couldn't be hidden. I never noticed it so much with Monica until the last four or five months though.'

'So, you think that the beatings only started recently then?' Dan asked.

'I doubt it,' she replied with a bitter smile. 'Men who beat women, beat women. However, I think that it had definitely gotten worse in the months before John Hashley died. I wasn't the only one who noticed it but the rest all turned a blind eye. I tried to speak to Monica about it but she blanked me out and pretended that everything was wonderful just like the rest of them. John Hashley was the next thing to God at Sanguine Salvatoris, or the next thing to Father Peverett, I should say. Anyway, Monica definitely drew the short straw when she married him. John Hashley was an angry man and, unfortunately, I think that he took his anger out on his poor wife.'

'Have you any idea what John Hashley was so angry about?' Mac asked.

Amelia shrugged, 'I've no idea. As I said, I didn't really know the man but, even in such a sanctimonious hole as that, you still hear rumours.'

'And what were the rumours?'

'That John Hashley was having an affair,' she replied lowering her voice.

'Any idea who with?' Mac asked getting a lot more interested in what he was hearing.

'No, I'm sorry. I doubt that it was anyone at Sanguine Salvatoris but he was apparently overheard when he was talking to one of the fathers about separating from his wife.'

'But wouldn't that go against everything that Sanguine Salvatoris stands for? 'Family first' and all that?'

'Oh, absolutely and that's why the rumour was so shocking. Sanguine Salvatoris as an organisation, believes that marriage is a sacred vow made directly to God and that it's a life sentence. They don't even believe in separation as an option if a couple is having problems. So, they have to stay together even if this means being in a living hell for one of them. That one is usually the wife.'

'Did you believe the rumour?' Dan asked.

'To be honest, no,' she replied. 'John Hashley was so holier-than-thou that I couldn't conceive of him even looking at another woman, let alone climbing into bed with one.'

'Was that all you wanted to say to us?' Dan asked.

'Do you really believe that Monica killed her daughter?' she asked.

'That's what all the evidence is telling us.'

'I still find it really difficult to get my head around. Although, having said that, Monica hasn't been right lately. She stopped helping me about two months ago after she sent me a spreadsheet that was basically gibberish. I had to do the whole thing again myself. She made some excuse about needing new glasses but she didn't volunteer to help me again. She missed quite a few of the Servant's meetings too which was very unlike her. I called her once to tell her that the meeting has started and it was clear that she had totally forgotten all about it.'

'So, do you think that she might have been ill or something?' Dan asked.

'Yes, I do. Might that help her in court, as mitigation or something?'

'It might.'

Amelia picked up her glass and downed it in one.

'I certainly hope so,' she said. 'Monica was a doormat but she could be quite sweet too. She definitely doesn't deserve this.'

She rose and left them to it just as the sandwiches arrived. Mac found that he was hungry and ate his sandwich almost as fast as Amelia had downed her drink.

'So, what do you think?' Dan said as he pushed his plate away.

'Well, there was nothing there that you could hang your hat on but something she said really interested me.'

'The rumour about John Hashley having an affair, I take it?'

'That's right,' Mac replied. 'I find that I've been wondering about John Hashley a lot. His suicide happened just weeks before the murders and I can't shake the idea that there might be some sort of connection between the two events. A number of people have now told us that John Hashley was angry about something, angry enough to beat his wife so badly that she's been brain damaged. Perhaps this affair was the reason.'

'Go on,' Dan said.

'Well, John Hashley was seemingly a model husband and the head of a Catholic household. He was a devout member of Sanguine Salvatoris and he walked the walk with his religion through the responsibilities he took on as Luminary Number One and the vast sums of money he loaned the organisation. I remember reading somewhere about how people can create psychological masks for themselves. They sometimes come to believe more in the mask than their true selves and so they lose their real identity. It's possible that John Hashley did just that. The public mask he wore, as a good father and devout Catholic, might have been shattered if he'd met someone and started an affair. It would go totally against everything he'd believed in up to that point. The outward mask of respectability was obviously important to him but where love, and especially desire, is involved then people can do some very strange things. So, John Hashley might have found himself on the horns of a dilemma. If he couldn't walk away from his religion or give up his lover then another solution had to be found.'

'And he found that solution by crashing into a bridge at a hundred miles an hour. Yes, that certainly sounds plausible enough,' Dan said. 'What else?'

'Well, she confirmed that they have cameras all over the building, except for the top floor. Weren't you told something else?'

'Yes, when I spoke to Father Renfield he said that they only had cameras in the car park,' Dan confirmed. 'Come to think of it, he was very quick at getting the footage from the car park to us.'

'Yes, and it was quite damning too, wasn't it?'

Mac began to wonder about Father Renfield and especially how tall he was.

Chapter Twenty-Five

Father Manley was around five feet ten inches tall which immediately interested Mac. He had grey hair and was of a slight build with a pronounced stoop. His lined face had a familiar look that told of a life full of suffering and anguish. Mac had seen this look before in the portraits of saints that had hung on the walls of the churches of his youth. His voice was soft with each word being pronounced precisely as it should be.

'It's appalling what has befallen the Hashleys, especially John,' he said with apparent sincerity.

'I believe that it was you who introduced John Hashley to Sanguine Salvatoris,' Dan asked. 'Is that right?'

'Yes, that's true. I first met John well over twenty years ago now. Once upon a time, when he was still a schoolboy, I used to be his parish priest and we grew quite close. I could see that the religious life appealed to him and it was my hope that he would one day enter the priesthood. However, God had his own plans for John and he eventually elected to go to university to study Business and Management instead. I watched his career from afar go from strength to strength but I used to worry about his spiritual life. Then, around ten years ago or so, we met again. John had just joined the Catholic Society of Businessmen and I had been booked to give them a talk on the aims and vision of Sanguine Salvatoris. It went down very well and several of the audience came to talk to me afterwards. John held back until they had all gone and then he came over.'

The priest stopped as emotion threatened to overcome him.

'I didn't recognise him at first,' he continued. 'The spindly schoolboy had grown up and filled out. He was now a man and a man who was making his mark on the world too. He immediately took up my offer to introduce him to Father Peverett and, after that, Sanguine Salvatoris became the focal point of his religious life.'

'From what we've heard, he worked very hard for your organisation,' Dan said.

'He did. I sometimes wondered how he managed to spend so much time on our affairs and still keep his business on an even keel. His energy was amazing and it seemed that he could sometimes make things happen just by the force of his will. Without John's help we certainly wouldn't be sitting here in this beautiful building, that's for certain.'

'Did you ever visit John at his home?'

'His house in Hertfordshire?' Father Manley asked. 'No, I never did but there was no reason to. If ever I needed to speak to John he always came here.'

'We've heard from several people that, before he died, John seemed to be angry about something. Have you any idea why?'

The priest slowly shook his head.

'I'm sorry but, even though we were friends, he rarely confided in me.'

'Who did he confide in?' Dan asked.

'About personal matters? No-one as far as I'm aware, except his confessor possibly. Perhaps that was part of the problem. John had never been good at talking about his emotions and how he felt about things. If he had been able to open up to someone then things might have been different. He killed himself, didn't he?'

Father Manley looked up at Dan, his eyes imploring him to disagree.

'There's been no formal verdict yet but that's what it looks like. Have you any idea what might have made him do such a thing?'

The priest slowly shook his head.

'I could see that he was troubled but John was the type of man who kept things bottled up. I think that, because he was so good at managing his business, he felt that he should be able to manage his feelings in the same way. That's not always possible though, is it? We all reach points in our lives when we need the help of others. If only he had reached out.'

'How well did you know his wife?' Dan asked.

'Not well at all really. She worked with the Servants while I'm the chaplain to the Luminaries. However, she seemed to be a meek and godly woman, I suppose. Is it really true that she killed her own daughter?'

'That's where all the evidence is pointing,' Dan said again.

The priest slowly shook his head again.

'On the surface, they seemed like the perfect Christian family but it now seems as if the Devil had wormed his way inside and had somehow corrupted them. It just goes to show that we must be ever vigilant against his wiles.'

'Do you really think that the Devil made John kill himself?' Mac asked.

'Of course. John was a good man, a paragon of lay piety in many ways. It's my opinion that it was the wife who, like Eve, was weak and introduced the evil one into John's life. Women are so morally inferior, don't you think?' the priest said with absolute conviction.

Neither Dan nor Mac had any answer to that one.

'Have you ever read a book called the Malleus Maleficarum?' Mac asked.

'Oh, of course,' Father Manley replied with a smile. 'The Hammer of Witches. That comes from a time when they knew how to fight Satan on all fronts. As a society, I'm afraid that we've regressed somewhat since then. I've heard that the dead girl was a witch. Is that true?'

'Well, she was interested in Wicca.'

'Oh, so little loss there then,' Father Manley said with a curl of his lip. 'In India they used to have a practice called *sati*. When a man died, they used to throw his wife onto the funeral pyre too. The British banned it in the 1830s but I often wonder if they were wrong to do so. In John's case they could have put both his wife and his daughter on the fire and saved a lot of misery.'

Mac found that he was glad when the interview was finally over.

The all too obvious misogyny of the organisation resonated with Mac. He felt that it was no coincidence that they had two witches had been killed with a hammer but what exactly was the link?

He felt as if he was seeing the ghostly outline of something but he couldn't quite make it out.

'Are you alright, Mac?' Dan asked.

'Oh, I'm fine. How long before the next one?'

'Another twenty minutes or so.'

'Let's go and have a look at the accommodation area,' Mac suggested.

They were followed to the lift by a young man who was dressed as if he was going to a business meeting. He appeared on the top floor just after they had arrived and ran after them.

'I'm sorry but you're not supposed to be here,' he said breathlessly. 'This is a private area. Only those who live or who are staying here are allowed.'

'And you are?' Dan growled.

'Luminary Matt Peake.'

'And you've been told to follow us by Father Peverett, I presume?'

Matt didn't deny it.

'Well Matt, can I very respectfully ask you to PUSH OFF!'

Dan's raised voice caused the young man to take a big step backwards. His face went pale and it was clear that he didn't know what to do next. After dithering for some seconds, he rushed off in the direction of the lift.

'Is this place getting to you?' Mac asked with a big smile.

'You could say that. If I'm honest I'm starting to feel a little claustrophobic.'

'Yes, me too.'

'So, why did you want to come up here?' Dan asked.

'Just to have a look around plus it appears that there aren't any cameras and microphones up here.'

They walked slowly around the circular walkway. Mac looked over the railing, the ground floor seemed a long way down from here. The rooms were arranged in little clusters of four each of which led off a short corridor. At the end of the corridor there was a fifth door. Mac thought that it might have been a bathroom but a sign on the door said that it was a 'Prayer Room'. They continued walking.

'Father Manley appeared so reasonable at first,' Dan said with a scowl.

'Yes, I thought that too,' Mac replied. 'Even though I've read quite a lot about Sanguine Salvatoris and their fundamentalist approach, hearing it said out loud surprised me too. I'd guess that, if he'd been born a few hundred years ago, he'd probably be happily burning witches for a living.'

'He's in the frame, isn't he?' Dan asked.

'Well, he's the right height and he certainly seemed to blame Monica Hashley for her husband's death. He was no lover of witches either so perhaps he saw a way of killing two birds with one stone.'

215

'Yes, kill Alicia and then frame her mother for the murder. Yet, he said that he never visited John Hashley at home.'

'Well, if he is our man, then he would say that, wouldn't he?' Mac said as he peeked down another corridor.

It was exactly the same as the first. He looked around and counted the corridors.

'There's at least forty-eight rooms here plus an awful lot of Prayer Rooms.'

'It's like a small hotel really, isn't it?' Dan replied.

'Anyway, I was just thinking about how this organisation is all about the men. It describes itself somewhere as holding on to 'old-fashioned values' but, unfortunately, one of those values seem to be extreme misogyny.'

'Yes, it seems like they only just about tolerate women here, don't they?' Dan said. 'Do you think that has anything to do with the murders?'

'Yes,' Mac quickly replied.

'In what way exactly?'

Mac shrugged, 'I wish I could tell you that. It's just that, ever since Chris James mentioned that book 'The Hammer of Witches', I just haven't been able to get it out of my head. Is it just a coincidence that Rhiannon and Alicia were killed with a hammer? I'm beginning to doubt that.'

They walked on.

'This walkway's quite exposed, isn't it?' Dan said. 'Bed-hopping doesn't look like it would be all that easy, unless the rooms were on the same corridor, I suppose.'

Mac stood as still as a statue and looked down one of the corridors. Dan stopped and looked too.

'Do you think that they'd have a register of who stayed here and in what rooms?' Mac eventually asked.

'I'd guess that by law they'd have to have something, even just to comply with fire regulations,' Dan said. 'What are you thinking?'

'That rumour about John Hashley having an affair. I know that Amelia Gambrinus said that it couldn't be anyone in Sanguine Salvatoris but what if she's wrong?'

'I see where you're going. It would have been more than handy to have a lover on the same corridor just a step away. They might refuse to let us have the information though, after all we haven't got a search warrant.'

'Yes, you're right there,' Mac said. 'Let's not mention it to them for now then. Ready to go down?'

Mac noticed some movement on the opposite side of the walkway. Matt Peake was still keeping an eye on them but from a healthy distance. Mac waved for him to come over. He approached them cautiously like a dog who had just been kicked.

'We're going back down now, Matt,' Mac said. 'Do you want to accompany us?'

He got into the lift looking as if it was about to explode and happily left them at the door of the room they were using for interviews.

'That lad could do with some assertiveness training,' Dan said as he sat down.

'Who's next?' Mac asked.

'Father Renfield then Father Peverett again and finally Father Ryan at around five o'clock. With any luck we should have time to grab a coffee after we're finished with Father Peverett.'

Mac guessed that Dan would want to compare notes too. As the minutes ticked by, he found that he was almost looking forward to meeting Father Renfield.

Chapter Twenty-Six

Father Julian Renfield slid noiselessly around the door and sat down. He immediately looked at his watch, thus informing them that his time was valuable. Dan pulled out his notebook and began writing, glancing up at Renfield from time to time. Mac had to suppress a smile as he could see that Dan was writing down a list for that evening's shopping.

Renfield looked at Mac and he looked right back which made the priest squirm slightly. He knew that Father Julian Renfield was around thirty years of age but he looked even younger. This was partly due to his clean-shaven fresh-looking face, which Mac guessed had just been exfoliated and scrubbed. It was helped by a recent haircut, in which the sideburns had been delicately razored and each hair had been gelled to perfection. And then there was his suit. It was black just like the other priests but, while their suits were just suits, this one had been tailored to hang perfectly around his slim body. The shoes were black but fashionable and the subtle aroma of an expensive aftershave wafted across the table.

Mac felt as though he had learned a lot before a single question had been asked.

Renfield turned his face towards the window and Mac had a sense of déjà vu. He reminded him of someone.

'My apologies,' Dan said as he put his notebook away.

Renfield nodded and a smile quickly appeared and even more quickly went.

Was Renfield feeling tense? Mac couldn't make his mind up. However, the stillness and stiffness with which he sat made it look as if he was on the defensive. This interested Mac. His eyes never left Renfield as the questions were being asked.

'We're here to get some background information on Monica Hashley and also on her husband John,' Dan said.

'Why John?' Renfield asked.

He had a slight Northern accent. Manchester perhaps, Mac thought.

'You'll find that out as we go along,' Dan said. 'I've been told that you were both Monica's and John's confessor. Is that right?'

'Yes, that's right and I, of course, will not divulge anything that was said under the seal of the sacrament.'

'That's understood,' Dan replied. 'We've uncovered a lot of evidence that seems to definitively point in a certain direction. However, we need to do our due diligence and ensure that we have uncovered everything relating to Monica and John Hashley that we can. This organisation was a large part of their lives and we're hoping that we can find a few more clues as to why the murders of Alicia Hashley and Rhiannon Brodeur were carried out as they were.'

'So, you're just dotting the I's and crossing the T's then?' Renfield asked.

'That's about it,' Dan replied. 'That's why there's just the two of us here today.'

Mac saw Renfield relax a little.

Well done, Dan, Mac said to himself.

'What was Monica Hashley like?' Dan asked.

'She was a good woman or so I thought. However, after John died, she changed.'

'In what way?'

'She became more withdrawn and quite angry at times. I asked her why but, at first, she wouldn't tell me. Then, around two weeks after John died, she brought me something, something that we both found extremely disturbing.'

'What was that?' Dan asked.

'A notebook that was owned by Alicia. She called it a 'Grimoire' which is a book of spells used by witches.'

'Was she worried at her daughter being a witch?'

'Yes, but there was more to it than that, I think. There were prayers written down in the book in which Alicia seemed to be thanking a heathen god for the death of her father,' Renfield said giving them a disbelieving look. 'I didn't know Alicia that well, I suppose, but I would never have thought it possible.'

'So, Monica was angry at her daughter?'

'Yes, almost irrationally so, I think. I initially put Monica's anger and confusion down to John's passing but now I'm not so sure. I think that she may well have been ill in some way.'

'Mentally ill?' Dan asked.

'Possibly. Whatever it was, she wasn't acting like herself.'

'Do you know anything about a book called 'The Hammer of Witches'?'

'Of course, I read it when I was in training,' Renfield smoothly replied. 'Mediaeval nonsense at its best.'

'Monica had a copy of it in her car, one that was taken from your library,' Dan said.

'Really?'

Renfield was trying to feign surprise, however, Mac felt that his voice went a little higher than was strictly necessary.

'Yes, really.'

'I had no idea that she did that. I don't remember mentioning the 'Malleus Maleficarum' to her when we talked but, of course, she could have always found it in the library for herself.'

'What did you say to her?' Dan asked.

'I can't reveal anything we discussed but I can tell you that it certainly had nothing to do with that book.'

'Do you think that Monica Hashley could have been angry enough to kill her own daughter?'

'I honestly wouldn't have thought so at the time but, from what I'm hearing…' Renfield said punctuating his sentence with a shrug.

Dan looked over at Mac. He was asking him if he wanted to carry on.

'How well did you know John Hashley?' Mac asked.

'Fairly well, I'd guess,' Renfield replied.

'Would you say that you were friends?'

'Yes, I'd say that.'

'Tell me about it.'

Mac found that, sometimes, an open question can lead to unexpected answers.

'Well, Father Peverett has been kind enough to entrust me with certain responsibilities…'

'Effectively, you were his deputy. Is that right?'

'Only in some things. To explain, since our dear Saint Miguel passed away, Father Peverett has become something of a leader for our movement on the world stage. That being the case, he can't always give as much time here as he would have liked. I just help him out now and again.'

'Would these responsibilities have included working with the Luminaries?' Mac asked.

'Of course.'

'So, you would have worked quite closely with John Hashley as he was the Number One Luminary?'

'Yes, that's right. You're asking quite a lot of questions about John…'

'Please just answer the questions,' Mac said. 'So how did that work? I mean with John having a business to run as well.'

'Well, he would often spend a few nights here during the week so we could work in the evenings. His office isn't too far away from here, so it was handy for him.'

'I take it that he always used the same room?'

'Of course,' Renfield replied. 'As Number One Luminary he always had a room at his disposal. Monica used the same room too when she was in town.'

'As you've probably heard, we've had a look upstairs. We were just trying to figure out Monica's movements on the night of the murders. What was the number of her room?'

Renfield hesitated slightly before answering.

'It was number twenty-four.'

'And who else had rooms on that corridor?' Mac asked.

'Well, two of the rooms were kept free for visitors and the other room...well, it's mine.'

Mac guessed that Renfield had hesitated to give himself time to think. He also guessed that Renfield quickly concluded that the police would find this out sooner or later and so it might look better if he volunteered the information now.

'So, Monica Hashley appeared to have left the building around seven o'clock in the evening and then returned just after one. Did you see or hear her either going or returning?'

Renfield shook his head.

'I normally don't go to bed until eleven or so and I'm a very sound sleeper.'

'What were you doing that evening?' Mac asked.

'I was in the library doing some research...'

'What was the research about?' Mac quickly asked.

Renfield answered just as quickly.

'I was looking for information on anti-Christian attitudes in some Middle Eastern countries. Father Peverett was doing an article on the subject for the Vatican News site.'

Mac felt as though he had just sent a really good serve over the net at tennis only to have it smashed back at him. Renfield was good.

'Was there anyone else in the library?'

'I don't remember seeing anyone. The library's usually very quiet in the evenings. That's why I like working there.'

The best alibis are ones that are plausible and can't be broken, Mac thought.

'And after that?'

'I usually spend an hour or so in the prayer room before going to bed.'

Mac didn't bother asking if anyone else had seen him there. He felt that Renfield was getting a little suspicious on having to answer questions about his movements, so he switched tack.

'That's a shame,' Mac said. 'We have enough video evidence for a conviction but it would still have been nice if we'd had an eye witness to Monica Hashley's movements that night.'

'I understand that but, I'm sorry, I can't help you there.'

'You said that you and John were friends, did you ever visit him at his house?' Mac asked.

He watched Renfield's face carefully. The question had obviously made him uncomfortable.

'Yes, once or twice, I think. If we were falling behind, John might invite me back for the weekend so we could catch up. He would then drop me back here on Sunday when he came to attend mass.'

Mac had to again suppress a smile.

'I take it that you met Alicia when you visited?'

'Well, only at mealtimes really and not always then. She didn't seem to be all that sociable and she kept to her room most of the time while I was there.'

'Thank you very much, Father Renfield, for your time. You've been most cooperative,' Mac said.

'Oh, is that it?' Renfield said looking surprised.

'Yes, we have what we need for the case,' Mac said with a smile.

Renfield left giving them a look that was part puzzlement and part relief. Mac watched him closely as he walked through the door. He would be willing to bet that Father Renfield was exactly five feet ten inches tall.

'When is Father Peverett due?' Mac asked.

'In about twenty minutes,' Dan replied.

'So, we'll have around an hour and a half before Father Ryan is due to see us.'

'A coffee and a donut would suit me,' Dan said. 'I don't know why but every now and then I really fancy a donut.'

'I think I saw a donut shop when we were out before,' Mac said.

'I saw it too and that's what started me thinking.'

Mac went to the loo and washed his face to wake himself up a little. Father Peverett was already there when he returned.

'I was just telling Detective Superintendent Carter that I have to be somewhere in fifteen minutes,' the Father said apologetically. 'I hope that doesn't inconvenience you too much.'

'No, I'm not sure we've got too many more questions to ask anyway,' Mac said as he took his seat. 'It's been really interesting talking to Father Manley and Father Renfield. It's not really anything to do with the investigation but we never asked them any questions about their backgrounds. How did they end up here at Sanguine Salvatoris?'

'Well, Father Harold Manley was one of my first converts as it were,' Father Peverett replied. 'We started the movement in a small room at the back of a church in the East End where Harold was one of the parish priests. He's been an ever-present within the organisation ever since.'

'I'm just wondering why he isn't your deputy instead of Father Renfield?'

'Well, Harold has always been more interested in the spiritual side of the organisation, that's why he's chaplain to the Luminaries. He's never been interested in the administrative side of what we do and I've found that you have to be good at multi-tasking to be in a leadership role.'

'And Father Renfield is good at that side of things?' Mac asked.

'Oh yes, he's very meticulous,' the Father replied, 'plus he has youth on his side. I'm hoping to be leading Sanguine Salvatoris for a few years yet but it's nice to think that it will be in good hands when I do finally retire.'

Mac looked closely at Father Peverett as he asked, 'How did you happen to come across Father Renfield in the first place?'

Interestingly the Father looked down as he answered, avoiding any eye contact.

'He was recommended to me by an old friend. He was the head of a seminary in a place called Urmston...'

'That's just outside Manchester, isn't it?' Mac interrupted.

'Yes, that's right. It's not far from Salford.'

Mac's ears pricked up on hearing this.

'Anyway,' the Father continued, 'I was told that Father Renfield was a bright young man who was very keen to work in our organisation and so he joined us for a few months, some six years ago now, and he's been with us ever since. As my role has expanded within the organisation, Father Renfield has taken over some of my responsibilities which is a godsend as I feel that I can trust him.'

'Is he related to you in any way?' Mac asked.

'No, no of course not,' the Father replied looking downwards again.

Mac had no more questions for him.

Dan gave him an enquiring look after Father Peverett had gone but Mac just nodded towards the door.

'Come on, those donuts won't wait forever.'

Outside Mac inhaled deeply. The air inside felt as though it didn't have enough oxygen in it. They didn't talk until they had turned the corner and started walking towards the main road and the donut shop.

'So, what was all that about? The painting, I mean,' Dan asked.

Before they had left Mac had gone over to the painting of Monsignor Etxeberria and the young Father Peverett and had looked at it for some time.

'I'll show you when we're seated,' Mac replied. 'That was a very interesting session, wasn't it?'

'Yes, but I somehow get the feeling that you got a little more out of it than I did,' Dan replied.

'All will be revealed,' Mac said with a smile.

Chapter Twenty-Seven

They had managed to get a table well away from everyone else so that they could talk freely without being overheard. The coffee was strong and the sugar-glazed donuts were satisfyingly sweet. After the donuts had disappeared, Dan sat back and looked at Mac.

'Come on then, let's have it,' he said.

'What did you make of Renfield?' Mac asked.

'Well, he was the right height and as smarmy as they come. He certainly seemed more than happy to drop Monica Hashley in it.'

'Yes, his suggestion of Monica's anger and irrationality would certainly add to the case against her, if we didn't know better that is. I think he knew that she was brain damaged and he was smart enough to have looked up what that might mean.'

'You mean about the fact that sometimes people with brain damage can sometimes become more aggressive?'

'Yes, he's smart alright but he gave us something the minute he opened his mouth.'

'How come?' Dan asked.

'His accent is from the North. Manchester probably.'

'And?' Dan said looking puzzled.

Mac took his phone out, selected a photo and handed it to Dan.

'That's the painting you were looking at,' Dan said.

'Father Peverett's changed a lot since that was done but just zoom in on his younger self and let me know what you think.'

Dan's brow crinkled with thought as he looked at the painting. Then Mac could see the penny drop.

'And that's why you asked whether Renfield was a relative,' Dan said.

'Yes, there's definitely quite a resemblance between Renfield and the younger Peverett, isn't there? What you probably don't know is that, when I was getting some background on Sanguine Salvatoris from Father Farrell, he mentioned the reason why Father Peverett was sent to Spain in the first place.'

'Let me guess,' Dan said. 'He got a girl pregnant.'

'Spot on. I think that Renfield is Peverett's son and all that about him being recommended is just a lie.'

'Well, we should be able to confirm that soon enough,' Dan said as he pulled out his phone.

He called Martin and asked him to investigate Renfield's background and to get the Manchester Police to do some discrete digging at the church in Salford that Father Peverett had been a parish priest at.

'Renfield's our man, isn't he?' Dan said as he put his phone away.

'Yes, I think he might well be,' Mac replied.

'Tell me why you think that.'

Mac sat back and thought for a while.

'I'm going to make an assumption here but I think that it's a valid one based on what we know. The story certainly makes more sense if I do, so here goes. John Hashley was unhappy, we know that, and I think that something happened that made him even more unhappy. I think he might have fallen in love with someone.'

'Who?' Dan asked looking puzzled.

'Renfield.'

'Well, I never thought of that one!' Dan said with some surprise.

'Well, we always assume that people are straight, don't we? I think that John Hashley thought he was too. He had the perfect family yet he was still angry and I wonder if he even knew why at the time. I think that John Hashley was gay but he could never admit it to anyone, not even to himself. So, he decided to bury his feelings by putting on the mask of a straight Catholic family man. He did it very well too and he probably even convinced himself for a time. That was until he met someone that he had feelings for, someone who also had feelings for him too. They had plenty of opportunities to get together, both at Sanguine Salvatoris, where they somehow managed to have a whole corridor to themselves, and also when John Hashley took Renfield home.'

'You think that they had sex there?' Dan asked.

'I'm almost certain of it. Renfield said that he'd been there once or twice but I'd guess that he visited a lot more often than that. However, I think that John Hashley's religion was important to him too and what he was doing with Renfield was diametrically opposed to everything that Sanguine Salvatoris, and he, stood for. Their focus on the family and their entrenched opposition to any relationship other than a straight one was what he had totally bought into but he had now betrayed all that. I think that this made him even more angry and, perhaps, his anger being directed at his wife can be explained a little by her being part of the mask he had to wear, a mask that denied his deepest feelings. He couldn't reconcile the mask he wore with his feelings and so, in the end, taking his own life might have seemed the least painful road to take.'

'It's easy enough to see how Renfield might have carried out the murders,' Dan said. 'Monica Hashley obviously trusted him. All he would have needed to do was to slip a sleeping pill into a drink and then take her coat, phone and car keys and pretend that he was her. Why do you think he did it though? He told us that Monica was angry at what Alicia had written in her notebook, do you think that he was really talking about how he himself felt?'

'I think that he was angry at what he read in the Grimoire but I don't think that it was so much about the prayer. Here, let me find it...'

Mac looked for another photo on his phone.

'Here, it's something else that Alicia had written in her Grimoire,' he said as he passed the phone to Dan.

I saw them. I saw them at it and it was so disgusting. They were like animals. God help me but it can't be true. I can't stand much more of this.

'Christ!' Dan said. 'She saw John Hashley and Renfield having sex, didn't she?'

'That's what I think too. At first, I thought it had something to do with her father's violence but it didn't quite make sense to me at the time.'

'So, Renfield would have had a raft of motives for killing Alicia; his anger at her prayers, the fact that she knew about him and her father and not forgetting the money. Sanguine Salvatoris would come in for a very nice windfall too if Alicia died.'

'If I'm right then Renfield's sexual proclivities, if they ever became public, would have spelt the end of his involvement with Sanguine Salvatoris and possibly even the Catholic Church. So, he found that he could kill several birds with one stone. Killing Alicia kept his secret safe and it also meant that that the organisation he would one day inherit would become even more richer and more powerful...'

Mac was stopped by Dan putting a finger to his lips. Then, a few seconds later, a shadow fell over the table. Mac turned and looked up and then up again. A very tall man was looking down on him.

'You're the policemen investigating the murders of those two girls, aren't you?' he asked in a very deep and very Australian accent.

He wore a black suit and a white dog collar. He was in his late thirties and his craggy face and broken nose spoke of violence.

Most likely on a rugby pitch, Mac thought.

'Father Ryan?' Mac guessed.

'Can I join you?'

Mac slid up on the bench seat as far as he could but, even so, he felt a bit squished in. Father Ryan wasn't just tall, he was broad with it.

'I take it that you didn't want to talk to us back there for some reason?' Dan asked.

'You bet. They've got cameras all over the place and, although they say they only use them now and again, I don't believe it. I'm afraid that there's not much I can tell you but at least I don't have to watch every single word I say.'

'Tell us about yourself,' Mac asked straining to turn his head around enough to make eye contact.

'Well, I'm only here until next week. Thankfully, in seven days I'll be back home in Perth. The one in Western Australia, I mean.'

'Why were you here in the first place?' Dan asked.

'There's already one in Sydney but they wanted to start a branch of Sanguine Salvatoris in Western Australia. My bishop knew that I was interested and so he sent me here as a sort of intern, I suppose.'

'And what did you learn?'

'That some people in Sanguine Salvatoris are lower than a snake's belly,' he replied with some bitterness.

'Why exactly do you say that?' Dan asked.

'Well, I believed all the hype they put around about the importance of families and people standing on their own two feet but I soon found that the whole place is rank with hypocrisy. I mean look at the way they treat women, it's like something from 'The Handmaid's Tale'. If they had their way fifty per cent of the population would be second class citizens.'

Father Ryan's anger was plain to see.

'How well do you know Father Renfield?' Mac asked.

'Well enough to know that I couldn't stand the bloke even before....'

'Even before what?'

'Look, there are things that I can't tell you. Well, just about everything really,' Father Ryan said giving them a frustrated look.

'So, there's nothing you can tell us that might help us?' Mac asked.

'Search me,' Father Ryan said as he gave them a strange look. 'All I can say is Matthew 7:7. Best of luck guys.'

He left two very puzzled policemen behind him. Mac was slightly quicker at getting his phone out.

'What was that? Was he giving us a clue or something?' Dan asked.

'Yes, I think that he very well may be,' Mac said before he started reading from his phone. 'Matthew 7:7 Ask, and it shall be given you; seek, and ye shall find; knock, and it shall be opened unto you.'

'Seek and ye shall find?' Dan said. 'And he said 'Search me' in a very peculiar way too.'

Mac said nothing. Indeed, he didn't move for well over a minute.

'I think that he's got something,' he eventually said. 'Renfield might be a cold-blooded killer but he's a Catholic cold-blooded killer. I think that he would have wanted to have his confession taken as soon as possible so that he could be absolved from all his sins. What if Renfield chose Father Ryan to take his confession?'

'Well, that would mean that, even though he knew Renfield had blood on his hands, he would never be able to say anything about it or even allude to it in any way without breaking the seal of the confessional,'

Dan replied. 'Not only that but he'll be safely away on the other side of the world in a few days.'

'I think that there might be another reason why Renfield chose Father Ryan. He told us that he couldn't stand Renfield and it's likely that this dislike was reciprocated. Once Renfield had confessed, Father Ryan would have to carry the knowledge with him for the rest of his life without being able to do anything about it. A sort of curse really.'

'So, what do you think he's got?' Dan asked.

'I've no idea but it's obviously something that will speak for itself. It's my guess that he's somehow got his hands on some evidence that might implicate Renfield in the murders.'

'So, what do we do next?' Dan asked.

'I think that we should do as he asked,' Mac replied. 'Search him and everyone else in Sanguine Salvatoris.'

The Full Moon *represents 'The Mother' who gives birth to all that is good in the world. We must thank her in the open air where we can see her face and she can see us. This is when our prayers are asked and answered and, if done correctly, then all knowledge and truth will be ours..."*

Diana L. Selene, Wicca – The Deep Magic of the Wondreth Coven

Chapter Twenty-Eight

Sunday

Mac had enjoyed spending Friday and Saturday night at home sleeping in his own bed. He also did his due diligence by his friend Tim by attending the Magnets both nights for some long-delayed talk and refreshment. Perhaps, 'enjoyed' wasn't quite the right word though. He had found himself growing increasingly restless as the time crawled slowly by until Sunday morning finally came.

Thankfully, he had slept well and was awake at six and in the station before seven. Only Martin was in the room and he was hard at work. He was unshaved and dishevelled and he looked exhausted. After saying hello, there was nothing for Mac to do but wait. Like Martin, forensics had worked through the weekend and they had promised to have an initial report ready for them sometime today. Mac kept checking his inbox every five minutes until he was interrupted by Dan entering the room.

'Anything?' he asked hopefully.

Mac shook his head. Dan looked as frustrated as Mac felt.

'Have they even said what was in the bag yet?' Dan continued.

Another shake of the head.

'I called them just after I got here and Bob Yeardley said that he could either talk to us or work but not both at the same time and more or less put the phone down.'

'That's unlike Bob but I suppose working eight days straight at top speed will do that to you,' Dan said. 'I feel for Martin too. After all the work he's put in, I'm going to give him a couple of weeks off when all this is done and dusted. If I was him, I'd take myself off to somewhere nice and warm.'

Mac thought of Cyprus, where he had been on holiday earlier in the year, and he felt a sudden pang of longing. He'd had to scrape the ice off his windscreen before he drove in and a wicked wind had chilled him to the bone while he'd been doing it. Sunshine and a warm sea to swim in seemed just what he needed right now.

Dan got them all a coffee and sat down. Mac could see that Dan was nervous but then so was he. Pretty much everything hung on what was in that plastic bag.

Mac had been planning to go with Dan when they searched the headquarters of Sanguine Salvatoris early on Friday morning but his back had other ideas. He had been due to meet Dan and the team at the station at four thirty as the raid was scheduled for seven. About two hours before his alarm clock was about to go off, he was woken by someone yelping with pain. It was himself.

The muscles in his back had gone into spasm and the pain was excruciating. By the time the first spasm had eased off, he felt tears running down his face. Then it happened again. The spasms very gradually eased off but Mac knew he would be good for nothing that day. The ferocity of the spasms had surprised him but not the fact that they had happened. He had been pushing himself too hard over the week or so since the murders and he knew that there would inevitably be a payback of some kind.

He had caught up with Dan on Friday evening at the station. The raid had been entirely successful in as much as they had been able to preserve all the data from the CCTV cameras, computer servers and so on. This was what Martin had been working on over the weekend. However, Dan's first thought had been to go directly to Father Ryan's room. The priest didn't seem all that surprised at seeing Dan again. On a small writing table there sat a large plastic bag. Without touching it, Dan looked inside only to see another plastic bag that had been tied with a knot. All Dan could do was call forensics and then watch them as they took it away.

He had looked over at Father Ryan before he left and asked him if he'd be in any trouble.

'I'm not sure,' the priest replied with a stony expression, 'but I'll take whatever's coming.'

Dan had been convinced then that whatever was in that bag was important. However, the long wait for the report had made him begin to doubt himself.

'Do you think that we'd have enough evidence against Renfield if Father Ryan's mysterious bag proves a dud?' Dan asked.

'Possibly but it's all circumstantial, isn't it?' Mac replied. 'A good eye witness or a bit of blood evidence would come in really handy.'

'The Chief Constable phoned me just before I came here and not for the first time,' Dan said as he started pacing up and down. 'He's getting all sorts of phone calls from MPs and even a couple of Government ministers.'

'It looks like Father Peverett is rallying the troops. I guess that he's realised that his life's work is hanging in the balance.'

'He was frothing at the mouth when I spoke to him during the raid,' Dan said. 'He all but sentenced me to eternal damnation.'

'Well, I suppose you can sort of understand that. He's still not aware that Renfield's in the frame, I take it?' Mac asked.

'Not as far as I know but the DNA test we took from Renfield might have given him a clue. Anyway, I'm not sure that the prosecutors will think that we've got enough. We need whatever's in that bag,' Dan said with a hint of desperation.

'I take it that the Chief Constable hinted that he might not take all the blame if the prosecution fails,' Mac said.

Dan nodded.

Mac wasn't surprised. It was rare for anyone to get to the top of the greasy pole by accepting responsibility for anything. He found himself crossing his fingers and silently praying at the same time.

There was nothing but cups of coffee punctuated by long silences for the next two hours. In that time several members of the team, who had all been given the day off, managed to pop in and they all asked the same question that Dan had. Jo and Gerry Dugdale were still there when the initial report finally came in.

Dan scanned the report while everyone looked at his face. He looked worried until he came to a section that he read carefully a couple of times.

A smile spread on his face as he said, 'Father Ryan came good after all and with bells on.'

Dan got out his phone and issued a single terse instruction.

'Bring him in, kicking and screaming if that's what it takes.'

It was an altogether less stressful wait this time. Just over two hours later they watched Renfield as he was being marched into an interview room. By this time the whole team had arrived and had gathered around the big screen.

Mac watched Renfield carefully. At the moment there was just him in the room and a uniformed officer standing in front of the door. Renfield was looking anywhere except at the officer. He must have been aware that he was being watched as he was hugging himself and trying desperately to keep it together. His rapidly tapping foot gave his unease away though.

They were all waiting for someone from the legal firm of Kenge, Dodson and Fogg to arrive. Mac had looked the firm up on the internet. They were at least one hundred and eighty years old and they came with an impeccable reputation. However, he couldn't find any evidence that they were specialists at criminal law so he was a little puzzled as to why they had been summoned.

Eventually, Dan and Mac got the message that the solicitor had turned up. This was confirmed by the big screen going black as he held a conference with his client.

Dan picked up a cardboard file and riffled through the stack of photos inside. Mac knew that everything they needed was inside as they had checked it twice already. They made their way down to the interview room and waited outside until the solicitor had finished. A few minutes later the door opened.

'Here we go, Mac,' Dan said with a grim smile as they walked inside.

Mac nearly wished Dan luck until he realised with a smile that he didn't need any.

Chapter Twenty-Nine

The solicitor shook their hands as they came in and handed them both a card. It informed them that he was Sir Malcolm Carboy and that he was a Senior Partner at the firm of Kenge, Dodson and Fogg.

'In case you're wondering why Messrs. Kenge, Dodson and Fogg aren't here, that's because they all died around one hundred and fifty years ago,' the solicitor said with a smile as he sat down next to his client.

Mac guessed that he used that line a lot.

Sir Malcolm was around sixty years old with white hair that was receding above a narrow face. A pair of half-moon glasses were perched at half-mast upon a prominent nose. He wore a dark pin-striped suit with a floral waistcoat, white shirt and an old school tie. He looked just like solicitors used to when Mac had first become a policeman.

'To explain,' Sir Malcolm continued, 'our firm have represented Sanguine Salvatoris in all its legal matters for nearly twenty years now. Although we're not too au fait with criminal matters, Father Peverett asked me to personally intercede. He's sure that some mistake or misapprehension must have been made in this matter.'

'We'll see about that,' Dan muttered.

He started the recorder off and everyone introduced themselves. Dan then read Renfield his rights. Sir Malcolm looked a little concerned at this but said nothing.

'Mr. Renfield, before we start, have you anything that you'd like to say to us?' Dan asked.

'Just that I have no idea why I'm here. On Friday I had a DNA test taken against my will and this morning I was dragged from my room by your men and driven here. Are we living in a police state now?' Renfield asked his anger apparent. 'And, by the way, it's *Father* Renfield not Mister. At least give me that.'

'All will be made clear, Mr. Renfield,' Dan replied ignoring his request. 'We talked at Sanguine Salvatoris but I need to ask you if you have anything to add to what you've already said concerning the murders of Rhiannon Brodeur and Alicia Hashley?'

'No, I have nothing to add. I know nothing about those murders.'

'How good are you at carpentry, you know DIY and things like that?' Dan asked.

Renfield looked more than puzzled at the question and, sensing some sort of trap, thought about it before answering.

'I hated woodwork at school and I've never done any DIY, if that's what you're asking.'

Dan gave Mac a look. This confirmed Mac's view that the killer hadn't known how to use a hammer.

'Very well,' Dan continued. 'It's not usually the case that we reveal all the evidence against a suspect during the first formal interview but, with you, we're going to make an exception.'

Sir Malcolm looked even more concerned at this.

'Let's go on a journey, shall we?' Dan said as he took some photographs out of the folder. He laid one on the table. 'This is our suspect leaving Sanguine Salvatoris in London.'

'That's Monica Hashley,' Renfield said. 'That's her Gucci coat.'

'The suspect took Monica Hashley's car and then drove to her home,' Dan said as he laid down a photo of the Porsche at the entrance gate to the Drymanshouse Estate. 'At her house the suspect picked up a hammer, a plastic bag and a pair of scissors. They then drove to Radley Meadows, going via a detour so that no-one would see them and parked just before the entrance to a farm.'

Dan put down a photo of the figure walking by the road sign. The Gucci coat could be clearly seen.

'The suspect then waited in Radley Meadows for an opportunity to strike. That came when the rest of the coven left Rhiannon and Alicia by themselves. The suspect crept up from behind and then hit Rhiannon twice with the hammer.'

Dan then put down a photo of Rhiannon lying on her back. Renfield barely glanced at it.

'The suspect then also hit Alicia Hashley twice. She managed to stumble away but she died soon afterwards from her wounds.'

Dan put down a photo of Alicia lying face down.

'The suspect then pulled Rhiannon's dress up, cut her panties with the scissors and removed them, leaving her exposed from the waist down. The hammer and panties were later found in the spare wheel compartment of Monica Hashley's car.'

Another photo.

'The suspect then drove back to Sanguine Salvatoris, parked up and entered the building,' Dan said.

Again, the Gucci coat could be clearly seen.

'To enter or leave the building an electronic key must be used. We've checked and Monica Hashley's key was used to both leave and enter the building,' Dan said.

Sir Malcolm looked bemused as he looked over the photographs.

'But surely these prove that Mrs. Hashley carried out the murders, don't they? I mean there she is,' he said pointing to the figure in the Gucci coat.

Dan cleared the other photos out of the way and left just one in the centre of the table.

'At first, we thought that too. Everything pointed to Monica Hashley as being the killer. We were nearly ready to charge her when we came across this,' he said tapping the photo.

'But that looks quite unremarkable to me,' Sir Malcolm said with a puzzled expression.

'CCTV cameras are everywhere,' Dan said looking straight at Renfield. 'The suspect may have thought that they were safe walking down a road in the middle of the countryside but they walked by a camera fixed to a barn that's used for auctions. As they have to store some quite valuable items there overnight at times, they had to fit a CCTV camera in order to get insured. It points straight down the driveway to the road at the top and it caught our suspect as they walked by. From this we were able to accurately calculate the height of the suspect.'

Mac saw Renfield's face go pale. He'd gotten it straight away.

'The height of the suspect was five feet ten inches tall,' Dan continued. 'By coincidence that's the same height as you, Mr. Renfield. Monica Hashley is only five feet six inches tall. That's quite a discrepancy.'

He put down another photo.

'In the CCTV footage from the Sanguine Salvatoris car park that Mr. Renfield here kindly sent us, you can see that the Gucci coat doesn't fit too well either. There's least a couple of inches of wrist showing there and, even though it was very cold that evening, every shot shows that the coat wasn't zipped up. So, we knew that the killer was wearing Monica Hashley's coat but the question for us became just exactly who was inside it?'

Dan let this sink in.

'It had to be someone who was staying in the Sanguine Salvatoris building that night. Someone who knew Monica Hashley quite well and, as we think that the suspect gave her some sleeping pills to knock her out, it had to be someone she trusted too. Who better than her own confessor?' Dan said looking straight at Renfield.

'That's quite a charge!' Sir Malcolm exclaimed. 'I hope that you have some evidence to back that assertion up.'

'The first lie that your client told us was that the only cameras at Sanguine Salvatoris were in the car park,' Dan said. 'Fortunately for us, there were quite a few inside the building too and we found that they were all operational.'

He pushed another photo across the table. It showed a figure walking across the Sanguine Salvatoris' lobby towards the exit to the car park. The figure was dressed in black from head to toe and a hood obscured the face. A coat was being carried over one arm.

'I don't get any of this at all,' Sir Malcolm said his frustration showing.

'You will,' Dan calmly said. 'Just a few seconds after this person left the lobby through the door into the car park, another appeared walking towards Monica Hashley's car but now they were wearing her coat. The video is being worked on by some experts in biometrics from Hertfordshire University. They can measure faces and the lengths of arms and legs and so on to identify people but they came up with something much more interesting here. The person in that video has a slight limp. You walk with a slight limp, don't you, Mr. Renfield?'

'I don't know what you're talking about,' Renfield spluttered as his face went even whiter.

'They've got lots of footage of you walking across that lobby without a hood and with a slight limp. It appears that every limp is a little bit different and the experts are as certain as they can be that the hooded figure is you. We even know where and when you got that limp but perhaps you might want to tell us about that yourself?' Dan asked.

Renfield turned to face the wall.

'Okay, I'll tell the story then,' Dan said with a shrug. 'It seems that Mr. Renfield here got quite badly beaten up when he was at secondary school. He was just fifteen when it happened and it was quite a serious assault. He ended up with broken fingers, a fractured elbow and a leg that had been broken in three places. They couldn't quite fit it all back together and that's how you got your limp. The attack was recorded by the police at the time as a hate crime. Would you care to tell us why, Mr. Renfield? No? Okay, it was because you were gay. The boys who attacked you said that you had tried to 'touch up' one of them. You denied this at the time and the police believed you. However, you did admit that you identified as a homosexual and had known this for at least two years previous to the attack. Have you anything to say?'

Renfield didn't.

'So, as your room at Sanguine Salvatoris is opposite Monica Hashley's, it would have been easy enough to get her coat, phone, car keys and key card once you had knocked her out. You then drove to the Drymanhouse estate and used her phone to open the gates.'

'But honestly, how could he possibly have known how to do that?' Sir Malcolm interrupted.

'Your client told us another lie. He said that he'd only visited John Hashley once or twice at his house.'

Dan pulled another photo out. It was taken at the entrance gate to the estate and clearly showed John Hashley in the driving seat and, beside him, Renfield in the passenger seat.

'We've got another eleven like this one,' Dan said. 'You've been to Monica Hashley's house at least a

245

dozen times so it would be no wonder if you knew how to access the estate and the code to her burglar alarm.'

'But, but it's all very circumstantial, isn't it?' Sir Malcolm said grabbing at a straw. 'Anyway, what possible motive could Father Renfield have had to carry out such a heinous crime?'

Dan turned and gave Mac a little smile. Renfield sat forward and looked at the two of them with something like horror.

'We've got a whole slew of motives. Shall we go through them all?' Dan said. 'Firstly, Let's look at Alicia Hashley's Grimoire.'

Dan stopped at seeing Sir Malcolm's blank expression.

'It's a book of spells used by witches,' Dan explained.

Sir Malcolm nodded although he still looked a little confused.

'In this job we often find that guilty people accuse others of the exact same things that they have felt or done. Mr. Renfield appears to prove this point. In trying to provide a motive for Monica Hashley to kill her husband, he told us that she was angry at Alicia for what she had prayed for.'

Dan put down another photo.

'You can see here that she initially just prayed for peace in her house. She did this because her father was an angry man and he regularly took his anger out on his wife. So much so that she's currently in hospital recovering from an emergency operation. Even so, she will be severely brain damaged for the rest of her life.'

Sir Malcolm studied the photo but stayed silent.

'If the prayers had angered Renfield then you have to ask why? Surely, John Hashley was just a colleague, wasn't he? This second excerpt from the Grimoire gives us a clue,' Dan said as he laid down another photo.

Sir Malcolm studied this one too.

I saw them. I saw them at it and it was so disgusting. They were like animals. God help me but it can't be true. I can't stand much more of this.

'We think that this is what really made Mr. Renfield here really angry. He hadn't realised it but he'd been caught in the act. Isn't that right, Mr. Renfield?'

Renfield ground his teeth but said nothing.

'I don't understand,' Sir Malcolm said. 'What was it that she saw?'

'Alicia saw Mr. Renfield here and her father having sex together,' Dan replied.

'No, that's not right...that...that never happened,' Renfield protested. 'Never.'

'All those home visits weren't so that you and John Hashley could work together. It was all about sex, wasn't it? And, before you say a word, let me just say that we have two bedsheets, one from the guest room and one in the laundry basket. Both have ample evidence on them that sex had taken place and that the two people having it were you and John Hashley. It was lucky for us that Monica Hashley hadn't paid her cleaning service for a while and they'd stopped coming. The brain damage, I'd guess.'

Sir Malcolm turned and looked at his client before moving his chair a little further away.

Dan continued, 'After Monica Hashley had brought you the Grimoire, you knew that there had been a witness to your sexual activities. Of course, it wasn't illegal but it would have ruined your standing in Sanguine Salvatoris, wouldn't it? All that about 'Family First' just disguises the fact that the organisation is virulently anti-gay. And, being the heir apparent, you would have had a lot to lose.'

'What do you mean by heir apparent? Sanguine Salvatoris isn't run like that,' Sir Malcolm said.

'That's what you think. I'll let my colleague tell you a little story,' Dan said as he sat back in his chair.

Mac took over.

'Around thirty years ago, Father Peverett was an assistant parish priest at a church in Salford, near Manchester. While he was there, he managed to get a young woman pregnant. I should say child really, as the girl was only fifteen at the time. However, instead of Peverett being charged with statutory rape and going to prison, the bishop packed him off to Spain and then bought the family off. They were poor and had a desire to go back to Ireland but they didn't have the means. So, the bishop provided the funds for them to do just that. The baby stayed here though. He was given to a very devout Catholic couple called Mr. and Mrs. Renfield who brought him up. We heard that they were very strict with the boy but they gave him no love which might explain things a little, I think. Anyway, they changed his given name from Brendan to Julian and ensured that he was brought up as a good little Catholic boy should. He was a very bright child and, after leaving school with some excellent exam results, he found himself at the best seminary in the country, training to be a priest. He was top of the class there too and so Father Peverett could publicly claim that this was the only reason why he wanted Julian Renfield to join Sanguine Salvatoris.'

Mac let this sink in.

'I would guess that a number of people in Sanguine Salvatoris had an idea of the relationship between the two priests but, like the famous elephant in the living room, no-one ever brought it up. And so, Julian Renfield found himself in the pole position to become the successor to his father as the head of the organisation. If, has had been rumoured, Father Peverett moves up to become the new global leader of Sanguine Salvatoris, then Renfield would have quickly slipped into his father's shoes and would be running one of the most influential religious movements in the country.'

'So, I think we can all see that Renfield had a lot to lose if his homosexual activities ever came to light,' Dan said. 'He had been very discreet until he met John Hashley but something about the affair made Mr. Renfield less cautious for some reason. Love, I'd guess. We also need to consider exactly what Mr. Renfield was going to inherit. John Hashley left Sanguine Salvatoris half of his company, a company with an annual revenue of six billion pounds. This got the organisation out of a very sticky situation as its debts were piling up. John Hashley also stipulated in his will that, if Alicia died without issue, they would get the other half of the company too. So, Alicia's death not only meant that a witness to his homosexual activities would be removed but that the organisation he was about to inherit would be even richer and more powerful than ever. So, he had several motives all of which told him that killing Alicia Hashley would solve all his problems. Rhiannon Brodeur was unlucky, she was just in the wrong place at the wrong time. He also had the perfect patsy who would take all the blame, the poor brain damaged widow. I'd say that was enough, wouldn't you?'

'Yes, I can see that but...' Sir Malcolm said before being interrupted by Dan.

'Oh, I'm sorry, I nearly forgot. There's one more photo.'

He put down a photo that was of a set of clothes that had been carefully arranged on a long table. There was a black hoodie, a black T shirt, a pair of black trousers and a pair of black trainers.

'But I thought...' Renfield said before quickly cutting himself off.

'Yes, you thought that these would be in Greece by now being worn by a refugee, didn't you?' Dan said before turning to Sir Malcolm. 'To explain, Sanguine Salvatoris had let one of their rooms out to a Catholic aid agency. They were collecting clothing and other personal items for Middle Eastern refugees being held in Greek camps. A truck came and took them away the evening after the murders but, luckily, someone rescued these.'

'Ryan!' Renfield hissed. 'He's broken the seal of the confessional.'

'I can't comment on that,' Dan said. 'He never said a word to us or anyone else about the confession that you made to him. He just preserved the evidence and hoped that we might somehow stumble across it. If that's breaking the seal then I guess he felt that whatever punishment he might face was preferable to seeing someone like you as the head of a religious organisation. A man that has the blood of two innocent children on his hands.'

'They weren't innocent,' Renfield said with a raised voice. 'They were evil. They were the whores of Satan.'

This outburst caused Sir Malcolm to move his chair even further away from his client.

Dan ignored the outburst and turned to Sir Malcolm.

'In case you're wondering, these clothes were worn by the killer of the two girls. We know this because of the blood spatter. Unfortunately for the killer, when he first hit Alicia with the hammer, it wasn't a clean hit and it ended up tearing her ear lobe. This caused quite a lot of bleeding and we think that Alicia must have shaken her head, possibly to try and clear it, spraying blood droplets over the clothes the killer was wearing. The trousers are the best. They have Mr. Renfield's DNA on the inside, and only his, and two nice big drops of Alicia's blood on the outside. This irrefutably places Mr. Renfield as being inside the clothes and at the scene of the murder when it happened. Is that enough, do you think?'

'Err...er...' Sir Malcolm said as he stood up. 'I'm afraid that my firm is not adept with dealing with criminal cases. I think that Mr. Renfield here should get himself another solicitor. Immediately.'

Sir Malcolm left without another word.

'The first rat has left the sinking ship,' Dan said.

'Sanguine Salvatoris won't sink,' Renfield said with some anger.

'Oh, I think it will,' Mac said. 'Even though Alicia is dead, it definitely won't get her half of the company as a crime was committed in order to make it happen. As for the other half that was bequeathed to Sanguine Salvatoris, any decent lawyer could contest that and I've heard that Monica Hashley has a very good one indeed. John Hashley made his last will just a few months before he died. It could be claimed that it was made under duress and that he was being manipulated at a time when his mental health was questionable. Not only that but the witnesses were all members of Sanguine Salvatoris which wasn't a good move either. In his previous will his wife got fifty per cent of his estate whereas in the new one she was cut out completely. As she is now in a position of needing life-long support due to the injuries directly caused by her husband, I think that it would be hard to find a judge that wouldn't throw the will out. Not only that but Monica Hashley's lawyers would then be able to call in all the loans that her husband made to you. That will leave Sanguine Salvatoris up to its neck in debt and, after the news of your arrest gets out, do you honestly think that anyone will lend it more money? No, I think that Sanguine Salvatoris is sunk and you did it, Mr. Renfield. All by yourself.'

Renfield's face had now turned grey as the truth of his situation was sinking in.

'Anyway, I think we're done here,' Dan said. 'Mr. Renfield, I'm now formally charging you with the murders of Alicia Hashley and Rhiannon Brodeur and also of perverting the course of justice. You will be held here pending a hearing. I also suggest that you get some legal representation pretty quickly.'

Dan then ended the interview. He left the room but Mac sat there for a while looking at Renfield who had his face in his hands.

'They were evil, Mr. Maguire,' Renfield said between his fingers. 'You must see that.'

'Evil? Why, because they believed in a different god to yours?' Mac replied. 'They weren't evil, they were two young innocent girls who were just trying to make the world a slightly better place. Anyway, I don't believe in the concept of evil. In my job I've seen the things that people can do to each other, the most terrible things that you could imagine, but I never thought that they were evil. Life can warp you, especially when you're young. Some murderers have had the most wicked things happen to them when they were children and you can almost understand why they did what they did. However, there are some who get warped by life and then work very hard to warp themselves even further. You're one of those people, Mr. Renfield. You killed two beautiful and innocent young girls to further your own interests but I don't think that you're evil either. Just very warped.'

'What's going to happen to me?' Renfield said quietly as if to himself.

Mac answered him.

'There will be a hearing and eventually a trial where you will be found guilty and sentenced to life imprisonment. If you ever get out, you will be an old old man. You have sinned, Mr. Renfield, sinned most heinously but, don't worry, you will have plenty of time to reflect on what you've done.'

Mac left him with his head in his hands as he went towards the door. As the door closed, he could hear the sound of sobbing.

Who was he crying for? Mac asked himself. Not for the girls and probably not for his father or even Sanguine Salvatoris.

Mac knew that he was crying only for himself.

The Waning Moon...*The 'Crone' or the 'Old Woman' represents the wisdom of the Goddess. It is wise to reflect upon our experiences and to learn from the messages that have been sent to us. We must also begin to prepare for the New Moon and the beginning of another cycle..."*

Diana L. Selene, Wicca – The Deep Magic of the Wondreth Coven

Chapter Thirty

A short while afterwards Mac said his goodbyes to the team. All that was left now was the paperwork and Mac had never been a fan of that. He left Tommy until last.

'How's Bridget doing?' he asked.

He had become so preoccupied with the investigation that he had almost forgotten about his daughter's pregnancy.

'Oh, she's fine. Bored stiff but fine,' Tommy said. 'Amrit will be with her now. How are you coping without her?'

Amrit was a friend of Bridget's who, in a former life, had been a nurse. She had been looking after Mac for a while now, cleaning the house and making sure that he didn't poison himself by eating out of date food. She was now in charge of Bridget for the duration of the pregnancy.

'I don't know really,' Mac replied. 'After all, I've hardly been home. Anyway, I'll be okay. Tim said that he'll give me a hand.'

Tommy just nodded at this. Mac could see that something was worrying him.

'Come on, spit it out,' Mac said.

'I'd never be any good at poker, would I?' Tommy said with a rueful smile. 'Now that the case is more or less finished, I was just thinking about the two girls. They were so young.'

'And you were thinking about how you'd feel if it happened to your child and even the thought of it scared you silly.'

'That's spot on. How could you have known that though?'

'Oh, because I've thought exactly that myself many times myself when someone's done something horrific to a child, especially when Bridget was young.'

'So, what's the answer?' Tommy asked.

'There isn't one,' Mac replied with a shrug. 'You learn to live with it but, when they're ill or they've had an accident, you'll worry like mad. It comes with the territory. The only thing I'd say is try not to worry until you know you have something to worry about but I'll wish you luck with that one.'

'It makes you wonder why people have children at all, doesn't it?' Tommy said with a bleak expression.

'You'll find out why soon enough. You will never have as much fun as you will have with a child or know as much love. Whatever the downsides, it's more than worth it, believe me.'

Tommy obviously did as a smile returned to his face.

'Thanks, Mac. I think that I needed that.'

'Anyway, don't forget that I'll be around to help too, doing my grandfatherly duties.'

Mac wasn't quite sure what those duties might entail just yet but he was going to do them whatever they were.

Tommy was right, Bridget was bored. She had that same look on her face that she'd had as a child when she wanted to go out and play with her friends but all she could do was stare out of the window at the rain falling outside. A few games of backgammon lifted her spirits a little, especially after she'd trounced her father. He hadn't even been trying to let her win.

At the end of the day, he found himself once again in the comfort of the Magnets with a pint in front of him and his best friend Tim sitting opposite.

'So, you did it again then,' Tim said.

'Did what?'

'Cracked the case.'

'No, it wasn't just me' Mac replied, 'Far from it really, I had plenty of help.'

He didn't mention where some of this help had come from.

'I've been thinking though, you know, about what people believe,' Mac continued. 'Christianity is supposed to be all about love and helping each other but you'd never have guessed that from an organisation like Sanguine Salvatoris. Yet, Rhiannon Brodeur seemed to have a lot of love for other people and she really tried to help them when she could. So, who was the true Christian here? Certainly not Peverett who defined his religion by who he excluded and definitely not Renfield that's for sure.'

'He was a bit of a slippery customer that Renfield, wasn't he?' Tim asked.

Mac could only agree.

'He nearly had us all fooled. Poor Monica Hashley is still in hospital and I doubt if she'd ever be deemed capable of standing trial so, if we hadn't found that crucial bit of evidence, Renfield would have got away with it.'

'Well, that camera had been over your heads every time you walked in and out of that barn so how did you notice it in the end?'

'I looked up at the sky and there it was,' Mac replied only lying slightly. 'I've always found it strange that it sometimes takes just one bit of contradictory evidence to blow a case open. Once you start looking at the evidence from a different perspective, it suddenly all makes sense.'

'Well, I wish our manager would look at our mid-field from a different perspective. We might get somewhere if he did.'

They were once again off on a night-long conversation examining the finer points of football as it related to their favourite football club, Aston Villa.

Mac was feeling tired but peaceful too as he gave Terry his last walk of the day. His mind wandered from the case to football to Bridget and back again. Then he had a thought and he pulled out his phone. It told him that today was October 30th.

The days had flashed by and, with some surprise, he realised that tomorrow would be Halloween. Mac used to think that the notion of spirits walking the earth was a bit far-fetched but now he wasn't quite so sure.

As if to emphasise that point, he had that feeling again. Terry was pulling hard on his leash and whining softly. Even though he didn't want to, he looked up.

In the darkness of the cemetery entrance an even darker figure stood. Even though he couldn't see her eyes, he knew that the apparition was looking straight at him. His mouth felt dry and his knees shook. The wind suddenly picked up and whirled around. It whirled tighter and tighter picking up leaves and throwing them into the air. When the whirlwind reached the spot where the apparition was standing, Mac heard a loud sigh as the whirlwind threw leaves high up into the air before it abruptly disappeared.

The apparition had disappeared too. The leaves fell slowly to the ground and Mac knew that he would never see her again. Terry had stopped whining and was now pulling Mac towards the nearest lamppost.

'Thanks,' Mac said still looking towards the cemetery. 'Thanks.'

The End

I hope that you've enjoyed this story. If you have then please post a review and let me know what you think. *PCW*

https://patrickcwalshauthor.wordpress.com/